C0-AVN-715

ROBERT L. PHILLIPS, M.D.

# WALTZ AND OTHER STORIES

*Books by Félix Martí-Ibáñez*

WALTZ AND OTHER STORIES

ALL THE WONDERS WE SEEK: THIRTEEN TALES
   OF SURPRISE AND PRODIGY

THE CRYSTAL ARROW: ESSAYS ON LITERATURE,
   TRAVEL, ART, LOVE, AND THE HISTORY OF MEDICINE

CENTAUR: ESSAYS ON THE HISTORY
   OF MEDICAL IDEAS

ARIEL: ESSAYS ON THE ARTS AND THE HISTORY
   AND PHILOSOPHY OF MEDICINE

A PRELUDE TO MEDICAL HISTORY

MEN, MOLDS, AND HISTORY

THE EPIC OF MEDICINE (*Editor*)

THE PAGEANT OF MEDICINE (*Editor*)

HENRY E. SIGERIST ON THE HISTORY
   OF MEDICINE (*Editor*)

*In Spanish*

ENSAYO SOBRE LA PSICOLOGIA Y
   FISOLOGIA MISTICAS DE LA INDIA

SURCO (*Essays*)

OBRA (*"My Work in Public Health"*)

YO, REBELDE (*A Novel*)

AVENTURA (*A Novel*)

# WALTZ
# AND
# OTHER STORIES

*by*

FELIX MARTI-IBAÑEZ

*Clarkson N. Potter Inc. / Publisher*
NEW YORK

© Copyright 1952, 1963, 1965, by Félix Martí-Ibáñez.
All rights reserved, including the right to repro-
duce this book or portions thereof in any form.

Library of Congress Catalog Card Number: 65-17791

Manufactured in the United States of America
First Edition

*With ever-growing admiration,*
*to Verna Sabelle, Aida Obler,*
*and Betty Hamilton, who through*
*many years have been*
*my devoted companions*

# CONTENTS

# WALTZ AND OTHER STORIES

# WALTZ

 Iт was not quite mid-
night, but the roulette room at the casino in Nice was
already practically deserted. At the only open table the
croupier called out *"Rien ne va plus"* as solemnly as
if he were proclaiming the Day of Judgment. The tiny
ivory ball was already spinning and skipping, pursuing itself endlessly, when Madame Olga Chaillon's
sun-tanned arm slithered like a golden serpent over
the green felt and placed her bet.

1

*"Cinq, noir, impair et manque,"* chanted the croupier.

Turning to her companion with the air of an empress, Madame Chaillon looked at him with imperious deep-violet eyes and said, "Raoul, I've run out of chips."

Her companion gave her a strained smile, and his small white teeth above his squared black dinner coat made him look like a domino piece. "So have I, *chérie,* quite a while ago, and what's worse, I have no more money with me."

"Always the same stupid story," she muttered angrily, inserting a cigarette in a diamond-studded holder.

"Tonight you have lost more than ever, Olga."

"All the more reason to continue."

"The hotel is very far from here," he protested, lighting her cigarette.

"Nothing is far in Nice," she snapped, leaving the table.

He watched her walk away—tall, statuesque, magnificently haughty, a toy for an Asiatic king. Her golden hair was wound in a thick roll at the back of her head, and her neck and shoulders, emerging gracefully from a low-cut décolletage, had exquisite lines of liquid softness. Her full-blown sensuous body was clearly outlined by a shimmering gold silk gown that seemed to have grown on her, like feathers.

"Olga," he called, following her to the next salon, where an orchestra was playing. "If you wish, I'll go to the hotel."

2

When she looked at him all the stars in the sky of Nice seemed to glow in her violet eyes.

"I'm sure we're going to win, Raoul. I'll wait for you here," she said, sitting down on a sofa.

Raoul stared at her as if he could not tear himself away. "Your eyes are irresistible and you know it," he whispered.

"I've been told that so many times, my dear Raoul. I'm beginning to despair of ever meeting someone who'll say something different. Not that it doesn't sound lovely when you say it," she added politely. "But hurry, darling."

When he had disappeared down the stairs, Madame Chaillon looked around the room. A few people were dancing, but the air already bore the sadness peculiar to the month of October in Nice. The casino was beginning to look like a castle at the end of the season, when only the servants remain, quietly moving to and fro, covering the furniture, putting away the silver candelabra.

The woman's gaze, following the diamond-studded line of her cigarette holder, was suddenly arrested by a great mass of gray-streaked dark hair. A man sat at the other end of the sofa, his eyes fixed with a distant look on the sparkling crystal chandelier hanging from the ceiling. His bold, dark-skinned profile, sharply silhouetted against the glowing background, had the impassivity of an Aztec idol.

Now Madame Chaillon all her life had been moved by an intense curiosity about men. She could be as passionately interested in their personalities as in their bank accounts. Raoul was away attending to her present financial needs, and this handsome stranger with the faraway look intrigued her.

"Would you please tell me the time?" she asked him, her voice caressing, her body slightly leaning forward as if poised to spring.

The stranger turned and their eyes met. His remained indifferent, betraying no admiration, no acknowledgment of her beauty. They were beautiful eyes, large, set wide apart, of a warm green, like grapes in the summer sun. His swarthy face, embroidered by sun and wind, might have been that of a seaman. She had met many men in her life, but never one so strange, so remote, so unapproachable.

Before the stranger had time to answer her, a large clock nearby solemnly began to strike midnight.

"Man's invention forestalls him," he said. "Midnight, the hour when spirits wander abroad." He paused. "Tonight they're celestial spirits, enveloped in bewitching clouds of perfume."

"This sounds more promising," thought Olga. And suddenly more than anything else she wanted this man to become interested in her.

"I wanted the time, not a compliment." Her voice

4

was deliberately cold, but her body, leaning closer to the stranger, betrayed her interest.

"And I had no hopes of finding anything here besides my own dreams. But night is always kind to poets."

"Are you a poet?"

"No, but *you* are poetry."

"You're being carried away."

"Not at all. I'm sincere. I would like to ask you a favor. Will you dance with me?"

"I don't dance with strangers."

"Oh, but I think dancing is a waste of time. Most people dance so that they need not talk. What I meant was, will you *talk* this dance out with me?"

"I'm afraid I don't understand."

"I mean that I neither wish to dance nor am I able to. You see, I lost a leg in the war and its substitute permits me very little in the way of acrobatics. But I should be so happy to talk this dance with you."

"I'm so sorry. Yes, I'd love to talk this dance with you. It's a waltz, my favorite music."

But they remained silent for a while. The waltz swirled around them in soft waves, at first gently and then, gaining momentum, stronger and faster, until they were completely engulfed by the whirlpool of music.

"Let's not introduce ourselves," he said, looking at

her with unyielding eyes. And she, accustomed to sub-
duing men with just one glance from her violet eyes,
was all the more intrigued.

"We'll talk while the waltz lasts," he continued,
"and then we'll part, like two cars passing each other
on a lonely road at night, leaving behind only the
memory of their blazing lights. I'm glad it's a waltz.
The waltz is the most heavenly of all dances. It is the
celestial spheric empire of romance. It makes one crave
to leave the earth, to become a winged creature and
soar into space. Have you ever noticed that people
waltzing look like birds trying to fly for the first time?
I love waltzes, all waltzes. Chopin's waltzes are sprinkled with moonlight and the dust of white lilies; the
majestic waltzes in grand opera conjure visions of
vast Gothic cathedrals; the sentimental waltzes at
country fairs make young girls sigh and dream far into
the night—and the elegant waltzes at court balls, all
pomp and glitter—I love them all. But waltzes can also
be cruel. There was a cruel waltz in my youth I shall
never forget."

He paused. The waves of the waltz swelled and
rolled through the warm air, encircling them, engulf-
ing them. Olga's eyes were riveted on the stranger's
luminous green eyes that seemed determined to ignore
her beauty, which had ruined so many men.

"It was in this same casino," he went on, with a tom-
tom-like resonance in his voice, "too many years ago.

6

In those days people staked *louis d'or*. Gold epaulets, diamond studs and tiaras, shimmering brocades and satins, towering plumes—all these gravitated to the tables. I was a young student then, so young that I believed I could capture in the net of my youth the wayward butterfly of Fortune. I gambled and lost.

"Next to me sat a woman. She was in her fifties. On her body a battle was raging between youth's slenderness and the plumpness of middle age. Her hair was bleached a bright gold, and her faded blue eyes were already framed by a web of fine lines. She played with that arrogance that wealth imparts to some people. For each humble one-hundred-franc chip I played, she tossed down a handful of gold pieces. And cruel Fortune smiled at her, while it mocked me and brought ruin upon my head. Without realizing it, we became fascinated by one another, she probably because of the anguish on my face every time I lost, and I because of her reckless stakes and fabulous luck.

"Three hours and several thousand francs later I had lost every franc I owned in the world, while in front of her small heaps of gold glittered like a pirate's booty. With empty pockets, I staggered to my feet and went out on the balcony for some fresh air. After a few seconds I smelled her perfume next to me. In her hands her small purse bulged with the money she had won. She spoke to me kindly, but I was angry at myself for having lost and at her for having won. When she asked me to have a glass of champagne with her for better luck, I accepted.

"She told me that she was alone and very wealthy. She was at that age when women, aware that autumn has come and is slowly shrouding them in its withered mask of gold, desperately search for the greenness of a young man's love. We went to her hotel. On her balcony, remembering all the time that I had no money for rent or food, I spoke of love to her. She came to my arms and the moon above seemed to be mocking me. It was then that I heard the waltz. The melancholy notes floated through the air, fusing with the moonlight, whirling around us, drenching us in nostalgia. I remembered again that I was penniless; I thought of my broken dreams, my studies in Paris. The blue sorcery of the waltz merged with the moonlight. Suddenly, bursting with fury, I pushed her away. I called her old, fat, ugly. I cried out that all her money could not buy one single kiss, one single caress of mine, and I rushed out of her room happy, as though I had had my revenge on Fortune. As I flung open the door, the woman's sobs reached me mixed with the wailing strains of the waltz."

The stranger was silent again. Olga, like a timid butterfly, was caught in the magic web of his words, hypnotized by the unflinching look in his baffling eyes.

"I have collected many waltzes in my life," he went

8

on, a fleeting smile softening the roughly carved features.

"One night in Algeria, while on sentry duty under a merciless white moon at a post of the French Foreign Legion, I was suddenly seized with the *cafard*. I stripped off my clothes and under the glaring moon I danced naked on the cold desert sand, intoxicated with Pinot and nostalgia. The distant howling of hyenas was my only music, but to my feverish mind it was the wail of a waltz played by *tziganes*.

"And I remember the waltz of the winds over the ocean, the waves whirling like leaves, and the waltz of the winds through the forests, the leaves whirling like waves.

"There was also the fatal waltz I danced in Brittany with a peasant girl in an abandoned cottage. The phonograph we were playing was so old it made the waltz sound like the wail of someone in pain. With that feeble spurt of music we wanted to drown out the torrent of explosives that enemy planes were dropping on the village. And then a bomb blew up the cottage, the girl, the waltz, and all possibility of my ever dancing again."

Olga, sighing, moved closer to the inscrutable eyes. Suddenly Raoul's head appeared at the top of the stairs.

"My friend is coming back," she anxiously whispered to the stranger. "Take me away with you and we'll continue talking about waltzes. Now, tomorrow, any time you say. I'll meet you wherever you say. Tell me where. Please hurry, Raoul is here and he'll be furious if he sees me talking to you."

The stranger's eyes suddenly sparkled with a grain of sunshine. "Your friend? Good, madame. The waltz has ended. Perhaps he'll be kind enough to take me downstairs, where my seeing-eye dog waits for me. But before we say good-by, tell me—what color are your eyes?"

## IT HAPPENED IN PARIS

ONE DAY LAST FALL, AR-
mando Lesseur and I were having lunch at Maxim's.
At our table, a Moor clad in red velvet was performing
the usual aromatic ritual with his silver coffeepot when
Yvette Darland walked in.

Some people enter a room and no one notices them;
nothing happens; they are as invisible when present
as when absent—but there are others whose mere appearance causes something of a commotion. Yvette

11

Darland's entrances always caused a big commotion. The lights in the room seemed to burn brighter, as if they had caught the radiance in her wide blue eyes, and the air instantly became electrified. When Yvette swept into Maxim's, with its sumptuous crimson velvet hangings, its gleaming crystal chandeliers, its Baccarat glasses golden with champagne, and its impeccably attired bowing waiters, the restaurant suddenly acquired the romantic atmosphere of a Louis Philippe court ball.

Armando was lifting his cognac to his lips when he saw Yvette. The bubble-shaped glass with his two hands cupped around it remained suspended in mid-air: he looked like a priest of some pagan cult offering the chalice to his goddess.

Yvette, tall, magnificently curvaceous, a cross between a camellia and a tuberose, followed the maître, head held erect, haughtily indifferent to the frantic whispering of the women and the covetous eyes of the men.

Armando, fascinated, watched Yvette's every movement as she gracefully sat down on the chair the maître pulled out for her with the air of a king offering a throne to his queen. She tossed back her chinchilla stole, while half a dozen obsequious waiters hovered around her. The man with her seemed utterly indifferent to his surroundings. He was small, thin, colorless, the insignificance of his appearance magnified by the woman's flamboyant looks. The splendor of the bird of paradise emphasized the homeliness of the turkey.

"Who is that exquisite creature?" inquired Armando, finally recovering his voice.

"Don't you know?" I asked incredulously. "I should have thought that *you* would know Yvette Darland, the beautiful Darland, the terrible Yvette, the last reincarnation of the *femmes fatales* of the past century who made the lives of our grandfathers both heaven and hell—in short, the most expensive demimondaine in Paris."

"Stop! You have said enough. What a woman! Strange that I have never seen her before."

"After all, you have been back from Argentina only two months."

"Who is that idiot with her?" Armando asked, peering inquisitively across the tables.

"Benoît Duval, a retired architect. It seems he inherited a fortune not long ago and he is spending it fast and enjoying it."

"With that monkey face and that puny little body, what can a woman like her possibly see in him?" asked Armando.

"I can't imagine. I should have thought that Yvette was beyond Duval's reach. But then one can never tell about women. At least, I can't," I added smiling. "Anyway, it must have started recently. I have seen Duval here many times, but never with Yvette."

"I never saw him here before."

"Of course not. He had to come with Yvette Darland for you to notice him."

Armando's eyes were once again riveted on Yvette, who lifted an oyster to her lips with exquisite daintiness, as though she were going to kiss it, not eat it. Duval was engrossed in the wine list. Yvette's blue gaze slowly surveyed the tables. The room buzzed with the lively chatter of many people, the wine glowed in the sparkling glasses, and the aroma of spiced foods mixed with that of fine tobacco.

When Yvette's gaze reached our table, she stared curiously at Armando, and then an expression crossed her face as though she had diagnosed and classified him as an approachable and acceptable male. She then continued eating, and I could only think of Venus consecrating oysters with her divine lips.

"What a woman!" Armando repeated. "Such carriage! Regal! Definitely regal!" He meditated for a moment, as though he were shuffling memories, comparing values, his gaze lost in the blue smoke-spirals from his cigarette. When he looked at Yvette once more, his long tapered fingers were gently rubbing the rounded curves of his glass and he wet his lips in appreciation of either the cognac or some thought that had crossed his mind.

"For that woman," he murmured, "I would gladly spare some time from Maruchi."

14

"So, we have come to that already, Armando?" I said, feigning surprise. "Just married, very much in love with your wife, and already looking for greener pastures?"

"A dog never renounces his old tricks. I love my wife very much indeed, but this woman intrigues me." He sighed. "But I have neither the time nor the money. Besides, that imbecile with her probably sticks to her like a vulture."

Just then Benoît Duval looked at us. His eyes met mine and he nodded and smiled.

"What the devil" Armando exclaimed. "Do you know that man?"

"I met him once at the Club des Professionnels."

"This is incredible! My luck hasn't changed."

"Poor Maruchi," I sighed.

"Good God, man! My wife has nothing to do with this. I doubt that anything will come of this, but you understand, if one can enter paradise, why be satisfied with just looking in from the gates?"

As we were leaving, Armando whispered, "Come, do something. Let's not miss this chance of meeting her."

"I'm not interested," I laughed.

"So much the better. Do it for me, then. I'll never forget it if you do this for me."

But there was no need for me to do anything. Much to my surprise, as we neared his table Duval stood up and, smiling, offered me his hand. He inquired whether I would be at our club that evening as he wished to consult me about some publicity work for the club. From the corner of my eye I saw Armando avidly eyeing Yvette's décolleté, whose ivory whiteness contrasted with the blood-red Chateaubriand she was eating.

Duval and I chatted for a brief moment and then he turned to Armando and apologized. I introduced them.

The two men could not have been more different in appearance. Armando Lesseur, tall, dark, lightly gray at the temples, impeccably dressed, worldly and urbane, exemplified the dandies who once abounded in Paris and now can be found only in the comedies performed by the Théâtre Français. Duval, short, ungainly, with thinning mousy hair, might have been Armando's valet.

Duval presented us to Yvette. As I bowed and kissed the soft plump hand, she appeared less ethereal. She was like a luscious fruit with a waxen delicacy from a distance but a little too ripe when touched.

"Madame," Armando said with a gesture that must have been fashionable at Maxim's in more romantic days, "if the reputation for beauty of French women were not already established beyond question, you alone would do so this very instant."

"Monsieur is terribly gallant," she smiled, her enormous blue eyes sparkling at Armando.

16

"Only patriotic," he replied. "I am very proud that my country can claim the glory of your beauty."

Armando gave further proof of his gallantry by generously showering more flattery upon Yvette. When we said good-by, Duval's face plainly showed that he regretted having introduced us.

Outside, Maxim's gay, warm atmosphere was forgotten for a few minutes as we buttoned our coats against the cold mist that enshrouded the boulevards. While waiting for a taxi, Armando said, "I hope my flirting with Yvette Darland did not upset you."

"Not in the least. Duval is not a friend, whereas you are."

"Thanks. I knew I could count on you. Well, I have met her and I am sure I impressed her. But what shall I do next? It won't be easy."

"For you, Armando, this is but chapter one in your private encyclopedia on the technique of love."

"Don't take this lightly. It is a most difficult case. I have no desire to win Yvette with my bank account. I couldn't afford it anyway. I must arouse her interest in me personally. It will be worth trying."

"You will have Duval to contend with. And how about Maruchi?"

"Duval won't be difficult. He is the type that never realizes a woman is deceiving him until he reads it in the gossip columns. But I'll have to be careful about Maruchi. I don't want to estrange my wife. I must find a way to talk to Yvette. My God! I have it. My birthday party next Sunday. We'll invite Yvette and Duval. Suppose I ask Duval tonight at the club?"

"Well, I suppose you can, but I doubt—"

"I'm sure he will accept," Armando interrupted me. "They will be only too happy to come."

I had known Armando when he was a bachelor and the terror of Parisian husbands. The son of a wealthy bourgeois family, his engaging personality and polished manners had helped him to become one of the leading textile manufacturers in France. When he reached the pinnacle of financial success, he placed his business in the hands of managers and thereafter devoted all his time to becoming a man of the world, exploiting with relish the effect of his physical charm on women. In two or three years he became one of the most discussed bachelors in Paris. He had been involved in numerous amorous intrigues, one of which finally ended in a duel and forced his flight to South America, where he had extensive business interests.

I had occasion to go to Buenos Aires on a newspaper assignment and there I heard about his fabulous parties. I saw him often, for I was amused by his swagger, his amorous successes, and his immense vanity.

We were at a charity ball at the Chilean Embassy when he met Maruchi Mendoza, one of the most cov-

eted young social beauties in Buenos Aires. Although
Armando was forty-two and Maruchi only twenty-one,
they were instantly attracted to each other. Each felt
flattered to have captured the interest of the other. Any
understanding, however, between the daughter of one
of the leading Argentine families and the French Don
Juan was unthinkable. In France it might have led
to an affair; in Buenos Aires it ended in marriage, or
rather it began with marriage, for the well-chaperoned
Maruchi was never left alone with the Parisian, a fact
that made him hasten the wedding. Buenos Aires will
never forget the extravagant wedding at the Iglesia de
las Mercedes, the beautiful Maruchi trailing dozens of
yards of the finest white lace and Armando wearing a
pearl the size of a robin's egg on his silk tie.

I visited the newlyweds several times at their home,
a wedding gift from the bride's family and a veritable
palace. Always surrounded by a select group of cultured young friends, they drank tea and sweet wines,
discussed books, clothes, the theater, and their friends,
and joked a great deal. Sometimes Maruchi would sing
sad Argentine ballads in a voice thin and sweet, like
that of a young canary.

Maruchi was petite, but as sculptural as a Tanagra
figurine. She perfectly illustrated the relationship between a woman and a bonbon. Her body had the perfect proportions of a sandglass, with the sand evenly
distributed (Yvette had much more sand below the

waist). Her skin was alabaster-white, her mouth sweet but impudent. Her thick hair was ebony, and her huge dark upward-slanting eyes were always moist. She was cultured but never pedantic, extremely feminine, reserved yet uninhibited. She was a child-woman growing up. An experienced lover like Armando must have had wild dreams of teaching her the grammar of eroticism in a thousand different lessons.

Three months after bidding them good-by in Buenos Aires, I met them again in Paris. Armando had promptly renewed his old friendships. He organized Maruchi's life so that she was always pleasantly occupied but also carefully watched. Paris could hardly overlook a beauty like Maruchi, and Armando avoided all possible temptations by turning his chalet in Passy into a gilded cage where his wife enjoyed every privilege—and every restriction.

I arrived at the party early. Although summer was over, the garden was still rich in color. The servants were as formal as British diplomats. The salon was charming with its Louis XV furniture and an exquisitely arranged cold buffet. A battery of champagne bottles aimed their golden tops from frosted silver buckets. In a corner framed by tall palms, an orchestra waited for the signal to start playing. The party would be intimate, very exclusive, and very fashionable, as was everything of Armando's.

20

Maruchi and Armando greeted me warmly. I was the only one in Paris who had witnessed their entire courtship, from the moment the seed of love was planted to the harvest of their present happiness. Maruchi looked radiant in a gown of rose tulle. She reminded me of a porcelain doll atop a Swiss music box.

At the first opportunity Armando whispered to me, "Do you think they'll come?" His impeccable evening dress, waved hair, and excited manner seemed more appropriate to a wedding than to a birthday.

"Of course," I replied. "One is not invited every day to such a charming party."

"It isn't just that. I am sure I impressed her very much. She will make him come. I can't imagine a woman like Yvette resigned to idling away her time with a dull chap like Duval, even for money."

"Ah! The expert huntsman is applying his vast technical knowledge to the case."

"Perhaps," he said smiling. "But I'm giving my prey the opportunity to see both the advantages and disadvantages, so that she may escape before the chase begins—if she wants to. She will see me in my house, with my wife, and I shall win her under the very nose of her lover."

"That shows equal doses of generosity and gallantry on your part." My caustic tone had the effect desired.

"Oh, come, my friend!" retorted Armando. "Your

puritanism is shocking. Wake up! This is Paris. In Buenos Aires I would have never invited a woman like Yvette to my home, but here nobody cares, nor is it considered a humiliation for my wife. Yvette is not a streetwalker. She's the Pompadour of today. A few centuries ago she would have been the power behind the throne. Anyway, you know what morals are today. We wouldn't even speak to a pickpocket, but we think nothing of consorting with a high-finance swindler. Besides, Maruchi does not know what Yvette is."

"Here is your prey. Good luck!" I interrupted him as Yvette's golden head appeared near the palms at the entrance of the salon.

Armando, suddenly nervous, pressed my arm as though he were going to the battlefront instead of going to greet a guest.

Yvette and Duval appeared delighted when they entered the sumptuous drawing room, and they greeted Maruchi with engaging discretion. When I observed Yvette's gracious manners and reserved poise, the fears I had entertained for Maruchi's sake vanished. A convent-bred girl could not have been more circumspect. After the first wave of whispers and sarcastic smiles, everyone accepted Yvette (for such is Paris), and a circle immediately formed around her, the women hoping to learn the secret of her fascination, the men attracted by her sensuality, which flowed from her like water from a fountain. Armando kept buzzing around her like a bee.

When the music began, I asked Maruchi to dance, but she had already promised the first dance. I saw her go off with Duval. Then I approached Yvette and asked her to dance. To my surprise she accepted, which seemed to please Armando, who was trying to drive away her other admirers.

Yvette and I danced in silence to the music of a melancholy Argentine tango. Her body in my arms was like a beautiful ivory and gold statue come to life.

"Your friend Monsieur Lesseur is a fascinating man," Yvette finally said.

"I am glad you think so. He admires you immensely."

"His wife is very lovely," she added, with that generosity beautiful women display toward other beautiful women when they are sure of their own superiority. "She has beauty and youth, which makes her twice as attractive. Monsieur Lesseur must be a very happy man."

"Your friend, Duval," I said provokingly, "seems to agree with you completely."

Benoît Duval and Maruchi were dancing nearby. Duval's awkwardness was set off by Maruchi's graceful movements, but he seemed unaware of the sad figure he cut, captivated as he was by the little Argentine beauty.

23

Yvette laughed. "Duval is a great connoisseur of feminine beauty."

"He proved that in your case," I remarked.

"Thank you, but I was not referring to myself. I'm happy to see him enjoying himself. There are no problems between Benoît and me. We understand each other perfectly. We know exactly what each one wants from the other. Of course, Benoît can be very jealous."

"He has good reason not to shut his eyes at night and to keep them wide open in the daytime. No man would want to stop looking at you or to leave you unwatched."

The dance ended and Armando immediately took Yvette away. A moment later they were whirling to the music of a waltz. Maruchi and I followed close behind.

"Lovely party," I said to Maruchi. "You have arranged everything exquisitely. Paris will remember it for a long time."

"Thank you, but Armando attended to even the smallest detail. I'm so glad you are here. It brings back the good times we had in Buenos Aires."

"Do you miss them, Maruchi?"

"Yes and no. I had more freedom there, strange as it may sound. My life in Buenos Aires was less organized, more casual. Here everything is planned to perfection, and sometimes I find it a little too perfect. It is nice, though, to be loved and cared for by a man like

Armando. He knows everything and does everything so well."

"Even choosing a wife."

"You and Armando must have gone to the same school. Tell me about Monsieur Duval and Mademoiselle Darland. What a strange couple. He is a very intelligent man, yet so helpless and diffident in a thousand little ways. He filled me with desire to protect him. She is one of the most beautiful women I have ever seen."

"She said the same thing about you."

"I don't believe it. Are they going to be married?"

"I don't know, Maruchi. I doubt it."

"Why?"

"I don't know. It seems they are just friends."

"It would be good for them to get married. Such a plain, awkward man could profit by the help of a beautiful woman, while she in turn would benefit from marrying such an intelligent and sincere man."

"You make it sound like a good idea, but, frankly, I cannot picture them married."

"Oh, pay no attention to me. In my country matchmaking is a national pastime."

When we finished dancing, a group of admirers claimed Maruchi. Armando seized the opportunity to lead me to a corner.

"Everything is all set," he said, his cheeks flushed with excitement.

25

"What, already!" I exclaimed, with a note of sarcasm.

"Do be serious! This woman excites me tremendously and I know that she is very much attracted to me. I'm sure that if it were not for Duval she would ask me to her apartment."

"Does Duval keep her locked up?"

"Of course not, but right now Duval is indispensable to her. She can't afford to do anything that would vex him."

"What do you intend to do next?"

"I don't know. I must find a way to see her alone. I must be careful. It would be a deadly blow to Maruchi if she were to find out. And it would be a financial catastrophe for Yvette if Duval found out. You see, my friend, this is going to be strictly an affair of love. There will be no financial obligations attached to it."

I looked at him incredulously. "Are you sure this is not some fantastic dream of yours?"

"Quite sure. She was most cautious, but she plainly implied that she is not altogether indifferent to love when she finds the right man."

"That *is* a miracle."

"And I did it all in my first talk with her. I dare say I haven't lost the old charm. All for love!"

"Aren't you somewhat stretching the meaning of the word?" I remarked ironically.

"We'll call it love just the same. We really *are* attracted to each other, you know."

"Congratulations. May you both be very happy."

The last thing I remember of the party is Duval looking for his coat while Armando was whispering to Yvette, his handsome dark face close to her golden hair.

Soon after the party, my work took me to the Riviera, and the pink laurel and the violet waters of the Mediterranean made me forget Armando's amorous chase.

It was midwinter when I returned to Paris. The rain drummed with long crystal sticks on the canvas awnings of the cafés. A few flower stalls, huddled together under the Rue de Rivoli arcade, were the only note of color in the gray city. In the glass-enclosed sidewalk cafés on the Boulevard des Italiens, the embers in the braziers glowed softly.

One evening, as I was leaving the Café Cardinal, I saw Yvette Darland dashing to the door ahead of me.

"Mademoiselle Darland!"

She stopped and turned. The full scarlet mouth smiled and her blue eyes sparkled. "What a lovely surprise!" she said. "I didn't see you inside."

"A great misfortune for me," I replied, wondering just where she could have sat to pass unnoticed.

"I had dinner with some friends," she said, pushing

up the collar of her green coat. She reminded me of a fairy in an Andersen tale wrapping herself in a huge banana leaf. "I interrupted dinner to keep another appointment," she added.

"I should be delighted to take you there."

She smoothed the folds of her coat a little too studiously, heralding the forthcoming lie. "I'm going home. I'm expecting some ladies from a benefit committee and I must not keep them waiting."

We got into a taxi and she gave the driver an address on the Avenue Montaigne. The streetlights, the cars, the scurrying pedestrians, all swished by, blurred in the enveloping mist of rain.

"How is Duval?" I asked to be polite.

"He's well. He's in Bordeaux this week, attending to some business. He'll be back tomorrow. I heard you were on the Riviera writing some articles."

"Yes. I'm flattered you know."

"Armando told me."

"Armando!"

"Yes. He told me you would return in a few days and that he would ask you to my anniversary party."

"Anniversary? Of a wedding?"

"Heavens, no! Two attempts at matrimony were enough. It's the anniversary of my last divorce, an occasion that provides me always with an excuse to throw a party. Of course, you're invited. Duval will be most happy to see you. The party will be held at La

28

Lueur Bleue, a delightful spot on the Left Bank. Armando and his wife are coming."

We said good-by, and I stood watching her skip gracefully over the rain puddles on the pavement and disappear into a small house adjoining the Hôtel Petit Georges. In my mind's eye, minutes later, I could still see her coat swirling around her beautiful long legs.

By the time I arrived at my club, I wanted very much to talk to Armando. A cheerful voice like a cascading stream of crystal water answered the telephone. It was Maruchi, and her warm reception made me feel like a long-lost friend.

"When did you get back? How have you been? How is the Riviera?" she asked all in one breath.

I laughed, thinking at the same time that there was a change in her voice, though I could not quite grasp what it was. "I got back a couple of days ago. Right now the Riviera is being swept and washed by the mistral and rain, getting ready, no doubt, for the next season. The only green to be seen is on the tables of the casino and the only blue is in the neon signs."

"Then we're just as well off here. I'm so happy in Paris. I'm having the most glorious time."

"This is the first time I've heard you say so, Maruchi."

"It's true. I was dreadfully homesick for a while. But Paris grows more fascinating every day. Besides, Armando has become a little more reasonable. He's so busy these days that he allows me to go out alone. I have visited a number of art galleries. The Salon d'Automne is magnificent and at the Indépendants there are several wonderful new artists. Armando is out tonight. Business. He has been busy every evening this week. That gave me the chance to go to the theater and call on friends."

"The process of converting you into a *Parisienne* is well under way, Maruchi."

"You're right. Now I understand why they say that everyone has two countries—their own and Paris."

I put down the receiver very much puzzled. Maruchi sounded positively exuberant. Yet what she told me, added to my conversation with Yvette, left little doubt about Armando's "business" engagements.

It was not quite eight o'clock the following morning when the doorbell woke me up. It was Armando. He embraced me effusively, as if I had just returned not from Nice but from the Gobi Desert. I gathered that he felt very pleased with himself.

"I'm so happy that I cannot sleep," he explained, when I expressed amazement at his being up so early. "I feel ten years younger. There is nothing like big-game hunting to rejuvenate a man. In fact I have the energy of ten men, energy for everything: business, my home, Yvette. . . ."

"So it has happened? *Consummatum est?*"

"Well, not exactly. This is a difficult and complicated situation. I wouldn't be bothered with it otherwise. It's like a game of chess. I must watch my opponent's moves as carefully as my own. We have to be damned careful. Duval is very jealous of her. I don't care two straws about him. But Yvette does. He spends a fortune on her."

"Have you ever been alone with her?"

"Yes, every Thursday evening at her home. Duval attends some meeting or other. But this week he's in Bordeaux, and I have been seeing her every evening. Unfortunately, he returns today."

"I'm surprised you have made so little progress then."

"My dear friend, Yvette is not an ordinary woman. Everything must be *comme il faut.* The right time, the right place—these things are important to her. Anyway," he concluded quietly, "she has refused so far."

"If you had said that first, you could have saved the rest. She has refused so far. That is a big reason." I laughed.

"Do try to understand. If Duval should suddenly walk in on us—we can't afford to take chances. But she loves me, really loves me."

"If you can get her to prove it, you will have made the greatest conquest in Paris."

"I will. Soon, believe me. Yvette is giving a party. She told you."

"What is it all about?"

"It will be a masquerade. Don't you see? Yvette and I can get away unnoticed. Please do me a big favor. Take Maruchi home the night of the party. I would trust no one else. You'll tell Maruchi I had to take a sick friend home."

"And I suppose Duval will stay behind dancing with himself."

"Yvette will tell Duval that she is not well and wishes to go home alone to rest."

"It seems very complicated to me."

"Of course. That's why it's exciting. That's the way Yvette planned it. Let her have her way, so long as I get mine."

In the bathroom mirror before which I was shaving, I could see Armando through the open door sprawled in an armchair. The blissful look on his face made me remark, "What bothers me is that you, Maruchi, Yvette—all of you seem to be blissfully happy. I fail to recall another love triangle in which everyone was happy. Maruchi positively beamed over the telephone, Yvette was radiant last night, and you —you're riding on a cloud."

"You forgot Duval. He won't have any reason to be happy."

"If he doesn't find out, I don't see why he shouldn't be happy also."

"I should be most surprised if Yvette does not leave him once she has tasted love with me."

"Armando, you should have been born a sultan with a fully packed harem. You derive a devilish joy from stealing other men's women."

"I can't help it. Taking a woman away from another man proves my superiority. You can't possibly imagine the joy it will afford me to step on a bug like Duval. You have seen him many times. Can you remember his face exactly?"

"Frankly, I can't even remember the color of his eyes."

"Can you remember anything about him, anything worthwhile he ever said?"

"He is undoubtedly a bloodless, spineless creature."

"Can you imagine how sick of him Yvette must be! That's why, despite his money, I'll take her away from him."

When Armando left, it was as though the maddening buzz of an electric fan had suddenly stopped. His excitement had been contagious, but now I felt uncomfortable. It was a wretched business. I did not like it, nor could I guess how it would end. For dull little Duval, Yvette's betrayal, with all Paris laughing about it, would be a blow below the belt.

On the night of the party, I met Armando and Maruchi at their home. Maruchi looked as if she had escaped from a Watteau painting. Her shepherdess costume of white satin was most appropriate to her guileless beauty, and her flowered bonnet was a perfect frame for her lovely face and dark curls. She carried a little basket of flowers and a small woolly white lamb. She looked so charmingly adolescent that I could not take my eyes off her.

"I have made a very interesting discovery," she said, as she rearranged before a mirror the tiny asplike curls on her forehead.

"What is it?" I asked, somewhat alarmed.

"Benoît Duval is Yvette Darland's lover."

She said it casually, as if she were discussing her dress.

"I'm sure," she continued, "that this is no news to you. I wish we women could keep each other's secrets the way you men keep yours. Even Armando has said nothing to me about it. I must be either very stupid or very naïve. I can't see what's going on under my very nose. I should have known that in Paris a woman like Yvette would make a profession of her beauty. Not that it matters a row of pins to me. I like her just the same. But it intrigues me that she should choose a man like Duval."

I was about to retort that certain women do not choose but are chosen, when Armando walked in. We left immediately for La Lueur Bleue.

At the restaurant, while Maruchi was greeting a

friend, Armando whispered to me, "I sent Yvette a corsage of black orchids fit for a queen."

"How clever of you!"

"There is nothing that type of woman likes better than to be treated like a lady."

Just then Yvette and Duval walked in. In his black domino, he resembled a huge beetle. Yvette was a daring but exquisite version of Venus. Her clinging gold lamé gown revealed one of her magnificent shoulders and boldly outlined her breasts and hips. Her thick blonde hair, braided and punctuated with tiny gold stars, spiraled upward into a miniature golden tower. Against her creamy skin the full scarlet mouth was a negation of austerity in life and an invitation to consuming passion. The black orchids writhed on her bosom.

The room reserved for the party was small and plainly decorated. Except for a generous number of champagne bottles, an abundant cold buffet, a small orchestra, Duval had taken no pains whatever to provide a suitable background for his lovely Venus. The air smelled sickeningly of perfume and flowers. The room was crowded. The men wore black dominos and black masks; the women wore all sorts of disguises: there were ballerinas and Columbines, Little Red Riding Hoods, *apaches,* American pinup girls.

The orchestra began to play with a great deal of discordance. I saw Armando dancing with Yvette.

Her hair would have betrayed her even if she had worn a mask over her entire face instead of the strip of white lace that barely covered her eyes.

Armando had warned me that he and Yvette would disappear at eleven o'clock. I was to look then for Maruchi, explain Armando's sudden departure, and offer to take her home whenever she wished.

The music played incessantly. Conversation was impossible. The guests seemed intent on dancing frantically and consuming as much champagne as was humanly possible. I was beginning to wish I could leave when suddenly I realized that Yvette's golden tower had disappeared. I looked at my watch. Eleven five. The orchestra was playing frenziedly. I was about to look for Maruchi when a domino whispered in my ear, "It's time." It was Armando. Wiping the perspiration off his forehead, he added, "Everything is fine. Yvette left a little while ago. Where is Maruchi?"

A Little Red Riding Hood interrupted us. "Is one of you Monsieur Lesseur?"

We hesitated. She giggled as though champagne bubbles were tickling her nose. "I only wish to return Madame Lesseur's compact. She loaned it to me a little while ago. I saw her go out afterward. She hasn't returned yet, and I'm leaving."

"Maruchi—Madame Lesseur went out?" repeated Armando, as though he had not heard right.

"Yes. I saw her through the window in the powder

room. She got into a taxi shortly after Mademoiselle Darland left."

The masks were only ornaments. Everyone knew everyone else.

"She must have gone out for a breath of air," Armando said to me. "For heaven's sake, please be on the lookout until she returns." He started to walk away but turned back. "What luck!" he said. "I don't have to sneak out after all. Now I can tell Duval that Maruchi is not well and that I'm taking her home. Come, let's find him."

It was not an easy task to find Duval. We stopped every masked domino of the same size as our host. The result was always negative. The guests, wild with champagne, bombarded us with confetti and the alcoholic fumes on their breath. The musicians beat their instruments as if they felt only hatred for them. To the various smells in the air was added the dust from the confetti. Half-suffocated and perspiring heavily, I promised myself I would leave as soon as possible, despite the Egyptian queen with whom I had been dancing all evening.

Half an hour later we came to the conclusion that Benoît Duval had also disappeared. Armando, his face congested, looked at me with worried bloodshot eyes.

"I don't understand it. Where can he be? Something has gone wrong. Do you thing he became suspicious and followed Yvette? But how could he have found out?" His voice was strained and perspiration ran freely down his face. "We must find out what happened. Please don't leave me now. We'll go to my house first. I'll wait for you in the taxi while you go in. If you don't come out in five minutes, I'll know Maruchi is home. I shall then telephone Yvette to make sure she's alone."

It was pouring when we climbed into the taxi. The windows were closed and I felt as though I were imprisoned inside a metal drum on which someone was beating a wild tattoo. Armando sat on the edge of the seat, his mask pushed high on his forehead. His hair, carefully waved early in the evening, hung limp.

"I don't understand," he repeated, cracking his knuckles. "We planned everything so carefully. What could have gone wrong at the last minute? I don't understand."

The cab stopped before Armando's house. I jumped out, and wading through the bubbling puddles with the driving rain pelting my face, I crossed the garden and reached the door of the house. Violet, the maid, answered the doorbell.

"Violet, has Madame Lesseur come home from the party?"

"Yes, sir, she came home and went away again."

"Went away! Where to?"

"She didn't say, sir, but she took two suitcases with her."

"Two suitcases? Are you sure?"

"Yes, sir. She said should anyone inquire where she had gone, to tell him to ask Mademoiselle Darland."

"Mademoiselle Darland!" I repeated incredulously. "Are you sure?"

*"Par le bon Dieu,* monsieur. That was the message and not one word have I added."

I crossed the garden in three jumps, leaped into the taxi, and collapsed next to Armando. He seized my arm anxiously.

"She's not there, I know. Where is she? Where are we going?"

His clothes and hair disheveled, his face distorted by anxiety, his composure gone, no longer the self-assured man of the world, he looked ridiculous, even grotesque. I repeated what the maid had said. Burying his head in his hands, he moaned, "What I feared has happened. She found out. She has left me. My Maruchi! I have broken her heart. She might do something desperate. My Maruchi! She adored me and now I have broken her heart. Heaven help me!" And he looked like a little boy who has lost a toy.

I gave the driver Yvette's address. All the way there, Armando complained incessantly, denying everything, blaming Duval, blaming everyone but himself.

We ran up the stairs to Yvette's apartment. Feverishly Armando rang the bell. A dainty little maid, heavily perfumed, opened the door.

"Madame is expecting you," she announced before Armando had time to speak. We crossed the small rose-colored hall and entered a dimly lit drawing room, warm, intimate, fragrant. There were brocaded love-seats, deep, cushioned satin armchairs, a Chinese desk, fine ormolu-encrusted tables, tall lamps with colored silk shades, crystal vases containing anemones, and an artificial fireplace whose electric flames were reflected on the glass of some large photographs nearby. The black orchids she had worn at the party were on the mantel, where they drooped like dead spiders. On a cocktail table there were some glasses and a huge silver bucket with two bottles of champagne. Yvette, in a red silk dressing gown with a plunging neckline, her hair swept back and down over her shoulders, was reclining on a sofa, smoking a cigarette. The tip of her cigarette glowed like a scarlet eye, inquisitive and penetrating.

Armando rushed over to her. "Yvette, what happened?"

She pointed to a sofa haughtily, as if she were setting up a tribunal for us to be tried. She then poured three glasses of champagne and offered us ours. I took mine out of courtesy; Armando, his out of habit.

"What I am about to tell you," she said, "demands a lot of champagne. Come, come, don't stand there like tin soldiers. Sit down. Drink a toast with me."

"A toast?" asked Armando. "To what?"

"To the unexpected," she answered, smiling.

"Yvette," Armando implored, "I can bear this no longer. Do you know that Maruchi went home and then left? She said *you* would know where she was going."

"She exaggerated, Armando. I have no idea where she is. All I know is that she did not go alone."

"With whom did she go?" Armando cried.

"Benoît Duval."

Armando jumped to his feet. "Impossible!" His face had turned so red that it looked like a scarlet mask under the black mask still perched on his forehead.

"Why impossible, my dear Armando?"

"That absurd little man? That clumsy, scrawny little fool? Besides, they hardly know each other."

"How little you know!"

"I don't understand. And how come you are taking it so calmly? After all, you have been defeated as much as I have. And you are in a worse position than I am." Armando sat down again.

"I have not been deceived and my position is quite intact. The whole affair has not surprised me in the least."

"What do you mean?"

"I knew it was going to happen."

I started to get up, but she stopped me with a wave of her hand. "Please don't go. Armando is very upset and I would rather have a friend in the room, at least until Armando calms down."

"Yvette," Armando implored, knocking over his champagne glass, "I beg of you, explain all this."

"There is very little to explain, Armando. Your wife and Benoît Duval love each other. They have gone away, They'll be married as soon as you give her a divorce."

"That's impossible!"

"Nothing is impossible to lovers."

"Lovers? My wife and Duval? Nonsense!"

"You could almost call them lovers. Right now they're trying to cross the French border by car, train, or plane."

Yvette, I'm going mad!" Armando squirmed in his chair. "What is this diabolical conspiracy?"

"Calm yourself, my dear. It is not so terrible. This happens in Paris every minute, in France every hour, in the rest of the world every day."

"But not to me. How could that monstrous little creature—"

"You were going to do the same to him," Yvette interrupted him.

"It is not the same thing to deprive a man of his—"

42

She did not let him finish. Thrusting a box of candy under his nose, she said coldly, "Have a bonbon."

"Yvette, Maruchi has deceived me, Duval has deceived me, you have deceived me."

She took a dainty bite from a chocolate and leaned back on the sofa. "It was very easy. I'm dreadfully disappointed. Duval thought that you would not be able to resist the temptation of making me your mistress. He was right. He knew that you went to Maxim's every Thursday. He arranged for us to meet. And, of course, you decided to add one more to your interminable list of conquests."

"Yvette, I fell in love with you the moment I saw you."

"Armando, I took my doctorate in love at the Sorbonne of life. For you I was but another trophy to be added to your collection. Frankly, the idea of fooling an expert lover like you amused me tremendously, perhaps because I have been fooled by men like you in the past."

"I'm appalled that you lent yourself to such an unspeakable trick," he exploded, tasting the dregs of his humiliation.

"Duval once was a very close friend of mine, and a very generous one," said Yvette coldly. "I am only too happy to help him now."

"Do you mean that that party tonight, the party we had arranged to fool Duval, was really planned by him so that he could run off with my wife? That crawling worm—"

"It seems that women don't agree with you," Yvette interrupted him.

"But he hardly knew me. Why should he want to ruin my home?"

Stretching her arms across the back of the sofa, Yvette resembled a great crimson butterfly spreading its wings. "He had nothing against you," she said in a bored voice. "Duval saw your wife at the opera one evening and he fell in love with her instantly."

"I have always treated you like a lady, Yvette."

"That was a psychological mistake. Duval was clever enough to treat your wife, a perfect lady, like a woman. He did not hesitate to speak of love to her the very first day he met. You know now how successful he was."

"How dared he!"

"You asked us to your home to make fun of him. Duval went because he was in love with your wife. He planned it cleverly. He got you out of the way with a decoy and he then proceeded to offer your wife something you had never given her—a simple, sincere love. Duval is no fool. He knows women are attracted to a helpless man. Duval knows how to look helpless with excellent results. How tired Maruchi must have been of your stupid vanity, your colossal conceit, your boring perfection! Your superiority must have bored her to tears. It was inevitable that she should be attracted to a gentle, unassuming, considerate man like Duval. They make an ideal couple. Don't you agree? The best thing you can do now is to grant her a divorce."

"Yvette, you are a deceitful woman!"

"And you are a fool!" she retorted angrily. "I feel sorry for you. Your wife discarded you for a man like Duval. Why, Armando, why? Did he perhaps offer Maruchi something more than your Savile Row clothes, your waved hair, and your cloying words? Why don't you study the technique of the man you call a worm? You might learn a thing or two about a woman's heart."

"I suppose he's laughing at me now," he muttered, ignoring her words.

"You're wrong," she said, exasperated. "Duval had no desire to make fun of you. He was very much in love with your wife and he did everything in his power to win her love."

"Including making use of you to estrange me from my wife. I dare say she won't think so much of your precious Duval when she finds that out."

"How little you know women, after all! Maruchi thought Duval and I were lovers. Don't you see? The easiest way for a man to win a woman is to make her think she is taking him away from a beautiful and dangerous rival. Besides, Duval let Maruchi think

45

that he was the helpless victim of a calculating but irresistible seductress. She really believed that she was rescuing a lonely, unprotected soul. And when she found out—I don't know how—that you were chasing me, that was the final blow. You were running after me and Duval was leaving me to run after her. What would any woman do?"

It was after four o'clock when we left Yvette still reclining on the sofa, her sensuous lips parted in the contented smile of a woman who has traveled the sea of love many times.

Outside, the rain had stopped. It was cold, but we were grateful for the fresh air. Dawn, haggard and gray, was creeping through the wet pale sky. Paris, a drowsy silver Venus, was waking up to a new day.

As we stopped at the kiosk near my apartment, I asked Armando, "And now what, Armando?"

He looked at me with eyes still dazed, still unbelieving. "What? I don't know. Let things take their course. . . . Give Maruchi her freedom. . . . I still have friends. Who knows? Yvette is an understanding woman. Tomorrow I shall send her the finest yellow roses in Paris to show her that I bear her no resentment."

A truck driving by dropped a bundle of papers at my feet. Michel, the newsboy, pulled out a copy of the morning edition and handed it to me, smiling, "*Bonjour,* monsieur. Here we go, all over again."

## THE PAGODAS

THE MAIN THING IN LIFE," said Valderin, munching on the olive from his third Martini, "is to have lots of pagodas."

"Pagodas?" I asked indifferently, wondering who was going to pay the check.

"Yes, pagodas," Valderin repeated underlining the word with a sharp nod of his prematurely bald head. Turning around, he called out, "Waiter, two more Martinis, and make them drier," and to me, "Pagodas, old friend, lots of pagodas. It cost me no trifling amount of money and a good deal of pain to discover the Great Truth. But I am not selfish. I shall reveal it to you now, and it will cost you absolutely nothing."

He gulped down half of his fourth Martini and with long scrawny fingers picked out the olive. Spinning it between his fingers as though it were a world globe, he continued: "It all started one Friday evening last December. I woke up in that wretched furnished room I call home with a colossal hangover and exactly two dollars to my name. Yet the day before had been payday. I remembered vaguely that the previous night I had met a friend and his girl at a bar on Third Avenue. After the devil knows how many Martinis and an outrageously expensive dinner, they deposited me at my door hardly able to resist the law of gravity and with a gnawing suspicion that my charming friends had had a great deal of fun at my expense and were going on with the party by themselves.

"It was useless, however, to fret over the past. The present loomed in my mind in all its devastating tragedy. To be alone in New York with only two dollars and a whole week ahead before you can replenish your pocket is depressing enough, but when this happens on your day off, it is a catastrophe. I didn't even have enough money for a quiet little dinner and a movie to keep me occupied until the next day, when I could borrow a few dollars from one of my fellow workers at the World Press. You know," he intercalated, examining with great care the now naked remains of the olive, "I have discovered that married men with children are the only people who have money before and after payday." He dipped the olive pit in the remains of his Martini and put it back in his mouth.

"Brooding about the sad state of my affairs," he continued, "I washed and shaved and, sadly convinced that the only untangled thing in my life at that moment was my hair, I went out, my head still clouded, despite the numerous dousings with cold water, in a sickening mass of mist. I felt as though I were floating in a strange greenish world.

"It was seven o'clock in the evening. At five o'clock that morning I had felt I was dying. I remained in a complete stupor until noon. I slept until three in the afternoon and was quasi-paralyzed until six. That was the sad inventory of my life. Perhaps, I said to myself, some scrambled eggs and bacon will pacify my troubled stomach. To avoid the unfriendly look that ordering breakfast at seven in the evening invariably begets in a restaurant, I went to a grill nearby where the waitresses, having witnessed all sorts of strange things, are completely indifferent to everything.

"The grill was shrouded in a sickly purplish light. Somewhere in a jukebox Frank Sinatra was pleading for a remedy for pernicious anemia. At the bar sat two or three gloomy figures, their hands embracing glasses, their eyes riveted on the rows of bottles lining the wall opposite the bar.

"I sat at a small table in a corner, as far as possible from the jukebox, and ordered breakfast. I lived to regret it. The pungent wobbling pyramid of eggs and bacon the waitress set under my nose a few minutes later made my stomach skip and jump. I was about to dash out when someone yelled my name close to my ear. My poor head almost split in two. Through a bilious mist I watched the gross body of our friend Ayllen flop down on the seat opposite me.

" 'What are you doing here?' he asked.

" 'Can't you see? I'm waiting for a subway,' I growled, pointing to the monolith of bacon and eggs.

" 'That joke is so antiquated,' he said scornfully.

" 'Your question was not very bright either.'

"Ayllen rewarded me with a smile as vast and empty as a museum at night. 'You certainly are in a bad mood. And you look terrible,' said he.

" 'So my mirror tells me.'

" 'In fact, you look damned awful. You must have had a wonderful time last night.'

" 'Ayllen,' I interrupted him, 'I am dying, I am flat broke, and I have no desire to listen to your witty remarks. The place is not big enough for both of us. Good-by!'

"And he said, 'Valderin, I'm going to give you some

priceless advice. Now don't get excited! Let's have
dinner or breakfast or whatever in heaven's name you
are having. I'll pay, so the least you can do is listen to
me.'

"Somewhat mollified, I raised the white flag. Unfortunately, Ayllen had worked all day and was fresh
as a daisy—there is nothing more exhausting than one
of my *rest* days—and he wanted to eat and talk. I had
to sit and watch him devour one of those meals that
could kill a man in my condition—from soup to nuts,
including pork chops with fried potatoes! Worse still,
I had to listen to him.

" 'The trouble with you,' he began, guzzling down
the clam chowder, 'is that you have no imagination.
Therefore you must go on binges. Look at me! I never
go on binges, yet I have one roaring good time after
another. You see, I know how to ferret out New York's
sweet mysteries.'

" 'You! You know New York!'

" 'Better than anybody else.'

" 'I'll laugh for three hours when my head stops
aching.'

" 'Go ahead, laugh yourself sick. I'm telling you the
truth. There are two New Yorks, just as there are two
Hong Kongs, two Parises, two Londons. One is the
city everyone sees and knows; the other is the city I
alone see and know.'

"The odious smell of the pork chops made my stomach do a somersault and Ayllen's subtle conversation made my head spin.

" 'Ayllen, let's postpone the philosophizing until the New Year,' I begged.

" 'This isn't philosophizing, it's the very secret of happiness. I was a very unhappy man,' he went on, attacking the pork chops, 'in fact, wretchedly unhappy. Not any more. Like you, I'm a frustrated newspaperman. Like you, I make very little money. But I have a few free hours at night to stroll around New York. I want nothing more. There was a time when those few hours drove me crazy. A poet once called it "the five o'clock feeling," when you leave the office and there is no place to go, no one waiting for you. Today I'm free and happy. You know why? I have my pagodas.'

" 'Pagodas?' I echoed indifferently.

" 'Pagodas,' he repeated emphatically. 'Don't try to find a connection between the real meaning of the word and *my* meaning. A pagoda, according to the dictionary, is a temple somewhere in the Orient. But to me it's a secret, mysterious place, a Shangri-La that only I know and where only I find pleasure.'

" 'There is no such place in New York,' I sneered. 'Here we all do the same things, say the same things, eat the same things, and even have to listen to the same stupid things.'

"Ayllen ignored my sarcastic remark. 'Remember

Marcel Proust's story about the two faces of love? One man considered Helen a prostitute, another man saw her as a romantic girl and fell madly in love with her, yet she was the same woman. It is Einstein's theory of relativity applied to life—'

" 'Ayllen,' I interrupted him gently, 'here is your dessert. Concentrate on it, and stop talking before you get indigestion!'

"Brandishing a piece of cheese on his fork, he continued, quite unperturbed, 'It's so very simple. I see a face of the city that the other nine million people don't see. Briefly, my theory is that there is beauty in all things if one knows how to look for it. Like the Biblical story about the dead dog whose beautiful teeth were shining in the sun— Don't get up! I'll come to the point. God, how impatient you are! Don't forget that I'm paying the check. As I was saying, my secret is that I discover beauty everywhere in New York, no matter how sordid the place may be. For instance, this is a dismal place—but look at those rows of bottles on the bar. They glow like sacred liquids on a crystal altar. And look at that artificial orchid between two bottles of port on top of the cash register. The light shining through the bottles crowns the petals with a myriad of sparkling rubies. I sit here. I look at them. I dream.

" 'Take, for instance, Pennsylvania Station. Is there a more prosaic place in the world? Yet it is one of my favorite pagodas. There is a certain corner enclosed by glass on the lower level, near the entrance to the Long Island Railroad, which is deliciously cool in summer and very cozy in winter. Many times I sit there like a fish in a heavenly aquarium and, beer in hand, I watch the commuters come and go. Those on their way home scuttle by like frantic puppets, their faces taut with fear and worry. Will they miss their train and get home late? Will the wife notice the drink, or two, indulged in on their way from the office and start nagging again? Those arriving are in no less of a hurry. Their families safely tucked in at home, there is the gleam of adventure in their eyes, and their nostrils quiver with anticipation. They all scamper by like the actors in those old movies. And I just sit there, like a little god, watching them. While the outgoing ones are already tasting the bitterness of approaching family squabbles and the incoming ones have parched throats, I just sit there savoring the sweet foam of my beer. Do you begin to see the beauty of the pagodas?'

"The truth is that despite my agonizing condition Ayllen had awakened my interest, and by the time he had finished a second order of apple pie I had agreed to go on a tour of his pagodas.

"It was an amazing experience. As he showed me around his pagodas, he unveiled before my astonished eyes a New York that was new and strange and full of marvels, he veritably opened doors to vistas vast and uncharted, such as one envisions only in his wildest dreams.

"Let me explain. Every day after work Ayllen drinks a few beers at a little bar on Lexington Avenue because the waitress walks like Sophia Loren. He frequents a restaurant on Eighth Avenue because the dirty windows, the dense cigarette smoke, a wailing accordion, and a barmaid who looks like a female Jean Gabin all make him feel that he is in one of those *bistros* in a French movie where the girl usually gets herself knifed in the last scene. A walk along the East River takes Ayllen on a journey not on one but on two magic carpets upon which a jeweler has spilled his most brilliant gems: the sky above studded with stars and the river below glowing with the lights from buildings and boats. The bus he rides to work is his morning pagoda, because a whole string of young ladies with improbable but divine anatomies smile down at him from multicolored cardboards. He takes his shirts to a Chinese laundry because the smell of oriental cologne in the air transports him for a few minutes each week down the Yangtze River among sampans and junks; he passes misty blue mountains and houses like baskets, from which female heads peer out like tea roses. He patronizes a certain movie house only because the blonde cashier in her glass cage is always humming. He said that she is a perfumed canary singing exclusively to him!

"These are but a few of his pagodas. There are cafeterias where the smell of synthetic food is indistinguishable from the smell of agglomerated humanity, subways so packed that if a sardine saw them it would prefer the comparative spaciousness of a tin can, drugstores where people eat lined up in rows like cattle at a manger—places we all know only too well and can never detest too much, but Ayllen has turned them into pagodas. Until one night. I remember I ran into Ayllen at the usual bar.

" 'Ayllen,' I said, 'you are a great man.'

"He looked at me suspiciously. 'You want money.'

" 'I got paid today.'

" 'Then I don't understand.'

" 'You have convinced me. In fact, you've changed my life. At first I didn't believe in your pagodas, but now I have a pagoda. I don't know what I would do without it. I'm convinced that there are only two kinds of people, those who have pagodas and those who don't.'

"He looked bewildered; then he broke into loud laughter. 'I knew you would like the idea. You see, we all have complexes. The pagodas are our escape valves. You might call them a psychological catharsis. Everybody has pagodas, the banker in his clubs, the housewife at bridge parties, the laborer in bars. What these people really want is not bridge or whisky or conversation. What they really want is a pagoda. Four people can go to the same place and each one will have a different pagoda—'

" 'Stop,' I interrupted him. 'You don't have to convince me any further. I tell you I have a pagoda.'

" '*You* have a pagoda?'

" '*I* have a pagoda.'

" 'Let's go and see it.'

" 'We'll have dinner there,' I said, as we went out into the cold night.

"We walked a few blocks and then I stopped. 'In here,' I said.

"He looked at me, puzzled. 'Are you sure you want to go in here?'

" 'Positive. This is my pagoda.'

" 'All right,' he said sourly.

"The Sea Pilot is a seafood restaurant on Third Avenue. It has too many glaring lights and too many of the wrong people, the drinks have too much soda and too little whisky, and the smell of fish is so thick you can almost touch it. In other words, it's a horrible place.

"We sat at a table in a corner of the enormous room. More than a hundred people were struggling with shells and bones. The noise was infernal. The smell of beer and fish was sickening, and the blazing ceiling lights bored holes in our skulls. A perspiring, sour-looking waitress handed us a menu as gloomily as if she were offering condolences. We ordered and waited. Ayllen was sulky and silent. I was happy.

"When dessert was served, Ayllen suddenly snapped, 'Why in hell did you bring me here?'

" 'Did you like the food?'

" 'I hated it!'

" 'So did I.'

" 'Well, then?'

" 'This is my pagoda.'

' 'This is a hideous place—too many people, too many lights, it stinks and it's noisy.'

" 'But it is my pagoda. See that waitress?' I nodded toward a blonde waitress dressed in green, who was serving a dish of crabs in tomato sauce to a big fat man two tables away. Ayllen glared at me.

" 'I see her.'

" 'She has turned this place into a pagoda.'

" 'Are you serious?'

" 'More serious than a Russian diplomat.'

" 'I can't believe it!' he cried angrily.

" 'Why not? That waitress is as slender as a stalk of wheat and just as blonde, a little advanced in years perhaps, certainly over thirty-five, but I like them that way—women, like grapes, are sweeter when fall comes —and her face has all the melancholy of a lonely princess waiting for her prince to—' Ayllen threw his napkin on the table.

" 'You moron!' he cried.

" 'What?'

" 'I said, Moron, with a capital M. This sad princess of yours is the woman I divorced a year ago. She is a witch and a shrew. I had to invent the pagodas to forget her.' And he rushed out.

"Well, that's the story of the pagodas," concluded Valderin. "But don't think that Ayllen discouraged me. I'm going to dine now at the Blue Canteen, my new pagoda. There is a waitress there—she looks just like Kim Novak."

And draining the last drops of his Martini, he walked out, leaving me the check.

I walked up to the cashier. Eyes the color of violets, skin as white as alabaster, lips like ripe strawberries. She was shy, gentle, like a deer in the forest. I paid the check and went out. I too had found a pagoda.

# AT NIGHT THE SUN SHINES

Doctor," said the man, "I'm afraid I'm losing my mind."

My eyes wandered from the man's tortured face to his long thin fingers twitching nervously in the circle of light cast by the lamp on my desk.

"What would you think," he continued in an anquished voice, "if I told you that I owe my fame and fortune to a woman with whom I'm madly in love, yet I'm afraid she exists only in my imagination?

"You probably know my name. Millions of people do. Leslie Normand. You must have heard my blues 'At Night the Sun Shines.' The biggest hit in the last fifty years. Millions of recordings of it have been sold, a Broadway musical play is based on its lyrics and score, and a film will be released soon. Overnight I hit the jackpot; I became rich and famous. But nobody knows that it is not my song. That is to say, I composed it, but it was a woman who gave it body and soul and placed it, alive and vibrating, in my hands. I must find that woman, Doctor. But first, before I continue this mad search, I must make sure that I am not insane.

"It all began one Sunday last August. New Yorkers sweltered under a scorching sun. The heat had increased to the point of desperation the feeling of depression that had been heavy upon me all summer. I, Leslie Normand, forty years old, created dreams nobody wanted. For twenty years I had been hammering out sweet little songs on the piano, with foolish sentimental lyrics about love and suffering, the moon, the stars, God knows what! Songs into which I poured all my dreams and hopes, only to see them tossed aside by some fat, bald agent with a cigar stuck between his rotting yellowed teeth.

"Hot, tired, and lonely, I decided to go to Jones Beach. I joined the half-naked mass of humanity sprawled on the sand. The sun was a weight pressing down on my body, sinking into the burning skin. A

61

half-hour later, oppressed by the masses of sweating flesh all around me, I went down to the water and swam out as far as I could. When the metallic cold of the ocean had shaken me out of my stupor, I just floated. It was then that I saw the girl, her wet face beneath her blue bathing cap glistening under the sun, her eyes half-closed, her lips a crimson line.

"We were alone in the rippling blue waters, about a hundred yards from the beach. She glided by a few feet from me, her face serene; her body in a blue bathing suit was one more serpentine ripple in the blue sea. I saw a blue stone sparkling on her right hand. And then she was gone.

"I swam back to the beach and lay down on the sand close to the water. And as soon as I closed my eyes, the obsession returned and swallowed me up.

"Doctor, you don't know what torment there is in creating music. I have no talent other than composing, and even then I write only what highbrows contemptuously call 'popular music.' My whole world revolves around what to me is the greatest music of all—the blues. Perhaps my childhood in Chicago is responsible. Every night I wandered through the alleys in the Loop, peering through the windows into bars and cafés, and I would stand still until the early hours of the morning under the glaring lights of the dance halls, listening to the piercing music, my young heart filled with an anguish I could not understand. Later, sleeping on my cot, I would hear the music in my dreams.

"I was only a boy when I composed my first song, 'Dead Child Blues.' This was followed by 'Windy City Blues,' in which I tried in vain to capture the heart-rending sordidness of Chicago's slums: the flickering lights beckoning in the night, the shadowy streets where the hungry and the lonely lurk, dim bars where eyes stare vacantly through thick cigarette smoke, lovers in dark corners trying to keep warm with their love.

"I'm not trying to tell you the whole story of my life, but what I have said may help to explain how the obsession started. I tried to capture the obsession in my song 'At Night the Sun Shines.' Great cities like New York are cemeteries where people are buried alive under the weight of many a torturing fear: fear of the present and the future, fear of reality, of losing their jobs and all they possess, of love and their inability to love, of sickness, loneliness, starvation—in short, fear of life. Every morning these living corpses are wound up like mechanical toys and they go forth into subways and buses and then into offices and factories, and they push and rush and fret and worry and bicker and quarrel until, the day over, they return to the tomb whence they started. And they go to bed with the burden of their fears for a blanket. The following morning they start all over again.

"But there are those who are liberated when night

falls. They have discovered poetry in the great city. For them the traffic lights are rubies and emeralds; they seek the reflection of the moon in Central Park Lake, not in the neon orgy of Times Square; they roam the streets, wondering about the people behind lighted windows and making up their own stories; they press their nose against the glass panes of bars and cafés trying to guess what mysteries lie within the walls beyond; they pick up a fallen leaf in October and dream. They go through life with an insatiable curiosity and a romantic imagination that fill their hearts with the sound of music.

"It was for these people that I wrote my last blues. No one could possibly guess the months I spent trying to put down on paper the plaintive, passionate music that I could feel swelling and surging inside my head. But like a live fish, it kept slipping through my fingers.

"Well or badly, a writer can put down what he feels. This is not so with a composer. Either one writes down the music one feels or one writes nothing. Week after week I pounded the piano, five, six, eight hours every night, but the fragments of music were like the pieces of a puzzle that would not fit together. The music welled and swelled inside me, whole and complete, yet what my fingers beat out on the keys was all broken up, discordant, disconnected. I would play on and on only to realize in the end that it was all a mere fragment of my blues. Night after night all summer long, when I didn't pound the piano, I hummed the haunting melody till perspiration rolled down my face, dropping on the keys. Through my open window I could see the lighted windows of the building across the street. Like restless eyes that could not reconcile themselves to sleep, they remained on all through the night, incessantly taunting me, mocking me. Desperately I would continue scribbling on my music sheets, but my hands failed to capture even one measure of the great treasure of harmonies within me. A thousand fragments of the musical garment had to be knitted together. An emperor's cloak had to be made out of beggars' rags.

"On the beach that Sunday in August, my mind was to have no rest. As soon as I closed my eyes, the haunting melody possessed me still once more. Suddenly something flared up within me. At first it was like a tiny hole of light in a thick curtain. Then, as if someone had placed his fingers in the hole and ripped it open, a torrent of light poured in. Very softly I could hear the melody of my blues, flowing, continuous, complete, exactly as I had felt it for months, all the scattered links joined, all the threads of confused colors woven into a harmonious musical tapestry. Not daring to move, afraid of frightening the voice that was singing inside me, with bated breath I listened. Slowly it became clearer and clearer, more and more as I had dreamed it. Cautiously I opened my eyes. The melody went right on! It was as though someone were singing it right beside me. And it was true! Someone behind me was humming my blues, the blues I had not yet composed.

"Even before I turned my head I knew who it was that was singing. She was leaning back, her face lifted to the sun, eyes closed, hands buried in the sand, knees drawn up. The blue cap was lying on the sand. An aquamarine suddenly sparkled on her sandy hand. I stared at her stupefied. She slowly opened her eyes and leaned forward until her face was close to mine. Her eyes were incredibly blue.

"I stammered, 'The blues you were humming . . .'

"She looked away, her eyes reflecting drifting white clouds.

" 'They're very sad,' she whispered. 'They're the dreams of those who dream awake at night.'

"Despite the heat there was a cold sweat on my forehead. I said, 'It's a strange song. I've never heard it—complete.'

" 'No one has ever heard the entire song. It's a dream, and dreams are mysteries of which we get but fleeting glimpses. It's a melody that has no direction, like a bee endlessly zigzagging in the sunlight.'

"She was putting into words exactly what I had felt and lived through during those long summer months of work. My elusive melody was like the humming flight of the bee with its fantastic spirals and spinnings in the blue.

66

"As though talking to herself, she continued, 'And yet, the flight of the bee has a goal which only the bee knows. Its capricious spinnings are actually invisible roads leading to the honey.'

"She stood up suddenly. Her frail, long body was still that of an adolescent. I also stood up and handed her the blue bathing cap. She smiled and walked away. I quickly joined her and silently we walked toward the wooden steps leading to the bathhouses.

"Utterly bewildered, I finally asked her, 'Do you like blues?'

"'I don't know,' she answered. 'I don't have time to listen to music. I have very little time for anything. I'm constantly busy, night and day.'

"I asked her what kept her so absorbed all the time. 'Dreaming,' she replied. She said it very seriously and she looked strangely pathetic.

"We reached the entrance to the bathhouses. For the first time since we started talking I realized that we were surrounded by a bustling multitude. I smelled oily lotions on burned shoulders and tasted salt on my lips. She nodded at me and turned to enter the women's bathhouse.

"'Wait, please!' I begged her. 'We can't separate like this. I would like to see you again.'

"Wiping the last drops of water off her face, she asked, 'What is it you want?'

"I insisted that I must talk to her, but she said, 'Not

today. It has been too much already. It's enough for today.' She seemed to be talking to herself. She continued, 'But if you really want to see me again, I'll be here, at this door, next Sunday at noon. Good-by.'

"Before I could say anything further she disappeared through the door. I stood there for a moment, stunned, confused. Then I ran to my locker, quickly got dressed, and ran to the exit of the women's bathhouse. I sat down on a bench opposite the door and waited. Hours passed and I saw many women go in and out. In vain I searched for her face. Not until closing time did I admit to myself that she was gone.

"I returned to Manhattan in a state of fierce agitation. I had given up trying to find an explanation for what had happened, but I cursed myself a thousand times for not having asked her how and where she had heard my song. I tried to tell myself that I should at least rejoice over the fantastic miracle. But as I was about to open the door of my apartment, it came to me suddenly that the girl could not have heard my blues anywhere for the simple reason that I had not finished composing them!

"I sat down at the piano. Thanks to the girl with the blue eyes, I now had my complete melody. I touched the keys softly, like a father caressing the head of his newborn child. I feared that the sound of the piano would drive away the melody in my head. Once more I played and hastily scribbled notes on paper. I struggled for hours. When I finally looked up from my work, the lights across the street seemed to mock me. I had been hammering at the keys like a blacksmith, but I had scarcely written down the beginning of the melody. I had thought that I could run through the whole song that night, but I was stuck after the first few bars.

"The week dragged. I tried again and again to give body to the ghost of my blues, but my desperate attempts were in vain. The following Sunday was a bleak day. At nine o'clock I was already at Jones Beach, sure that it all had been a dream. A clock somewhere was striking noon when she appeared, clad in a blue dress with a dark-red belt, her light-brown hair, brushed straight back, hanging below her shoulders. She looked even younger than in her bathing suit. She carried nothing, and I guessed that she thought it was too cool to swim. Slowly we went along the walk toward the garden.

" 'My name is Leslie Normand,' I said after a few steps. 'Please forgive me for not telling you last Sunday. I was so stunned I must have seemed very stupid to you.'

" 'It doesn't matter. Names don't mean anything. They can be beautiful or ugly, important or silly, according to the people they belong to. We really should never hear a person's name until we know him well.'

"Just the same, I asked her name. She shrugged her

shoulders. 'Call me Anabelle, a poetic name, although no one has written verses to me.'

"We sat on the bench near great clumps of begonias. I couldn't cross the barrier that seemed to stand between the strange girl and myself. There was a disturbed look in her eyes that contrasted with the serenity of her face.

"I began to say that there was something I wished to ask her, but she interrupted me. 'You don't have to ask. You'd like to hear me sing again. I knew you wanted to see me because of the song.'

" 'Anabelle, how—'

"And again she interrupted me. 'Dreams are not personal property. When a dream goes forth into the world in the form of a story, a movie, a song, it becomes millions of little flames burning everywhere, kindled by that first fire. But a dream can also be shared even before it takes form. It's a beautiful song. It will make many people dream.'

"Closing her eyes, she began to hum my blues. I listened as in a trance, wondering whether it was my song or hers. There was a new depth in the music that I hadn't noticed before. I closed my eyes and my hand found hers. Waves of nostalgia swirled in my head: pale faces, candlelight, paths quivering with fall leaves, carriages silently rolling down streets gleaming with rain. When Anabelle stopped, the music went on and on. I knew then that it would never leave me again.

"We returned to the city together, talking very little. We walked along the Hudson on Riverside Drive, had dinner by candlelight in the Village, danced to soft music. She smiled when we toasted each other with champagne. Later we strolled through the deserted streets of the Village. It rained, but we didn't care. And then she said she had to leave and that I was not to go with her.

"I pleaded that I could not let her go alone at that hour, that I would take her home, that I had to see her again the following day. She pushed me away gently, and her eyes again had the strange, disturbed look.

"'You can't come with me,' she said firmly. 'You have your song. Now you must let me go.'

"I insisted that the song meant nothing to me, that I wanted to see her again, that it was only the beginning for us. Sadly she replied, 'This is the beginning for you. For me—I don't know.'

"'But this is all so strange. You have never told me how you knew my song.'

"She said she didn't know the answer to that.

"'It doesn't matter, nothing matters but you,' I insisted. 'I can't lose you now. You gave me my song, but now you're taking away something that means even more to me.'

"It was useless. She said that perhaps someday we would meet again. We would look for each other and find each other again. I felt powerless to hold her. She got into a taxi and I watched it drive away.

"Doctor, I have looked for Anabelle all over New York. I have returned to the places where we went together. I put ads in the personal columns of the papers. All in vain.

"The only hope left was the song. I had thought that once it was published, she might come to me again. You know the rest. The whole country is singing 'At Night the Sun Shines,' but still there has been no sign of life from Anabelle.

"Last night I noticed for the first time that the building across the street whose lights I had watched throughout the sleepless summer nights was a psychiatric clinic. That's why I'm here, Doctor. Day and night I'm obsessed by the thought that it was all a dream, a hallucination. I fear for my sanity. Please help me. Please, Doctor, tell me what to do."

There was a long pause. The man's hands were clenched on his lap. Night had enfolded the building in black velvet. A cool breeze stole through the half-open window, warning us of the approaching winter.

"I may not be able to explain everything," I said, "but I think I can explain some of it. Come with me."

Leslie Normand followed me silently down the hall into the elevator, and we went up to the fifth floor.

"Here we have several patients in partial seclusion," I explained. "Some have been interned by their families, others come here of their own free will. Sometimes they recover and never return here; at other times recovery is temporary, and after a few days in the world of light, the patient returns to the darkness of his psychosis."

We stopped in front of a door with a little window covered with white netting enabling one to look inside without being seen by the occupant of the room. Leslie Normand looked at me with puzzled eyes.

"Life can be even stranger than the fantasies you invent in your songs," I said. "Look through this window."

He did as I said, and when he turned back to me, his face was chalk-white.

"Anabelle!" he whispered.

I looked in myself. In the dimly lit room, a girl dressed in azure blue stood by an open, barred window, her eyes staring at the windows on the opposite side of the street. The aquamarine on one of her fingers beckoned at us with flashes of blue light.

"Anabelle Delorme," I said, gently pulling Leslie Normand away from the door. "She's an orphan with a moderate income that has enabled her to live here since she first noticed the symptoms of her illness. Professional ethics forbid my giving you complete details, but you love her and you should know the truth. Three months ago Anabelle left of her own accord. She came back one Monday at dawn. Since then she has spent most of her time looking through that window, silent, far away in her mysterious inner world."

"But, Doctor," Normand cried piteously, "is there any hope? Is there anything that can be done?"

"We're doing all we can. I really believe that you've done more good than all our treatments in the past two years. Your windows on the other side of the street must be on the same level as hers. Night after night Anabelle must have listened to you playing the piano. She listened to the desperate shreds of music you played all night long and her hypersensitive mind wove the melody that she sang to you on the beach. I can't explain the rest. Perhaps she saw you at your window, recognized you on the street, and followed you to the beach. Only she could explain that. But there is your 'hallucination,' the woman who completed your famous blues."

Color rushed back to Leslie Normand's face.

"Doctor,"—there was happiness in his voice—"if there was one miracle, there can be another. I'm going to help you bring Anabelle back to real life, and one day we'll create dreams together. She's no longer alone in her private dream world."

"You can help a great deal. It'll be difficult but not impossible. We'll bring your music back to her, try to evoke memories of you, awaken associations of ideas, create light within her."

## AT NIGHT THE SUN SHINES

At the door to the street Norman grasped my hand. "Time is not important to me, Doctor. I can wait."

Back in my office I opened a book, but I could not read. Soft distant notes floated in through the window, notes of infinite sweetness and nostalgia, as though the night itself were playing its mysteries on an invisible piano.

# THE TRAIL OF GALADON

WHEN I GO TO PARIS, I AL-
ways drop in at Harry's to see who is in town from the
States. Afterward I seldom bother to go back, since
Harry's is only a European extension of a Manhattan
bar. Every time I stop at Harry's I hope to run into
Mitzi, a very good friend of mine and, what is more
important, the proud possessor of the prettiest legs I
have ever seen on a newspaperwoman.

It was that magic hour when the Champs Élysées,

76

veiled in the pearly haze of dusk, is like a Pissarro canvas. The fall had carpeted the streets with golden leaves. When I entered Harry's, the first person I saw was Mitzi, her fascinating legs wound around a bar-stool and a big hat like a Saturn ring encircling her face.

"You, in Paris!" she cried, stretching out a small hand hardened from constant hammering on the type-writer. "What a delicious surprise! Tell me what's hap-pening in New York."

"Nothing ever happens when you're not around, Mitzi," I said, while the bartender, who had recog-nized me, was mixing my favorite drink.

"Manhattan certainly hasn't dampened your gallan-try."

"And Paris has only increased your charms."

"Enough of that!" Mitzi laughed. "What brings you to Paris?"

"Nothing in particular. I thought I might find some-thing over here to write about. I plan to spend a few days on the Riviera and then I must go to Rome to cover a psychiatry congress. And you, are you still keeping New York women informed on French fash-ions?"

"Just about. I'm a sort of one-woman fifth column trying to sneak a few styles over to New York before they're out on the market. The rest of the time I idle away at the Café de la Paix or here, flirting alternately

with Frenchmen and Americans. It's my way of con-
tributing to international understanding."

"Are you waiting for someone?" I asked her.

"I never wait for anybody. They wait for me. Today I'm with Bob Ventners of Universal. Right now
he's phoning some friends of his. We're having a drink
together while we wait for them. You know Bob. He'll
be delighted to see you."

"Another Martini, Mitzi?"

"My mother never taught me to say no to anything.
That's been the tragedy of my life."

We ordered fresh drinks, toasted each other silently,
and sipped.

"I have an important message for our friend Galadon.
Do you happen to know where he hangs his hat now?"
I asked her.

"I neither know nor care," she answered coldly.

"I hadn't heard that you two had quarreled."

"You've got to be crazier than Galadon to pick a
fight with him, and that is impossible. No, we didn't
quarrel. But I don't know where he is and I don't
care. When somebody makes trouble in your life—
and mine is chaotic enough as it is—you let him go
his way and set out in another direction."

"What happened between you two?"

"That's just it. Nothing really happened. You know
we used to meet here almost every evening for a drink
and later we would go somewhere for dinner. Since

we're both journalists—and wolf doesn't eat wolf—our relationship was strictly platonic. We amused each other. We had many laughs together. That was all. Not that Galadon, with his usual lack of tact, wasn't forever trying to talk me into an affair. Finally I stopped seeing him altogether."

"But why?"

"Galadon has become impossible. His nonconformity has gone to his head. While he was working for the paper he controlled himself somewhat, but finally he went completely wild. He did what he pleased, where he pleased, and when he pleased. If he had real talent he would be a Henry Miller, but he hasn't. He has become unbearably bohemian. No one will put up with his odd habits and his intolerable insolence."

Mitzi lit another cigarette with the stub of her last one. She then fished the olive out of her Martini and munched on it, her little nose wiggling up and down like a rabbit's.

"Let me tell you some of his tricks," she continued. "Bob can add a few more that cannot be told in front of a woman, even if she's a journalist called Mitzi.

"I'll never forget the last night we went out with Galadon several months ago. A week before, he had thrown a party to celebrate his being sacked by his paper. They got tired of paying his rent for nothing. After he was fired, he moved to a hotel on the Rue de Lappe, in the Bastille of all places! Actually it was a

79

combination of *bistro* and something worse. But nobody knew where he lived until he showed up here one night quite drunk and ordered champagne for everyone—we were eight, mind you—and then invited all of us to dinner the following evening. He said he would take us to a fascinating little spot where they had the best *poularde en demi-deuil* in Paris. We accepted, and he asked us to meet him at his hotel at seven.

"The same evening Galadon showed up here I had invited John Braun, a journalist from Transunited Agency, to join our group. Johnny and I had been dating for several weeks and were just beginning to take each other seriously. For the first time in my life I was considering giving up my bachelor girl life to become Mrs. Braun and mend socks and change diapers. I hesitated before introducing Johnny to our crowd. You know their brand of humor. I was afraid they might scare Johnny away. But I warned them that we were serious about each other and they promised to keep it clean. Johnny liked them, especially Galadon, who that night was more amusing then ever. He really sparkled, like a fresh bottle of champagne with the foam gushing out all over. Well, when we finally left here that night Galadon had already disappeared—without paying for the champagne, of course—in the company of a blonde nobody here will even talk to.

"The next evening we all met here to go to his hotel. Do you know the Rue de Lappe? No? It's right out of one of Jean Gabin's old films. You know, the sort of street where they finally knife Vivian Romance. Shabby *bistros,* sordid hotels, and other establishments I won't describe. We had a hard time locating the Hôtel du Chat Solitaire, but we found it—between two *bistros,* with another one on the ground floor which we had to cross to reach the hotel. You should have seen those hags! Macbeth's witches every one of them! And the filthy, drunken bums! The smoke was impenetrable and the smell of cheap wine sickening. It was a perfect frame for the proprietress: two hundred pounds of fat stuffed into layers of grimy cotton shawls and skirts.

"She sneered when we mentioned Galadon. She informed us that she doubted very much that he was presentable. He had been dragged in at nine that morning by a chauffeur and a woman, who dropped him at the door and left immediately. At noon he had come down and ordered champagne, and finally a waiter got him upstairs again.

"The five flights of foul-smelling, crooked stairs to Galadon's room were a nightmare. Why he should choose such a place was beyond our imagination. He couldn't be destitute, since he could afford champagne breakfasts. We decided that it was just sheer bohemianism and that there was nothing to do but ignore it.

"When we knocked at his door there was no answer. We tried the knob, and finding the door unlocked, we all walked in. Galadon was in bed, a bottle of champagne in one hand and a copy of Voltaire in the other. Around him, scattered all over the bed, floor, and furniture, were clothes and books and champagne bottles. A woman's skirt was draped over a chair.

"We stood around his bed, mystified and silent, like a crowd around an accident. He stared at us for a moment and then said, 'What the hell are you all doing here? I've never seen so many people in this room except in nightmares.' Under his messy hair, his unshaven face was a ghastly greenish color. There were large purple circles under his bloodshot eyes.

"When one of the boys reminded him that he had asked us to dinner, he howled with laughter. 'You didn't take me seriously? How stupid can you be! Well, it's out of the question now. I have a rotten hangover.'

"Another fellow told him angrily that he had made us come all the way out there for nothing and that there were girls with us. Three of the girls, secretaries from the Embassy, were staring wide-eyed at the dirty sock Galadon had wrapped around the naked bulb above his head. I didn't dare look at Johnny Braun.

"Finally Galadon said, 'Oh, all right, since you are here we may as well go and eat,' and raising the covers, he jumped out of bed naked. The secretaries ran out screaming.

"While we waited for him downstairs, one of the boys had a fight with a drunken sailor who pinched one of the girls. Johnny Braun had a long face. At last Galadon came down. He looked as if he had been embalmed for a week.

"When we finally left that hellish place it was raining and there were no taxis anywhere in the whole neighborhood. After walking the entire Bastille district looking for the fascinating little restaurant, Galadon finally admitted that he had forgotten where it was and that we should look for some other place. By then everybody was soaking wet, exhausted, and furious, but every time we went into a place, Galadon insisted that the atmosphere didn't suit his mood and we had to leave. Don't ask me why we simply didn't tell him to go to hell. I don't know. We've asked ourselves that question many times.

"We finally wound up having some putrid rabbit stew in a horrible little *bistro*. I pity the poor bunny that came to his end in that nauseating sauce! And Galadon was as dismal as an undertaker. He kept nagging us because we hadn't left him alone with his hangover. At dessert he perked up and began to flirt with one of the girls, until her boyfriend got mad and left. Soon after, Galadon went to telephone his hotel, he said. After a short while he returned and said that there was a message for Johnny Braun to return to his office immediately. As is customary among newspaper people, Johnny had given his office Galadon's address. We therefore suspected nothing. Johnny left in a hurry and soon after we thanked Galadon for the dinner and left.

"The next day when I saw Johnny he was very angry. He didn't mind, he said, paying for my dinner any time, but it was a beastly joke for me to make him pay for eight people. I didn't even know what he was talking about. He said that when he was putting on his coat at the *bistro,* the *patron* whispered to him that I had said that he should pay the bill to avoid any more trouble and that everything would be straightened out later. You can imagine how I felt.

"I ran into Galadon two days later right here, and I said things to him I have never said to anybody else in my life. He laughed. When I asked him why he had picked on Johnny, he said that Johnny had a stupid face. I just turned my back on him and haven't seen him since—and don't want to either. Here is Bob. He can tell you more."

Bob recounted a series of binges, fights, and perverted pranks Galadon had indulged in. They made Casanova appear a model of Victorian modesty.

"Why do you want to see Galadon?" Bob asked, when he had finished his lurid narrative.

"I have a message from his former boss and friend in New York. He wants him to go back to the paper and behave like a human being."

"I doubt very much that in his present state of barbarism he'll accept. But you can try. When you're in Nice, stop at the Agence Touriste-Trade on the Promenade des Anglais. Galadon is writing some articles for them. They may be able to give you his address. Nobody here has it. He quarreled with everybody."

Two days later I was having dinner at the Hôtel Negresco in Nice with André Cantoir, Assistant Director of Touriste-Trade. I inquired about Galadon.

"My friend," he said, after lighting his cigar with the precision of a terrorist setting off a bomb, "you're a writer, so nothing should please you more than to see confirmation of the saying, 'By their fruits ye shall know them.' Allow me to postpone my answer to your question until I have taken you to a certain place not far from here."

After dinner we walked down the Promenade des Anglais. It was drizzling and the sea breeze carried the first warning of winter. Cantoir asked me to have a cognac with him at a *bistro* behind the casino, a small café which from the distance shone in its dark alley like a Christmas tree. The words "Café des Américains," outlined in red and green lights, winked on and off above the door. Inside there was a small bar, as neat and tidy as a laboratory on inspection day. There were fall flowers on the small tables, mirrors with gilt frames, colorful signs of the approaching carnival, and a small white-and-blue-striped awning over the bar that gave it a festive air.

We sat down and ordered two cognacs. Cantoir then asked for the *patron*. Almost immediately this gentleman stepped out from behind a curtain and greeted us most graciously. Cantoir introduced me and we chatted for a while about the weather and the tourists. Finally, between puffs on his cigar, Cantoir asked casually, "Have you heard from Monsieur Galadon?"

The proprietor's face turned purple. "No, no, no, and I do not want to." He looked at me suspiciously. "Is monsieur a friend of Galadon?"

Cantoir lied obligingly. "No, he is not, but he is curious to know what happened the last time you saw Monsieur Galadon."

"Ah, Monsieur Cantoir, the headaches that *cochon* caused me! You cannot imagine. Look," he said to me, pointing at the canvas awning, the mirrors over the bar, the bottles. "The awning was ripped to shreds. The mirrors all had to be replaced and these are not half as good. The glass shelf was only cracked, but the bottles, monsieur, thousands of francs' worth of liquor lost, and only two tables were left standing."

"But surely Monsieur Galadon couldn't have done all that himself," I said.

"*Mais non,* monsieur, of course not. His friends did it. He incited them to do it. One of his little jokes! He came here one night, while he was working for Monsieur Cantoir. He had had a lot to drink, as usual. He ordered champagne and asked two girls at the bar to join him. They were *filles de joie,* certainly, but they were minding their own business, waiting for their boyfriends. I begged him to leave them alone. I explained that their boyfriends, two sailors, would be coming soon. I wanted no fights. He paid no attention, monsieur. When the sailors arrived, I warned them that he was drunk. I begged them to go away, to go and fight in the street. I wanted no trouble in the house. They left with the girls, but they told Monsieur Galadon that they would be waiting for him outside. Galadon is a big talker, monsieur, but he is small like a shrimp and skinny like an umbrella. I was surprised therefore to see him go out immediately after the sailors. He said to me as he left, 'We'll be back in half a minute and you can laugh at the battle of Bastogne.'

"I warned my two waiters, monsieur, but I was sure that he would never come back after a fight with the two sailors. Monsieur, I nearly died when I saw him walk in a few minutes later arm in arm with the two sailors. They walked over to me and one of the sailors said, 'So, you were a collaborator? And you dare insult the French navy! You Nazi dog!'

"They were drunk. It was useless to reason with

them. Monsieur Galadon's powers of persuasion must be fantastic! In five minutes the two sailors had turned the place into a battlefield. The two waiters had black eyes. The awning was in shreds. The mirrors, bottles, vases, everything was broken. And the obscenities they shouted at me! Of course, I locked myself in the washroom when the fight started." He sighed. *"Ce sale bohème!"*

Eight days later I was settled comfortably in a chair in a hotel in Geneva telephoning one Jean Petit, with whom, according to Cantoir, Galadon was now living. Through the window I could see a park, its maple trees clad in the golden splendor of fall. The gray sky threatened rain, and cold damp air blew in through the open window. A woman's voice answered in a French that rang with a healthy German accent. Shortly after, I heard Galadon's voice. He sounded as if he had just awakened from a profound sleep.

"Galadon, it's Charles," I said.

He was silent for a brief moment and then, "Charles? Charles who?"

"Me, Charles, the only Charles crazy enough to follow you to Geneva."

"Oh, it's you. What do you want?"

"To talk to you, naturally. Can you come to my hotel or meet me at a café?"

"No."

"Later, then?"

"No."

"You can't or you won't? What I have to say will interest you."

"Nothing can interest me in this damnable weather."

"There's money in it. You can go back to your old job."

"What a fiendish idea!"

There was a pause, and finally Galadon said, "You want to come here?"

"Sure I won't be intruding?"

"Oh, for God's sake! Come on over. The couple I live with are going to the movies and I can't go out now."

It was pouring when I arrived at 21, Rue Calvin. A sharp wind clawed at my face. The whole universe had turned into one great wet sponge. Glad to escape the bullet-like rain, I entered the house and climbed five narrow flights before I reached the Petits' door. I had to ring three times before the door was finally opened. Galadon casually extended a hand and pulled me in.

I followed him into a combination bedroom-study of moderate size. A small stove glowed in a corner. In another corner there was a daybed and nearby a table with a typewriter and papers scattered all over it. There were a few books on the bureau and a small basket of fruit. I sat down in the only chair, and listlessly he dropped on the daybed. The only light came from a lamp near the daybed and left most of the room in shadow. Everything was plain but comfortable. After the bleak weather outside it was a pleasant warm refuge.

I had not seen Galadon in nearly a year. He had not changed. Short, skinny, hair thin and graying, face pale and bored, small dark eyes restless behind thick glasses, like little mice in a glass cage.

His trousers were shabby, his sweater frayed. He wore no tie. No, he had not changed. Yet there was a new element in his appearance, an aura of tranquillity, a bourgeois placidity. I had never noticed it before.

"What brings you here?" he asked casually, as though he had seen me only the day before.

"I covered a congress in Rome and I'm on my way back to Paris. I just stopped over to say hello and give you a message from New York."

"From whom?"

"The paper."

"Are those bastards still alive?"

"They're still alive and they still remember you."

"Do I owe them money?"

"They want you back."

"After throwing me out?"

"It seems they're short of help."

He shrugged his shoulders and stretched out on the daybed. "You've been to Paris?" he asked.

90

"Yes. I saw Mitzi and Bob."

"I bet they told you some tall stories about me."

"They did."

"They make me sick! They're so sanctimonious. The most inoffensive joke sends them into a dither. Frankly, I'm glad I don't have to see them any more. Here I know no one and see no one."

"But what in the world do you do here? Are you working?"

"I haven't done one stitch of work in weeks. The typewriter, the books, the papers—all a camouflage. The only thing I read is a pornographic magazine mailed from Paris and the *Journal de Genève* to put me in the right mood for this godforsaken town."

"I don't understand."

"It's very simple. I have discovered how to be happy. I don't work, if I can help it. I have reduced my needs to a minimum. I don't need much food and I drink nothing but Vichy water, which is wonderful for my rotten liver. The only vice I indulge in is a visit to the *crèmerie* in the afternoon. The rest of the time I sleep."

"I don't believe it."

"All right, don't believe it. It's the perfect life. I used to live like a human being. One day it occurred to me that it would be wonderful to live like a cabbage. Not like any other vegetable, but like a cabbage. Cabbages are like elephants—solid, comfortable, in

91

perennial repose. I'm a Geneva cabbage and I'll go on being just that as long as I can."

"You must be joking. I'm sure you're working."

"Very well, I'll tell you what I do every day and then let's not discuss it anymore. My God, I haven't argued so much in weeks! I wake up at noon. I breakfast in bed on *café au lait* and brioches and I read the *Journal de Genève*. Have you ever read the *Journal de Genève?* Fascinating paper! It makes you feel that the rest of the world simply doesn't exist. Nothing makes the headlines but the local news: an old man who fell off his bicycle; the opening of a watch exposition; an anecdote about Prince Rainier, and so on. When I'm through with the paper I go back to sleep. At three o'clock they bring me tiny radish sandwiches, which I adore, a small steak with potatoes, a salad, a bottle of Vichy water, and tea with cream. At five I go to the *crèmerie*. There I sit until eight listening to the corniest sentimental music and watching the fat bourgeois cows of Geneva sip tea. Then I come back here, I have dinner, and I go to bed."

"You're crazy!"

"No, I'm happy. I'm contented. I'm at peace."

"Galadon, the Vichy water has gone to your head."

"So, it has gone to my head. Good. Enough of this. Tell me about yourself."

He was interrupted by a sound from the next room that startled me. It was a baby crying.

"There goes that brat again," Galadon said, with the air of a man who is resigned to a heavy burden. "Let's see what he wants now."

I followed him into a half-lit hall and into a dark room. Galadon turned on the light and I saw rose-colored walls, a large bed, a dressing table, clothes scattered all over the chairs, and in a corner a crib, where a blond pink baby with clenched fists was now crying with all the strength of his miniature lungs.

Galadon stared at him as if he were a strange animal. "Whose baby is that?"

"The family's. When they go to the movies I take care of him."

I was suddenly seized by a fit of laughter. "You, a baby-sitter?" I finally asked between peals of laughter. "You, the inveterate bohemian from New York, Paris, the Riviera, you, a baby-sitter?"

"I pay no rent," he said unabashed, "and I don't pay for the food either. All I do is mind the baby one evening a week."

He picked up a red slipper from the floor and waved it in front of the wailing infant, who went on crying.

"The little bastard won't stop. What shall we do?"

The baby's bottle was lying on the blanket over the crib. I pushed the nipple into the baby's mouth and the crying stopped suddenly, as though I had switched off a radio.

"You are a genius!" cried Galadon. "Well, now that

he has something to do, let's go back to my room."

"You take wonderful care of him."

"What do you want me to do? Nurse him?"

We went back to his room, leaving the light on in the baby's room.

"Do you want to go out for a while?" I asked Galadon.

"I don't usually, but we'll go out when these people come back."

"Who are they?"

"A Swiss couple. She's really half Austrian. They advertised in the paper for a boarder to help pay the rent. The poor sap is a watchmaker and doesn't make much money. They have two children and he's having trouble with the domestic finances."

"With what I imagine you give them they're probably no better off. I dare say you're living off them."

"Not exactly," he said, unruffled. "I do pay something whenever I get hold of a little money, or I buy things for the house."

"What things?"

"You're beginning to sound like an accountant. Come, let's get ready."

He changed his clothes. I noticed that his closet was in perfect order and every suit clean and pressed. Just as he was putting on his jacket, the doorbell rang. Galadon went to open it and returned with a man, a woman, and a child. The man was under forty, tall, and thin. His hair was carefully combed flat and he was fastidiously dressed. His entire appearance betrayed the proper citizen. She was a comely buxom blonde, with a flawless milk-white complexion.

Galadon introduced me to the Petits. Madame Petit greeted me politely but coldly, and then left the room with the child.

Petit said cordially, "A friend of Monsieur Galadon may consider this home his own."

"Thank you," I said. "It's a charming home."

"It's not what I would like for Maria," he said, "but one has to adapt oneself to the circumstances."

"Monsieur Galadon is most fortunate that he can live here with you."

Galadon was watching us as though we were two not very funny clowns. Finally he seized my arm and pushed me toward the door. I said good-by to Monsieur Petit, promising to return for tea sometime.

As we opened the door to the hall, Maria came out of her bedroom and placed her hand on Galadon's arm. I walked discreetly to the top of the stairs. Maria whispered urgently to Galadon, glancing at me with hostility. Without saying a word, Galadon pushed away her hand and joined me. She slammed the door behind us.

Outside the wind was blowing harder than ever and everything was drenched, but it had stopped raining. We walked in silence toward Rue de Florissant, where we took the bus. Finally Galadon said, "What's stopping you? Ask me. Go ahead."

"What am I supposed to ask?"

"Oh, don't be difficult. You're dying to know what there is between that woman and me. Very well, I'll be brief. Everything you're thinking is true."

"What about her husband?"

"He may or may not know. I am not sure."

"What if he does know?"

"It wouldn't matter. If he became difficult she would leave him."

"How do you know?"

"She loathes him. He's poor. He's dull. She didn't love him when she married him. She has been bored ever since. She's not from Geneva. Only Genevans can endure this dreadful monotonous life."

"Genevans and you," I sneered.

"I have my reasons."

"Maria?" I asked incredulously.

"Nonsense! I'm not in love. But I have a good life with her."

"Doesn't it bother you that you're living off the man you're deceiving?"

"It should bother him more and yet he keeps his mouth shut. I suspect that he knows about it, but he's in love with her and is afraid to lose her."

"It's a hell of a situation."

96

"It has been going on for months and it may go on for many months more."

"And then what?"

"I don't know. I'll probably get bored. I'll go away. Right now I like it here. You don't know how wonderful it is to live peacefully, to be served delicious meals in bed, to sleep as much as you want, to listen to a little music at the *crèmerie*—"

"And free sex right at home," I interrupted him.

"That's secondary," he said.

"Why don't you leave the house at least?"

"What? And have to pay rent? Besides, I like the husband. He's a nice chap, well read, too. He's always trying to show me around the museums."

We stopped at the Crèmerie des Ambassadeurs. Most of the tables were occupied by neatly dressed people, mainly families. The buzz of conversation mingled with the fragrance of pastry and strains of Beethoven. I ordered a glass of port and Galadon a pot of tea.

"Do you come here every afternoon?" I asked, looking around me.

"Every single afternoon."

"Doesn't this life bore you?"

"I'm perfectly happy here. I did many foolish things in Paris and Nice and wound up with ulcers. Here I have a quiet, pleasant home, something I never had before in my life."

"I can't understand what that woman sees in you."

"Neither can I."

"Has it occurred to you that you're destroying that woman's life?"

"If you're going to moralize I'll pick up my hat and relieve you of my presence. You always condoned my bohemian ways, but now that I lead the life of a good citizen—"

"A good citizen?" I almost shouted.

"Shall I get my hat?"

The evening came to an abrupt end when Galadon reminded me that a steak and a very special dessert were waiting for him at home. After all, he could not offend the family! Incredulously I watched him walk away and disappear in the thick fog beyond the *crèmerie* window, looking every bit the part of the model middle-class citizen.

The following morning I telephoned Galadon. I was leaving for Paris in the evening. Madame Petit answered the telephone.

"He's not here now," she said, "but he wants you to come over at three this afternoon."

Madame Petit opened the door when I arrived at five after three. She seemed more friendly.

"Will you come into Monsieur Galadon's room? He is not back yet but he should be home soon."

"I'm sorry," I apologized. "I thought he had said three."

"Neither he nor my husband will be back until three thirty. That's why I asked you to come at three. I wanted to talk to you alone."

We sat down, and she lit a cigarette. She must have been in her late thirties. Her blue eyes were incredibly bright and clear, and her startling white skin reminded me of fresh snow on a lake. A clinging dressing gown outlined the fleshy curves of her figure.

"Monsieur Galadon has told me about the offer from the paper. I beg a favor of you, monsieur. You have great influence over him. Please don't let him accept this job in New York. I plead with you as I have never pleaded before. For the sake of my home, persuade him to stay in Geneva."

With her hands clasped across her breast, under the feeble rays of the fall sun that filtered through the window, she looked like a stained-glass Madonna.

"Can you understand? I expect nothing from him. I ask him nothing. I only want him near me. I need him. He has brought me a happiness that I had never known before. He has stirred emotions in me that I, the mother of two children, had never experienced before. I can't let him go now."

"But really," I said, embarrassed, "I have no influence over Galadon. I don't believe anybody has. In any case, if he decides to leave, why don't you go with him?"

She blushed a deep pink. Without looking at me, she

murmured, "If I leave this house he will have no need for me then. I know exactly what I mean to him. My only hope is to keep him here, where he is comfortable. I know that he doesn't love me. But I love him. I need him. I'm past the age when a woman dreams of a Prince Charming. If the only way to keep him near me is to continue this nightmare of all three of us living in the same house, I'm willing to go on like this."

"But what about your husband?"

"My husband knows. He told me so last night. I threatened to leave him. He adores me and the children. He would consent to anything rather than lose us. If he ever opposed me, I would take the children and follow your friend to the end of the world."

"But you said that he doesn't want you outside of this house."

"I know, but I'm desperate. I don't know what to do. All I know is that if he remains here everything will be the same. Why, why did you have to come here?"

There was no need for me to answer. The door opened and Petit walked in. He nodded at me politely but coolly.

"I saw your friend coming, but I was carrying too many packages and couldn't wait for him."

When he kissed her on the cheek she became as rigid as a marble statue.

100

"I understand your friend is leaving us," ventured Petit, sitting down on the edge of the sofa while he cleaned his glasses with a handkerchief. With his long legs stretched out stiffly, his long scrawny body slouching forward, his gray eyes still watery from the cold outside, he looked like a dummy long neglected in a showcase.

"That's not definite," Maria said coldly.

"My dear, a journalist can't go on forever without writing. *N'est-ce pas,* monsieur? Besides, Geneva is too confined, too provincial. It stultifies the creative instinct in a writer. Here we only care about the sanctity of the home and children. We only want to live in peace, with no interference from the outside world."

He didn't finish. With an angry look at him, she walked out of the room. Fortunately, for I had nothing to say, the bell rang at that moment and Galadon walked in.

"Hello," he said to no one in particular. "Here is some candy for Tintin. Don't go, Monsieur Petit. My friend and I are only going to say good-by."

Petit muttered something about things he had to do, and making an obvious attempt to conceal his gloom, left the room.

"Galadon," I said, "Madame Petit spoke to me before you both arrived. She begged me to induce you to stay. She claims that her entire life depends on your staying here?"

101

"Of course I'll stay," he replied. "What did you think?"

"I thought you were going back to work."

"Me? Run around the streets and sweat blood for those howling fools in New York? You must be raving mad. I'm not going anywhere."

"Madame will be very happy, I'm sure. Don't you realize that you're standing on a volcano about to erupt? Wouldn't it be better to leave now? You will eventually. Why wait?"

"My dear friend, thanks for your interest, thanks for your advice, thanks for your message, thanks for everything, but you still don't understand. I told you I am no longer the man you knew. I am a cabbage. A forgotten cabbage in an abandoned garden. As long as no one makes soup of it, the cabbage is happy. Leave me alone with my provincial life. Let me play the little bourgeois. I wouldn't exchange this house for the best hotel suite in Paris."

"This isn't your house, Galadon. Remember that."

"Not the furniture. Well, if I find a minute I'll drop you a line in Paris."

A few days later, back in Paris, I received a note from Galadon hastily scribbled on the stationery of the Hôtel La Résidence, Geneva:

Dear Friend,

Well, it happened. Petit insisted that I marry

Maria and adopt the children. Damn the poor sap. I left, of course, and Maria left right after. She went to live with an aunt, taking the baby with her. Petit kept the other child. A beautiful life completely shattered. And all because the foolish man failed to realize that his wife interested me far less than the comforts of his home! I'll take that job now. You will find me at Harry's one evening next week. *Au revoir*.

G.

The following Thursday I went to Harry's. The first thing I saw were Mitzi's legs around the barstool. She raised her glass to me. She looked like a goddess raising her chalice to toast the return of her hero.

"Mitzi, you look devastating."

"Your greetings are monotonous, but flattering."

"Absolutely sincere, Mitzi. Without you, Paris wouldn't be Paris."

"They said the same thing about Mistinguette until she must have been a hundred."

"The only similarity between you and Mistinguette is that she had fabulous legs and so do you, but hers should have been in a museum, while yours are the aerodynamic marvels of tomorrow."

"Charles, you do more for my morale than a dozen Pernods. What have you been doing? I have never been so bored. John Braun finally gave me the gate.

He went back to New York. That's my fate. I take them by surprise, they make love to me, and then they vanish. I'm like the poor fisherman whose hook never catches anything. By the way, do you know who's here? Galadon."

"I have a letter from him in my pocket."

"He showed up here night before last. He begged me to buy him a Martini. He was ill after he drank it. It seems he has been eating and drinking nothing but radishes and Vichy water. He felt obliged to tell me the story of his life in the past few months. I guess you know it."

"Yes, and the people involved, too."

"It seems that the lady went to live with her aunt and the husband is now sorry that he didn't put a bullet through Galadon's head. But you know the Swiss—they never do anything against the law. Besides, the shot would have attracted the entire neighborhood. Galadon, as usual, escaped punishment."

"Do you think he'll ever go back to that woman, Mitzi?"

"Not on your life! He's back in that Hole of Calcutta in the Rue de Lappe. Once a bohemian . . ."

"The whole thing is fantastic. How do you explain those long months doing nothing, leading such a deadly life? He wasn't even in love with the woman!"

"Who knows?" Mitzi said pensively. "It certainly was all new to him. Good meals in bed, his clothes kept neat for him, a home, a woman, even children, all free, no responsibilties, no need to work. For the first time in his life he had all those things. And he's lazy and has no scruples. The tragic part is that this time he left behind not unpaid bills, or filthy clothes, or empty bottles, but a broken family, a home destroyed."

Mitzi finished her drink and lit a cigarette, which silhouetted her strong-looking profile against the bas-reliefs above the bar.

"But this time," she added, smiling thinly, "Galadon paid his share. Never again will he be a happy man. Where will he find a hotel in the Bastille where they'll serve him radish sandwiches and tea with cream in bed!"

## DARKNESS IS BETTER

Late one afternoon I
went to visit Leonardo Medini, the fan painter. It had
rained all day and there was a hint of snow in the
cold drops of water.

The long, dreary subway ride left me in a remote
station in Brooklyn. Outside, the shabby neighborhood
seemed to cower under the heavy, darkened sky. Gusts
of rain rushed at me and the wind clawed with sharp,
frosty nails. Raising my raincoat collar, I plodded on,

106

stumbling through the large puddles of water on the sidewalk.

The narrow street where Medini lived was flanked by dilapidated old houses. In the tiny front yards stunted, naked shrubs shivered under the pelting rain. Number 15 stood next to a vacant lot littered with rusted iron and garbage cans. In a corner under a thin tree, a dog lay motionless, wooden, doubled over like a dying sentinel; only his glassy eyes gleamed through wet, stringy hair. On the opposite side of the lot, a canal crawled away, its grimy waters bearing no reflections, as if cursed by God.

I crossed a small enclosure, where some plants drooped, drained of life and color, and reached the door of the house. Solidly built, the structure still had a certain dignity, like a great lady fallen into extreme poverty. I pulled a rusty chain. Before the tinkling of the bell had vanished through the rain, the door opened. A tall woman, startlingly pale in her severe dark clothing, looked at me for an instant and then, lowering her eyes, waited for me to speak.

I asked for Mr. Leonardo Medini and she said that she was his wife, whereupon I introduced myself and explained that a French client of the law firm I worked for had bequeathed to Mr. Medini the sum of one thousand and one dollars.

Showing no surprise, the woman motioned me into a small vestibule, saying, "Leonardo will see you immediately." Her voice was infinitely sad as she continued, "May I thank you for coming in person? It's very kind of you," and without waiting for a reply, she disappeared behind a dark-blue curtain that separated the hall from the rooms beyond.

I could hear the rhythmic beat of the rain against the walls as I removed my dripping raincoat and looked around me. There were two old chairs, a metal coatrack, and a table with a spotless but faded cloth edged with worn-out lace. A few daisies drooped in a plain vase at the center of the table. Everything gave an impression of poverty, a clean, dignified poverty, and I was glad that the money was going to help these people.

"Leonardo will see you now." She had pushed aside the curtain, and for an instant the dark-blue cloth framed her pale face, bright blue eyes, and the heavy plait on top of her blonde head.

In the next room a tall massive man waited, arms outstretched, hands wide open, as though he wished to embrace me. He had a wide leonine face, mahogany-colored, and a shaggy red mane that flamed about his face like a fire over a forest. His large blue eyes regarded me steadily. His lips were open in a wide smile.

"Come in, my friend," he said, in a voice that resounded like an organ, "and give me your hand."

I realized then that the fan painter was blind. I clasped his hand and he placed his other hand over mine, warming it instantly.

"Sit on the sofa," he urged, motioning toward a small wooden bench with a cane back. "There you will be comfortable. I prefer the large armchair, where the patriarch of the house traditionally sits." Without help from his wife, who remained standing and silent, he sat down on a small wooden chair that could hardly support his corpulent body. His movements were natural and relaxed, those of a man at peace with himself and with the world.

"You must be cold and tired," he continued. "A good cup of English tea will perk you up, and Martha will serve us her special buttered scones. Would you like that? But of course you would. There is nothing like a hot cup of tea on an afternoon like this. Only when we inhale that delightful aroma do we fully enjoy the blessing of being dry and comfortable while we listen to the rain beating outside."

Martha excused herself softly, and softly she left the room. The fan painter pulled out from a pocket of his tobacco-colored corduroy jacket an enormous curved pipe, which he deftly filled with tobacco. Its aroma immediately permeated the room, blending happily with his rugged appearance.

"You will find some cigarettes there on the table, in

the little lacquered box, and nearby a lighter that never fails. But if you prefer a pipe, we can share this excellent tobacco."

On a flimsy table covered with a faded but clean green mat stood a plain wooden box that once must have been a sewing kit. I pulled out a cigarette and lit it with the small metal lighter.

"Martha told me that Monsieur de Castignac sent you," he said, taking some matches out of his jacket pocket.

"Yes, Mr. Medini. I was requested to bring the message personally."

"No more of this Mr. Medini," he interrupted me with friendly brusqueness. "Just Leonardo. If it was good enough for Da Vinci, the greatest of all, it is good enough for a fan painter. Like kings and popes, we artists use only our Christian names."

He paused to light his pipe. I dared not offer to do it, since his movements were as sure as mine. I glanced around the room. Behind Leonardo a large window opened upon the vacant lot I had seen next to the house. The drab, gloomy background contrasted sharply with the massive figure of the fan painter, his wild red hair, the clear blue eyes, and even his voice, as rich in harmony as his words were in color. There were two more cane chairs in the room, a sideboard with plain white pottery and a little vase of artificial flowers, and two floor lamps with plain white shades.

A cabinet filled with books and a low table piled high with magazines completed the furnishings. But spread all over the light-gray walls were some twenty hand-painted fans, framed like pictures, and although time had aged them, the exquisite landscapes, seascapes, dawns in the country, sunsets, fishing scenes, all of intricate design and brilliant coloring, filled the room with charm and beauty.

"Are you admiring my collection of fans? All my visitors do. They are but a few of the many thousands I painted in fifteen years of work. I was the best fan painter in Paris, a talent I inherited from my father, who was the best fan painter in Milan. Strange thing, I never painted a picture. The fan was far more attractive to me because it has life, it moves and talks, it can feel and suffer. A painted fan may very well become a museum piece, yet it is always alive because the play of the ribs gives the effect of movement and vitality to what would have but two dimensions on canvas.

"I started to paint as a hobby in Paris, where my father sent me to study. Finally I made a profession of it. Oh, that made him very angry! He did not want me to start so soon and he stopped my allowance. But after many years of poverty, I attained fame in this unusual art, earned a great deal of money, and enjoyed life as it could only be enjoyed many years ago in Paris.

"My fans fluttered like colored doves in the hands

111

of the most beautiful women in Paris. They rested on alabaster décolletés, which in those days were the main subject of conversation in the artistic world; they enhanced the grace of ballerinas and singers and adorned the dressing rooms of actresses and the bedrooms of courtesans.

"When I became blind," he continued, without any trace of bitterness, rather as though he were relating one more event in his career, "I had to give up painting. I regretted it deeply, of course, but I had already spread my wings. Those wings still flutter in the hands of the beauties of yesterday, who still fan themselves with my creations, keeping me alive in their memories. At times it seems that the breeze stirred by the graceful play of their fans caresses my face.

"But let us return to the matter that brought you here. You mentioned to Martha a message from Monsieur de Castignac. Poor Monsieur de Castignac! He was one of my best clients. So romantic! He bought exactly one thousand and one different fans for the woman he loved. No two of my fans were ever alike. Thus their value lay in their originality, for each owner possessed something unique. Monsieur de Castignac placed at the feet of the most famous ballerina in Paris a gilded basket filled with one thousand and one fans. I counted them twice. They were of all types—of paper and silk, feathers and ivory, of silver and gold—every one of them painted by me. He told his beloved

112

that a different fan would fan their passion into a fresh blaze every night for a thousand and one nights. The idea so delighted her that she gave generously of her love. Of course, it didn't last a thousand and one nights. That was too many nights for a ballerina in the Paris of those days.

"When Martha read in a French paper several weeks ago about de Castignac's death in Paris, I had a premonition of this gesture."

I had listened fascinated to the fan painter. "We went crazy at the office, trying to figure out this strange legacy of one thousand and one dollars," I said. "Here is the check."

Taking an envelope from my pocket, I placed it gently in his hand. He accepted it with the dignity of an Asiatic emperor in a palace in Samarkand receiving a gold cup wrought by a vassal. Without opening it, he placed the envelope on the table.

"Many thanks," he said gravely. "This is further proof of Monsieur de Castignac's admirable nature. Even after death he is romantic."

"In that art you must have been by far his master," I ventured.

He laughed so loudly that it drowned out the drumming of the rain.

"No one in those days needed a master. The joy of living was enough. Today a man must convince himself that he is surrounded by beauty and kindness. For there is no romance in *what* we do, but in *how* we do it. There is no romance in the life we live, but in how we live it. It is not actions that are great, but those who perform them. Things are not so valuable and precious as the rich think they are, nor so sordid and miserable as the poor would have us believe."

Just then Leonardo's wife entered with a tray heaped with ordinary china and silverware, a steaming teapot, sugar, cream, lemon, buttered toast, and three small pieces of pastry, the kind one buys in any bakery. Though modest, it looked neat and appealing.

"This is the happiest hour on a rainy day," Leonardo said. "Outside, the wind and the rain isolate us from the rest of the world—the little river will certainly have swelled by tomorrow"—I remembered with a shudder the sluggish, grimy canal—"and here, Martha's incomparable tea and good company. If you please, let me have the silver tongs."

I looked at the table. Next to the cracked sugar bowl there was a silver-plated teaspoon. I handed it to Leonardo, wondering whether he was mad or whether, out of pity, his wife deceived him with imaginary pictures of opulence.

Gracefully, Leonardo scooped up some sugar and dropped it in his cup.

"In this room," he said, with a generous sweep of the arm, "Martha and I spend many happy hours every day. We have been doing this for the past ten years, ever since I became completely blind." This time there was a tremor in his voice when he said the word, and I saw his wife turn deadly pale. "We live on the income my father left me. Although small, it is for life, and there is enough to pay the rent for this house, which has miraculously remained low after all these years. I guess it is because the neighborhood has not prospered and the little parks"—I remembered the lot with the hungry dog—"are neglected. All in all, most of our time is spent in this room, which is our studio during the day—Martha and I make little metal play-things for a toy factory—and at night we read, talk, and dream. Our door is always open to our friends. In summer there is cold beer and in winter tea, or warm spiced wine when circumstances permit it. We chat, share the hearth with friends, enjoy ourselves, and are as happy in this private world of ours as sultans in their palaces."

His face was illuminated by an inner strength and peace, and I listened to him bewitched, while a doubt began to gnaw in my head. What was his wife think-ing? How did she feel about all this? Until now she had said very little. Instead, she had listened atten-tively to everything he said.

She sat quietly, her blue eyes glowing softly, as if she were grateful and contented; yet there was sensu-ality in the fresh, full mouth. She seemed to accept Leonardo's magic juggling of words as though she

115

were convinced that the spoon was really "silver
tongs," the "platter," as he had called it, was not an
ordinary plate, and the "table linen" which he asked
her to remove after tea was of fine Dutch linen with
frothy lace borders instead of a cheap cotton cloth.
Were both of them victims of the same illusion? Was
she, with her seeing eyes, as blind to reality as the
blind painter, or had he communicated to her his vol-
untary spiritual blindness to the drab reality around
them?

After tea, when she sat next to me on the sofa and
Leonardo suggested that we make ourselves comfortable on the "feather pillows," pointing to the old flat-
tened cushions, I suddenly realized that I also was
accepting the magic change from the real to the fantastic, from the modest to the sumptuous. Could the
fan painter really transform a dreary subway ride into
a caravan journey to Baghdad and a dilapidated house
in a dismal neighborhood in Brooklyn into a palace
in Damascus?

"While I was in the kitchen," Martha said, "I heard
your conversation with Leonardo about Monsieur de
Castignac. I, too, knew him and I believe his gesture
is a most delicate way of changing a simple legacy into
a friendly tribute to Leonardo's genius."

"It certainly is the most poetic legacy our firm has
ever handled."

"Yes," interrupted Leonardo, his face enveloped in

blue clouds of smoke, "Martha met Monsieur de Castignac shortly after I did. She was very young. She was a dress model at one of the fashion houses in the Faubourg St. Honoré."

"A small but exclusive shop," she explained. "We used Leonardo's fans. That is how we met. For two years we went around holding hands, strolling along the banks of the Seine, rummaging in the old bookstalls, gazing at the silver-gray sky of Paris, watching the autumn leaves fall in the parks, or just sitting on the benches in the Louvre until the guards asked us to leave. Leonardo was a beginner then, with very little money. Our love was as platonic as we were thrifty."

Martha's face looked suddenly very young, as if her memories had restored the bloom to her faded beauty.

"Martha," Leonardo recalled, "was then like a figurine of the finest porcelain, all light and music. We were married and we were radiantly happy. Almost overnight I became famous. We spent our money as fast as it came in." He shook his pipe into a copper ashtray and went on talking, smiling his eternal smile, as wide and luminous as a dawn at sea. "Then I began to lose my sight. Too many miniatures, too much work done under poor artificial light, too much microscopic filigree. It is true, I lost my eyesight, but I have retained light within my darkness."

Martha's eyes had clouded and her face had turned

117

pale again. She started to get up from the sofa, but Leonardo stretched out his arm and gently but firmly pressed his large hand upon her shoulder, holding her down. Leaning forward in his chair, he spoke again, fast and passionately, his words crackling like logs in a fireplace, as though he wanted to drive away something cold that had come between them.

"I am telling you this as a tribute to Martha—"

"Leonardo!" she implored.

"Calm yourself, my love. I only wish to relate to our friend—which he most certainly is from now on, since he has accepted our hospitality—that what might have been a fatal tragedy in our lives turned out to be merely a change of direction to new seas of supreme happiness. For as soon as the first days of despair passed and we realized that, thanks to the modest income we had, the terrifying economic problem was solved, a new philosophy of life took hold of me and filled me with satisfaction and contentment. Until that time I had been trying to create beauty through my art. I had been fighting the outside world, which in reality was ugly and at times sordid, by creating a world of illusion, which was the only one I could see. freed of the outside world, I began to live in that other world of illusion, which was the only one I could see. That is how real life should be. Good people should live in opulence, surrounded by beautiful things, hope, and kindness. Well, then, Martha and I would live in that world where the ordinary things of daily life are of gold and silver, the work of artists and geniuses. Instead of apologizing for our plain clothes and humble home, I would accept everything that surrounded us as fine and beautiful. Thus our lives, mine and Martha's, have graciousness and dignity. Martha has learned to accept and share this philosophy of accumulating infinite riches within the soul and scattering them upon those around us. For while enriching ourselves, we can also make rich those willing to share this wealth."

Like a magic storyteller, the fan painter went on talking. When the world on the other side of the window was finally blotted out in rainy darkness, I regretfully got up to leave. Leonardo offered me one of his old fans, which he said he would fetch from a chest in his room upstairs. Neither my protests that I could not accept it, for I dared not offer to pay for it, nor Martha's insistence that she would go up to get it were of any avail. He climbed the stairs alone, and we stood watching him, a blind, red-haired giant wrested from some mythological fable, feeling his way up the small staircase, trying perhaps to prove to himself that he was not helpless, that he was self-sufficient. We heard him open a door. Still under the spell of the fan painter's words, I turned to look at Martha. Her face was ashen and a shadow veiled her lapis lazuli eyes.

"What do you think of Leonardo?"

119

"He's the most extraordinary man I have ever met and he couldn't have found a better companion than you."

"I was afraid you might think that," she said, her voice full of tears. "I don't know why Leonardo spoke to you as he did nor why I'm telling you this, but I deserve neither praise nor admiration. There's something he omitted. He didn't tell you that when we met I was frivolous, lightheaded, a coquette, and this caused him a great deal of pain. When we were married, I promised to change, but I didn't. It was not until he became blind the second time that I began to see the world through his eyes—"

"I don't understand," I started to say, but Leonardo was now coming down, the fan, wrapped in tissue paper, in his hand.

"I now give you," he said, with the air of a king presenting a knight with a gold-hilted sword, "one of the finest pieces of my work. Keep it as a remembrance of your visit, which has brought me so many happy memories."

I warmly said good-by to them, promising to return. When I stepped into the dark street, the wind with its sharp knives slashed my face. Stumbling into the puddles of black water bubbling under the pelting rain, I again faced a cold, dark world. Turning my head, I saw Leonardo's huge figure silhouetted in the frame of the door, his wild hair, a vivid scarlet under the light, whipped by the wind like a flaming fire.

"Come back soon!" he shouted.

Although it was already late, I returned to my office, compelled by a strange curiosity. Perhaps the papers from Monsieur de Castignac would shed some light on the mystery of the fan painter.

It was eight o'clock. The deserted offices had that eerie stillness of after-business hours. The rustle of the papers echoed through the silent rooms. And then, among the correspondence, bills, receipts, and other documents received from Paris, I came upon the yellowed newspaper clipping. "The Painter of Light Goes into Darkness," the headline read. There was Leonardo's background, his marriage to a beautiful model, and his success as a painter of fans of incomparable style and unique coloring, just as he had told me. And then the painter began to lose his sight and finally became blind. The cataracts could be removed, the doctors said. And while Leonardo waited for light to be restored to his eyes, he became aware of another light in his mind. As the days went by this strange light pervaded his whole being and everything around him. Everything he touched and felt he saw in his mind full of light and color, possessed of a beauty he had never known before. To his friends he said he had never been so happy, that he was living in an incredible fairyland where his wife Martha was queen. The color and light that his blind retina could no longer see had finally exploded in the sensitive, poetic imagination of the fan painter.

Together with Martha and his dearest friend, Gustavo Ledoc, who lived with them while they waited for the operation to be performed, Leonardo spent several weeks of unique happiness. And then they operated on his eyes. He was alone the day the bandages were removed. He wanted to surprise his wife at home, he had said to the doctors. When he again could see the world around him, he rushed home, flung the door open, went directly to his study, picked up a brush, dipped it in paint, and splashed a silk fan with exultant strokes. It was then that he heard voices on the floor above. He dashed up the stairs. At the top, he stopped short. Reflected in the large mirror in the hall was the interior of his wife's bedroom. Cold sweat covered his body as love and friendship collapsed before his eyes.

"And this is light!" he screamed. And he jabbed himself in the eyes with the paint-soaked brush.

The second operation was unsuccessful, the clipping said. Leonardo's friend disappeared, and the blind fan painter and his wife sailed for America.

My forehead was running with sweat when I finished reading the clipping. But then I recalled Martha's pale face, submissive and tranquil, and the face of the giant, with his scarlet hair waving like a banner, at the door of the house he had turned into a castle.

A few minutes later, at the sandwich shop around the corner from the office, I ordered a cup of coffee. Helping myself to some sugar from a chipped bowl, I suddenly noticed that I was holding the cheap spoon between my fingers as delicately as though it were a pair of silver tongs.

# THE SECRET

I'LL BE BACK IN AN HOUR," said Brandon Grant, and without so much as a glance at his wife, he opened the door and went out.

Elaine Grant was standing by the window watching the sun sink into the quiet waters of the Pacific. It went down fast in this part of the world, like a gold doubloon dropped into a dark-blue velvet purse. It was incredibly beautiful, she thought, even more so than the first time she had seen it. It took her breath away then. It did now. Still, she could not help but reflect that it was exactly like those gaudy sunset post-cards that make one wonder how anyone could possibly have the bad taste to print such improbable garish colors. Abruptly she turned and faced the room.

Under the lighted lamp on the night table, the round clock, its black hands pointing to twenty-five of five and suggesting a long, droopy mustache, resembled a gloomy caricature of a Chinese face. Brandon would be back in an hour. But in an hour she would have left her husband, forever, in the middle of their second honeymoon.

Slowly Elaine glanced around the room. Memories of the night before rushed at her fiercely from every corner, making her cringe. On the armchair lay Brandon's tuxedo. She remembered Brandon in the dinner suit only a few hours before—tall, broad, mahogany-colored under the mass of red hair that curled ever so softly. The suit lay there now, empty, crumpled, but still exuding her husband's animal vitality. Her own gown next to it, dozens of yards of the palest blue tulle, seemed suspended in mid-air like a piece of fallen sky. On the dresser, at the end of a zigzagging trail of pink powder, was her ivory compact, open and overturned. She shivered. The mirror was broken. Nearby, her purse lay half-open, a pink handkerchief protruding through the metallic mouth like a mocking little pink tongue.

Elaine sighed. The party at the Manila Nautical Club had been most successful. Seven hours of uninterrupted dancing and drinking. On the way back to their hotel, she and Brandon had been tired and silent. Later, in their room, she had tried in vain to repulse his alcoholic amorous advances.

An hour, Elaine thought, walking over to the telephone near the bed. Her eyes quickly turned away from the rumpled bed sheets, and in the mirror across the bed she caught the disgust on her face. She stared at the tall, slender woman in the mirror, her blonde head emerging like a sunflower from the starched white collar. The soft scarlet mouth hardly betrayed her twenty-eight years, but the fine lines around the disturbed violet eyes already hinted at the approaching thirties. Three years of married life had stamped a haunted look on her face, and for the first time Elaine saw how very tired and weary she was from fighting the unknown.

"Front desk," she asked of the operator. "This is Mrs. Brandon. Will you kindly reserve one seat on the six thirty plane to San Francisco and send for my bags in half an hour. Yes, one only. My husband will remain here a few days longer." The sharp click of the telephone as she put it down was like the final stroke of a pen signing a farewell letter.

Once more Elaine glanced around the room. Only a few feet away, she thought, perhaps not even that.

Despair mounted in her throat and a sob was forced out through her lips. Somewhere in this room, between these four walls, the secret was hidden. And she knew she had to find it. Nothing else would allay the unendurable torment. To go away, never to see her husband again, was not enough. The secret was like a hideous viper nestling securely in her soul, and it had to be driven out and destroyed, or it would continue gnawing at her, poisoning her life, no matter where she went.

The secret! Five years. One thousand eight hundred and twenty-six days. Thousands upon thousands of hours. What had he done with them? Why did he refuse even to mention them, preferring to condemn himself utterly before her eyes with his silence? In her husband's tempestuous life, so rich in adventures and changes of fortune, the five years were an unexplored island that disappeared like a fog in a sea of conjectures. The "lost" five years had kept her awake many nights, her mind racked by wild suspicions, and had finally changed her life into a hideous nightmare.

Elaine walked over to the wardrobe and flung the doors open. The old familiar smell rushed at her, the smell of tobacco and old leather and salt and iodine, the smell that had so enchanted her that night in Detroit when she met Brandon at a Christmas dance organized by the employees of the automobile factory where she worked.

127

"Brandon Grant, world vagabond," her friend had said jokingly, when she introduced them. And she was immediately captivated by the vibrant face, sea- and sun-scorched to a deep mahogany color, and by the faraway look in the crystal-blue eyes, which spoke of remote seas and lands.

"Elaine." Brandon whispered her name softly as they danced. "It sounds like the silver bell that we sailors hear on the high seas when we dream of land."

His strong arms about her, her face close to his dark face lined by strange scars, hardly aware of the music, Elaine felt herself being swept away by the mysterious stranger, while her fiancé, a young, good-looking electrical engineer with apologetic manners and a nice bank account, stood by helplessly watching them. For the first time in her life Elaine tasted the sweet joy of yielding to strength. Brandon's plainly cut blue suit no more concealed the strong man of the sea than her fiancé's skillfully padded suit concealed the flaccid physique of the city dweller.

For Elaine hated weakness. After much illness and sorrow, both her parents had died when she was a child. Life with her neurotic aunt in Detroit had been far worse. As soon as she was old enough to work, she went to live alone, vowing to be strong always and to dominate when others were weak. Her closest friend had been a weak girl whom she had dominated completely. Her sweetheart, whom at first she thought she loved, had finally disappointed her when she discovered his physical weakness.

Brandon carried her away in his strong arms while they danced, out into his strange, strong, wild world. The red-haired giant was wholesome and fragrant, spattered by sea foam and moved by roaring winds.

When the music stopped, they went out on a terrace overlooking the city. It was snowing, and Brandon insisted that she wear his jacket over her shoulders. His arm around her, they watched the city lights winking in the distance through the fluttering snow. The white flakes danced madly around them, but Elaine never felt the cold wind. Brandon's jacket smelled of tobacco, leather, tar, salt, and iodine, and Brandon's arm was strong and warm.

"Elaine, do you like living in Detroit?" he asked her.

"I hate it. I feel like a robot in this perennial procession of automobiles."

"I understand. I hardly touch land before I start dreaming of the sea again. I know this means giving up a home, but the sea is in my blood. It's my whole life."

"Why 'giving up a home'?"

"Because no woman would have me. I'm a seaman who comes home only for a few days every two months. Only when I'm too old to sail will I retire. I shall settle down in a little house by the sea, so that I may watch it until I die."

"A woman in love would gladly accept that life." Elaine heard her own words as if someone else were talking. "A few days of happiness would fill the months of waiting with memories and they would keep the half-empty house warm until your return."

They looked at one another through the wild curtain of snowflakes. Towering over her in shirt sleeves, his red hair shimmering through the film of snow that covered it, he reminded her of the proud Vikings in the stories she loved to read as a child.

"Elaine, will you be that woman?" And the snow, like nuptial rice, fell over their first kiss.

In the hotel room, Elaine, impatient at her memories, began to search through her husband's clothes. The familiar smells were no longer a mysterious symphony. The magic had disappeared. Instead, they evoked disagreeable incidents. They reminded her of the sea, which she now hated, for it had finally come between them.

Elaine searched rapidly through the drill jacket, the cotton jacket, the fishing jacket. Impatiently she pushed back the flap of the last pocket. Why did men have so many pockets? Then she turned to Brandon's suitcase. The contents of the battered case were like a colored film of the roving life of its owner—a morocco leather wallet from Africa, a tobacco pouch of caribou hide from Greenland, slippers from Persia, a Chinese dressing gown with fearful red dragons, a leather belt exquisitely hand-tooled from the Argentine pampas, a silver flask with an inscription in Guarani from Paraguay, a long, slender pipe from Kabul—all sorts of odd things that Brandon had collected in thirty-three years of roaming around the world.

This was not the first time that she had rummaged through his belongings. In the first months after their marriage she used to open his bags upon his return from his trips and pull out every object he had picked up in the exotic lands where his boat had stopped. Squealing with delight, she would examine them and smell them and try to guess where he had been and how he had come by them, while he sat nearby, smiling, his eyes caressing her. Thus she had opened the doors into his fantastic life, and from the moment they left Detroit, through their honeymoon and the succeeding months in the little house overlooking the bay in San Francisco, the home port of Brandon's ship, there had been one fascinating revelation after another about the man she had married.

"Like the Chinese," Brandon had said, "we were married first and got acquainted afterward."

They had tacitly agreed to let the knowledge of each other's past life grow in the course of their marriage. The nights of tender passion had alternated with days that were an incessant journey through the past of the beloved. In a few days Brandon knew all about Elaine's life, but he was a never-ending mystery to her. An unusual box, an odd pocketknife, a strange wallet, each souvenir evoked some episode in his life. A bullet hole in a silk handkerchief decorated with bullfight scenes had disclosed the years Brandon spent sailing back and forth to the ports of the Spanish Levant, carrying arms to the Loyalist forces, in the course of which he had been shot at by a German plane. A delicate Siamese pipe had started him on the story of the years he had smuggled arms to the Chinese revolutionaries at the beginning of their civil war. A string of white beads with which Arabs keep their fingers occupied to curb excessive smoking was entangled with an old love in Algiers.

Thus, in a disorderly fashion, Brandon's past had flowed in from every port in every sea—exotic, fascinating, dangerous, alive with adventures, changes of fortune, fights, escapes, even encounters with the law, in which he had always managed to elude punishment by a microscopic margin of luck, astuteness, or ability. And during the long periods of waiting in the small house overlooking the bay, Elaine had amused herself solving the puzzle of his past, patiently assembling the pieces of his hazardous life, integrating snatches of conversations, a story here and a story there, fragments of this and that, into an orderly, coherent pattern. Many were the hours she had spent in her lazy solitude building a chronology of Brandon's life, putting in order the chaos of information she had elicited, linking together periods seemingly isolated in a void, trying to fill in the vague silhouette of her husband.

Then one day she had realized that the puzzle was complete except for one piece. Frantically she had tried to remember, but in spite of her efforts she could not find the missing piece—one empty, blank period, glaringly white in the colorful panorama she had patiently re-created. With pen and paper she mapped out Brandon's life—actions, places, dates. And she discovered that from the time he had run away from a farm in Oregon at the age of thirteen to board his first ship, to the present, there were five consecutive years she could not account for. For those five years she could find no clue whatsoever in either his stories, his personal belongings, the scars in his face recording duels, fights, and even torture by Amazon Indians, or the white lines on his neck, those branding marks that turned purple in moments of anger.

The weeks following her discovery were sleepless, almost tortured, and on the day Brandon finally came home she knew she would break the unwritten law between them and ask him about the five years.

Brandon's homecomings were always as though the Pacific had erupted into the peaceful little house.

Dropping his bags on the floor, he would pick her up in his arms, pressing his scarred face against her soft cheeks, his lips searching avidly for hers. The startled house echoed with his booming voice and the air grew misty with the huge puffs of smoke from his pipe. She always had the sensation that he brought the sea, with all its tumultuous depths and palpitating mysteries, in with him. The days after his arrival were a continuous holiday, filled with much laughter, and walks and picnics under the trees, where their passion would bloom again.

One afternoon, Elaine, seated on his lap, her fingers entangled in his red hair, said half in earnest, half in jest, "Brandon, I have pieced together your life year by year, but there is one piece missing, the five years prior to the two years before our marriage. Where were you? What did you do in those five years?"

His blue eyes became as hard as steel.

"Elaine," he replied coldly, "we have never questioned each other about our pasts and we are not going to start now."

"Does it annoy you, darling?" she asked, somewhat hurt.

"No. I just don't like it. I won't allow anyone to interrogate me about my life."

"But, darling, marriage means sharing everything. It's not just curiosity on my part. I only want to know everything about you so that I can feel we are truly one."

134

He stood up, forcing her to her feet.

"The past is dead and buried. I won't stand for any more questions. When we got married you didn't care about my past. Your curiosity now is impertinent." His tone was fierce and there was hatred in his eyes.

"I don't understand," Elaine exclaimed, puzzled and frightened. "Are you afraid it might change things between us? You could have robbed, murdered, anything, and I would still love you."

"Then, if what I did does not matter, there is no need for you to torment yourself and me any longer."

When Brandon left a few days later, they parted without the usual tenderness. He was silent and aloof, and she was hurt, frightened, and miserable. From then on she had lived in a constant mental tumult. She had imagined and discarded countless explanations for the five lost years. Had he been in some foreign prison? Was he a criminal? Perhaps he was married to another woman, whom he still saw during his long absences. In the daytime her mind was a swarming hive of suspicions; at night it became a jungle of frightening nightmares in which Brandon played monstrous roles, surrounded by beautiful women who taunted her and demanded the return of their husband.

She had tried to question him again, to renew the conversation, but he always answered with the same steely look, the same strange grimace of hatred, and absolute silence.

In desperation she consulted police records, read every newspaper in the library for the five missing years, until she was utterly exhausted by the fruitless search. Brandon's arrivals now brought only interminable silences alternating with violent quarrels, and rancor rose in Elaine's heart like a silent tide of sinister waters. If Brandon preferred to destroy their happiness rather than tell about the five years, then he must have done something so monstrous that he dared not discuss it. But what could he have done? What horrible crime had he committed that he was afraid to tell her who adored him and would help him to carry any burden? Or was there another woman who still played a part in his life?

The battle ranging in Elaine's mind appeared to have its effect on Brandon also. He lost a great deal of weight and looked worried and haggard. Often in the middle of a conversation his eyes would become vague and he would suddenly stop talking. The sea no longer entered the little house with him; instead most of him seemed to remain away, with the sea.

One day, when she had finally decided to leave him, he came back and told her that they were going to Manila on a second honeymoon. There they would find a solution to their problem, he promised.

All through the trip he tried desperately to be as he was during the first months of their marriage. The sea, the winds, the distant stars seemed to whip his passion back to life. After two weeks in Manila, Elaine could bear it no longer. She had hoped that the trip would change everything, but she knew now that she must leave him or go insane.

That morning at breakfast Brandon had received a letter. His face had turned deadly gray. If only she could find that letter.

Furiously Elaine tossed down the leather case with Greek symbols that she had pulled out of the suitcase. It was useless. She would never know what had ruined their marriage. Elaine saw her image blurred in the mirror and only then did she realize that she was crying. Rage swelled up in her throat and sobs shook her body. Brandon had allowed her to open all the doors to his fabulous past but one, and behind that door he had taken refuge, shutting her out with her misery. He knew, for she had told him that morning, that if he did not open that door their marriage would have to end.

"I'll never let you go," he replied. "No matter what happens, you'll remain with me—for the rest of our lives."

" 'For the rest of our lives.' " His tone had made her shiver. Shivering now, she entered the bathroom. She hurriedly went through every jar and bottle in the medicine chest, the small leather box with the razor, the soapbox. Suddenly her throat went dry as she stared into the box containing the tube of shaving

137

cream. Her tearful eyes smarted and she could hardly lift her hand to brush off the tears. Leaning against the wall, clutching the carton in her hand, she slowly pulled out a small roll of papers. There were three letters, one dated in Manila two days before: the other two, also from Manila but of an earlier date, were addressed to Brandon at the Nautical Club in San Francisco.

Vaguely while she read the letters she heard the dripping of the faucet, the thumping inside her chest, and then the telephone. She staggered to the bed and picked up the telephone, staring all the time at the top letter, on which the drops of perspiration rolling down from her face were blurring the ink.

"Mrs. Grant, shall we send for your luggage now?"

She heard her own voice, strange, choked. "Never mind."

"But, Mrs. Grant, you'll miss your plane."

"Never mind," she repeated, once more reading the words blazing before her eyes: ". . . and we urge you to report immediately for further analysis, to determine whether you should renew the treatments received during the five years you were interned in this leprosarium."

"Never mind," she said once more, "I'm staying." And in the mirror across the bed she saw the horror in her eyes as she repeated her husband's words. "For the rest of our lives."

# THE PERFECT LOVER

MY WIFE HAS A LOVER.
There is nothing I can do," the young man added
with quiet desperation. "I don't know who he is. Besides, I love her. That's why I've come to you for
legal advice."

He stared with hopeless eyes at the blindingly
bright summer sky beyond the window.

"Tell me everything," I said.

His fine blue eyes looked at me, but he still seemed far away when he spoke.

"I was a struggling painter in Greenwich Village when I met Rima. Like many others in the Village, I had dreams of fame and glory, but I seldom had enough money to buy a decent meal. I lived and worked in the attic of an old house on Charles Street. There were days when I worked feverishly, spurred by visions of fame and wealth. And there were days of despair, when I did nothing but wander through the Village, hoping to find someone who would buy one of the paintings that covered the cracks in the walls of my studio. And then I met Rima.

"It was a hot afternoon in June. Tired, discouraged, with sweat rolling down my face like drops of rain down a windowpane, I pushed aside brushes and paints and went to the window, gasping for air. It was two o'clock and the street, ablaze under the fierce sun, was deserted. Suddenly I saw a black and red skirt fluttering like a butterfly along the street. I had but a glimpse of a pale face under a small straw hat and masses of shining blonde hair before she disappeared into the house opposite my window. Her clothes were elegant, and there was an air of mystery about her. She wasn't the type of woman one usually sees in that part of the Village.

"Two or three days later, on my way home from the art shop, I bumped into her. Looking into startling

140

golden-green eyes, I mumbled an apology. Saying nothing, she stepped aside and hurried into the same house as before.

"Two days later, I was sitting at the window at about the same time when I saw her again scurrying into the building across the street. I realized then that I had been waiting for her.

"It now seems but a brief moment to me, yet our courtship lasted six months. The day before our wedding we were sitting at Luigi's bar. From the wall above the bar, Dante and Beatrice smiled cryptically down upon us. I was remembering the first time I had seen her and said, 'Rima, I used to watch you go into the house across from my studio. I could only see that your face was very pale and your hair very blonde. Who would have guessed then that one day we would be getting married? I love you, Rima, I love you. I can't live without you.'

"She finished her drink absent-mindedly and then said, 'I love you, too. I didn't think I could fall in love again. I was sure that there would never be anyone else. And then you came along and knocked down my little house of cards.'

"'Rima,' I started to say, but she interrupted me.

"'I know what you're going to ask me. Don't. I cannot answer you. You know my past, my present is happy, and my future looks bright. I divorced a wealthy architect who never understood me. Now

141

I'm going to marry a starry-eyed painter. We're going to be very happy. Don't ask for more, and everything will be all right.'

"I wanted to believe her, but I could not put out of my mind her visits to the house across the street before she met me. I found myself constantly wondering whom she could have gone to see there three or four times a week. I tried to find out, but all the superintendent could tell me was that the apartment was rented to a blonde woman and that he had never seen anyone else go into the apartment. I myself had always seen her go in and come out alone.

"We first talked to each other one afternoon. I followed her into a drugstore and sat next to her at the counter. She asked me for a match. She was twenty-six, five years younger than I. Her face was like that of a Raphael Madonna, but her figure had all the sensuality of a Matisse odalisque.

"She disliked talking about herself. When she did, she was always vague. She told me she came from Chicago. Her parents had died when she was eighteen and she had gone to work in an office. Then she came to New York, and she had been working in a leather-goods shop on Fifth Avenue for two years when she met Peter Bowen, an architect. They were married, and she divorced him a year later. That was all I knew about her."

"At first I didn't mention her visits, which stopped

soon after we started seeing each other. But one day as we were looking out my window, I said, smiling, 'Did it ever occur to you that I might have formed a bad impression of you?'

"She looked at me coldly. 'Why, Gerald? Because of my visits to the house across the street? I should think a Village artist would be a little more broad-minded.'

" 'Rima, I'm in love with you,' I said pleadingly.

"She said something about understanding, and when I replied that I could not understand what was a mystery to me, she turned away abruptly, picked up her bag and gloves, and walked to the door, saying, 'In that case ours will be an unfinished story.'

"I was frightened. I ran after her and put my arms around her. I begged her not to go, to forgive me. I told her I had no right to pry into her past, that I should be grateful instead that she was risking her future by marrying a starving artist. Repeatedly I told her that I trusted her.

"Fortunately the word 'starving' turned out to be a figure of speech. We were married, and Rima brought me good luck. A Madison Avenue gallery gave me a one-man show, and I sold several paintings and even received enough commissions to keep me busy for at least a year. Above all, I had Rima.

"We rented an apartment overlooking the East River, but I kept my studio and I worked there from eight to ten hours practically every day. I didn't even stop for lunch. More than anything else, I wanted to be famous for Rima, for my love had reached limits no longer human, perhaps because there was something in Rima that persistently eluded me, something I could not fathom, that made her remote, unattainable.

"Such was my happiness with her that I could not understand how a man could ever be happy again having known and lost Rima. I never thought about her first husband. To me he was merely an incident in her life, the same as going through school or having measles. But her visits to Charles Street continued to torment me. I couldn't stop wondering who the man had been and where he was now.

"I tried several times to get her to talk about it, but she always changed the subject. One evening we sat embracing on our terrace, watching the lights of the river. A few minutes before, I had tasted such sweet and tender passion in her arms that I felt completely fulfilled and contented. Yet it was at such moments that her visits to Charles Street tormented me most. I could feel the old ache stirring inside me, growing slowly, gnawing at me fiercely, goading me to question her, to find out who the man was, otherwise I would never again have peace of mind, I would never know complete happiness. Suddenly I asked her, 'What is your idea of a perfect lover?'

144

"She hesitated, as if she were afraid to speak. Finally she said, 'You won't understand, you may even get angry, but I'll tell you. When I was a very young girl I used to have recurrent dreams about a strange, fantastic world. I never found out where it was, but it was a remote land, for there were odd things and odd people, and there was always a man, an unreal sort of man. I never saw his face clearly, but he told me that he had wandered all over the world, tasted all the pleasures and joys, experienced all possible emotions, and finally, like Parsifal looking for the Holy Grail, he had come to me.'

Her words plunged me into a feeling of depression bordering on despair. I felt that I was left out, that there was a barrier between us that I would never cross. And the ache inside me deepened.

" 'Have you ever been in love before?' I asked her.

" 'I thought I was in love with my first husband, but I was wrong.'

"Suddenly she pushed my arms away and looked at me angrily. With kisses and caresses I appeased her, but my jealousy grew fiercer than ever.

"Next day I couldn't work. I stood at the window in my studio, staring at the house across the street. Suddenly I decided to go there. I wanted to see the walls that had sheltered her and another man. I gave the superintendent a tip and he took me upstairs. I thought my wife had given up the apartment. You can imagine my consternation when the man told me that it was still rented to a Mrs. Bowen. She came twice a week, he said, always alone. He had never seen anyone else go up.

"It was an old studio with a large fireplace, very much like mine across the street. The furniture was old and cheap-looking—two armchairs, a studio bed, several odd tables. But how I noticed them I shall never know, for scattered all around the room—on the mantelpiece, on the tables, on numerous shelves on the walls, and even on the floor—was the most fantastic collection of curios and *bibelots* I had ever seen, literally hundreds of objects of all kinds and shapes: figurines, boxes with strange symbols, bells, ikons, little dragons and winged horses, pagodas, idols, ashtrays, countless odd and exotic things from all parts of the world. Yes, the whole world, the six continents and the seven seas, was imprisoned in that room!

"I left the room deeply disturbed. When I got home we had a brief but sharp argument. She explained that she had had a lease for two years which would expire in a few months, but if I insisted on being so ridiculously jealous, she would go to the trouble of canceling it the following day. Her eyes were two bright cold emeralds.

"She canceled the lease, and for a few weeks we were happy once again. But now I know she has a

146

lover and I would like you, as a lawyer, to help me."

"How do you know?" I asked.

"Two weeks ago," he said, "I came home early. Rima was out. When she returned she refused to tell me where she had been. Two days later, I saw her hurrying home ahead of me, yet she told me afterward that she hadn't been out of the house all day. Finally I decided to spy on her. This afternoon I followed her to Macdougal Street. I saw her go into a house near Houston Street. She's there now. I want you to come with me and be a witness. You'll keep me from doing something foolish, and we can put an end legally to a situation that is driving me insane."

Gerald Sandes and I got into a taxi and crossed the Village under a blazing July sun. We got out on Macdougal Street, and Gerald pointed to an old three-story house across the street. Boxes bright with geraniums lined the windows. At one of the windows on the top floor sat a blonde woman staring at the sky.

Perspiring, we climbed the dank-smelling wooden stairs. On the third floor there was only one door. Gerald pushed it open without knocking. The woman at the window jumped to her feet. I recognized the blonde hair, the emerald eyes. All around us was the most amazing collection of knickknacks—a strange, exotic, fantastic world, as Gerald had said.

"Rima, what are you doing here?" Gerald's eyes avidly searched the room.

Her cold voice seemed to increase the heat around us. "I will not tell you. You have no right to interfere if I don't hurt you with this."

"But you *are* hurting me, Rima. How long have you been coming here? Whom do you meet?"

"I have been coming here for a month," she answered. "As for whom I meet, it's useless to explain. You would never understand."

"But Rima," Gerald cried out, "aren't you happy with me? What is it you want? You did this to your first husband and I thought it was because you didn't love him. But how can you do it to me after claiming you love me so much?"

Like a madman he darted from one place to the other, examining everything in the room. She had returned to her seat by the window. She was like a wax figure. Gerald suddenly seized a figurine from the mantelpiece and smashed it against the floor.

"What are all these things?" he shouted. "Spinsters' baubles, childhood toys, schoolgirl souvenirs? Is this the world of dreams where you meet your lover? I swear I'll kill him when he walks in!"

"He will not come in," she said, without turning.

"You warned him!"

"You could never kill him, Gerald. No one could kill him."

"Rima, for the last time—"

"Gerald, you may have a divorce if you want. Go now!"

We left the room. Gerald descended the stairs as a condemned man approaches the scaffold.

The landlady stopped us at the door to the street.

"Are you looking for someone?" she asked.

"No, thank you," replied Gerald. "We have been up-stairs."

"Where?" she demanded.

"On the third floor. I don't see that it concerns you. Excuse me," and he started to open the door.

But the landlady continued, "You saw that poor girl on the third floor? I'm so sorry for her. She's so beautiful and she fixed her room so pretty. But she's always alone. She comes twice a week and she sits at the window for hours and then she goes away. I asked her once if she was waiting for someone. She said no and that no one was to go up there. No one! And now you say that you were up there."

We went out. As we crossed the street I looked up. The sun was blinding, but I could see Rima among the geraniums, her head leaning against the window frame, her eyes staring at the sky, her mind wandering in the dream world where she met her perfect lover.

## *SILENTLY THE IVY GROWS*

ALL I COULD SEE OF THE man before me in the hospital bed were his lips, half of one cheek, and two pale-blue eyes which fever had turned into drops of phosphorescent liquid. But the man's spirit breathed vigorously underneath the geometric pattern of bandages, and the hand that took the cigarette I offered was steady. A moment later, a slow, toneless voice began the story. In the stillness of the sunlit morning, the voice gradually darkened

150

with terror the immaculate whiteness of the room. At the foot of the bed the fever chart recorded a steep peak and sudden descent. Blue smoke wove a curtain between us. And Alvin Carey spoke.

"Doctor, I shall tell you in a few minutes what happened over a period of almost one year. It all began on a Sunday. Georgia and I loved Sundays. Somebody once spoke of the golden quality of Sundays. Even if the rest of the week has been gray, Sunday is always a golden day—golden not only on certain calendars where they are framed with a border of gold, but also in the feeling of rest and peace that permeates the air. Georgia and I were always completely happy on Sundays!

"That Sunday, at about five in the afternoon, we began to get dressed for Sonders' party. Our Park Avenue apartment, radiant with sunshine, was like a gilded gallery, and for a moment we considered staying home to enjoy the rest of our Sunday alone.

"Georgia and I usually spent Sundays working, I revising what I had written during the week and she editing and typing my manuscripts. At dusk we would switch on the lamps, play the stereo, mix Martinis, and pass the hours talking and reading and daydreaming.

"But attendance at Sonders' party was obligatory if I was to remain on friendly terms with him. At least, that's what Georgia said. Ever since he rejected my collection of short stories with the flimsy excuse that his firm published only novels, I felt that something had come between us. His reason for rejecting my manuscript was too absurd to be true. If my stories were good—and they are—why not change his stupid editorial policy and publish them, which, if not money, would certainly bring his publishing house prestige? At that time I wanted to break with Sonders, but Georgia convinced me that it would be childish and impractical.

" 'Do you want to go to Sonders' party?' Georgia asked me.

" 'About as much as I want to attend a funeral,' I answered. 'I haven't seen Ralph in six months and I could go another six without seeing him. The people at his parties are intolerably dull and his cocktails taste like penicillin.'

" 'Come on, Alvin,' she urged, 'don't be difficult. It is important for you to be friendly toward Ralph. We'll only stay half an hour.'

"She kissed me softly on the lips, then, locking her arm in mine, led me to the door.

"The party was everything I had feared. Sonders' apartment on Central Park South was packed with people—too many bad authors, whose works for some unearthly reason Sonders delights in publishing, and too many old hens cackling admiringly around them, lots of smoke and noise, and horrible Picassos hanging on the walls, as if Sonders had invited characters from Dante's *Inferno* to the party. And, worst of all, the first incident of the tragedy.

"Sonders rushed up to me displaying all his teeth and shook my hand vigorously, as though nothing had happened. Georgia unfortunately greeted him with equal enthusiasm. They kissed and hugged and positively beamed at each other.

"When he left us to greet other guests, I whispered to her, 'Let's not overdo it.'

" 'Alvin, be reasonable,' she entreated. 'We are his guests and we should return his friendliness.'

" 'Friendliness!' I flared up. 'Hypocrisy! He does not like my stories but he likes me as long as you are along.'

"Georgia's blue eyes fluttered like two frightened bluebirds and misted with tears.

" 'You're such a foolish child,' she said quietly, 'but perhaps that's why I love you.' She gave my arm a little squeeze and sailed away into the chattering crowd.

"The party became unendurable, as the air grew more stifling and the presence of the admired and the admiring more intolerable. I asked myself repeatedly why had Sonders invited me, since I did not belong to his clique, unless it was to humiliate me. But this would not really have mattered, had it not been for Georgia's behavior. At first she had not wanted to come to the party, but once there I could not tear her away. Every time I looked for her in the oscillating jungle of heads I spied her flaming red hair close to Sonders' gray head. And when her group circulated around the room, as groups will circulate at every party, and finally reached me, I saw her lips whispering close to Sonders' face.

"On the way home we had our first real quarrel since we were married.

" 'What were you doing all evening so close to Sonders? And you didn't want to go to the party!' I reproached her.

" 'I was trying to patch things up for you,' she protested.

" 'Nobody asked you to do that,' I said angrily. 'Your behavior was most indecorous.'

" 'My behavior may result in their publishing your stories.'

"I could see that she was deeply hurt, which I considered most unreasonable and exasperating. 'According to that idiot,' I shouted, 'they only publish novels. Besides, if it requires that you flirt with him, I'd rather not have the stories published.'

" 'I was not flirting,' she screamed. 'If anybody was, it was you. I ruined my entire evening trying to pave the way for you for a new interview with Sonders and you dare to accuse me of flirting! And what were you doing kissing Victoria Henners?'

154

" 'Victoria? You're talking nonsense. She merely gave me a peck as she was leaving.'

" 'I saw you kissing each other twice and the first time was not when we arrived.'

" 'You're being absurd. You take everything so seriously. That's Victoria's way. She always acts like that."

" 'Well, then, if you don't want me to take your little flirtation with Victoria seriously, you shouldn't get upset about my little talks with Sonders.'

"That was all. But that night we didn't speak to each other again. I lay awake most of the night fretting over Georgia's strange behavior and unfair accusations.

"Several days later there was a cat show and Georgia, who loves cats, asked me to meet her at the exhibition.

"I arrived a little before the appointed hour. Georgia, on the other hand, was late. And she was always so punctual! It was then that my suspicions began.

"Half an hour later I was tired and sick—tired of waiting and sick of cats. Their smell, their purring suddenly became unendurable. I was about to dash out when Georgia sauntered in, elegantly dressed, her hair and mouth two bright red flashes between the dark-blue hat and dark-blue suit.

" 'I have been waiting half an hour in this infernal place,' I said sharply.

" 'I'm so sorry, darling. They kept me waiting at

the hairdresser's. I shouldn't have asked you to meet me here.'

"I didn't believe her, but I made no comment. In silence we strolled around the cages, suspicions furiously racing one another in my mind, while the horrid little beasts behind the bars stared at me with a gleam of mockery in their glinting eyes.

"My suspicions were to be confirmed then and there. Georgia sneezed, and when she pulled a handkerchief out of her purse, a gray card slipped out. I recognized the gold monogram as I picked it up.

" 'Georgia, where did this come from?' I cried.

"She flushed. 'Sonders gave it to me at the party. It's an invitation to a literary gathering next week.'

" 'Why didn't he mention it to me?'

" 'Because you left without saying good-by. I forgot to show it to you.'

" 'But you said nothing to me. I'm sure that if I hadn't seen it accidentally, you would have never mentioned it.'

" 'I told you that I forgot. You can't possibly believe that I would go to a party without you?'

"At that moment it flashed through my mind that Georgia had arrived late because she had been with Sonders and that he had just given her the invitation. I stared at her fixedly. She didn't flinch. The amazing limpidity of her blue eyes was not marred by any feeling of guilt. Behind her, a Persian cat watched me with wise, pensive eyes, his long tail curled up into a large question mark.

"During the following weeks I watched the sad process of destruction of the delicate crystal that is marriage. In a man's relationship with the woman he loves and marries, he one day discovers a fine crack that mars the perfection of the marital pattern. Slowly the crack grows wider and wider, until finally, at the slightest touch, the crystal breaks into numerous fragments.

"One morning the mail arrived while Georgia was out shopping, and I noticed an envelope addressed to her from a New York bank, which was not the one we both used. Puzzled, I opened it and found inside a receipt for a deposit of one hundred dollars. When she returned I confronted her with the receipt.

" 'I didn't know you were opening my mail,' she remarked sarcastically. 'Evidently you tolerate no secrets between husband and wife. I told you some time ago I would deposit the money Aunt Mariette sends me from time to time in a separate account so that I can buy clothes for our trip to Europe.'

"I dropped the matter without further comment, but I knew that she was not telling the truth. We had postponed the trip indefinitely. It was hard to believe that she would be saving so far in advance. It seemed more logical that Georgia, feeling estranged from me, had considered the possibility of a separation. Observe how unfair she was. It bothered her that I opened her mail, but it never bothered her that I might be hurt by the bank incident.

"Yet a few days later when I arrived home she was wearing a sulky look on her face and her lips were grimly set. On the cocktail table lay a blue envelope. I immediately recognized Victoria Henners' bold handwriting. Since Sonders' party we had been carrying on an innocent correspondence and, all in fun, wrote to each other in rather affectionate terms.

" 'Congratulations,' said Georgia. 'You have a devoted admirer. Her life will be unendurable if you don't fly with her to Havana. As far as I'm concerned, you can take off right now.'

"Imagine her taking a joke like that seriously when she herself was leading a secret life! I clothed myself in an armor of silence, which her sharp tongue could not pierce.

"That very night the first frightening incident occurred. As I was shaving, the razor slipped from my hand, inflicting a deep cut on my cheek. Normally Georgia, who had just brought some clean towels into the bathroom, would have screamed and rushed out of the room, for blood makes her faint and the idea of pain drives her hysterical. Instead, she stared at me fascinated while blood ran down my neck.

" 'Don't stand there like a fool!' I shouted. 'Get me something to stop the blood.'

158

"She opened the medicine chest mechanically and handed me the styptic pencil. The fascinated expression in her eyes was to haunt me for a long time. When the bleeding stopped, I asked her for the penicillin ointment. She said she didn't know where it was. In vain I searched through the medicine chest, where it's usually kept. While I was searching in the closet, one of her purses fell to the floor and the tube of penicillin rolled out.

" 'What does this mean?' I asked.

" 'Oh, I'm so sorry! I haven't used that purse for months. The penicillin has been there since I took it to Aunt Mariette's when she cut herself with the scissors. I had completely forgotten about it.'

"That gave me much to think about, so much, in fact, that in an attempt to fathom her strange behavior, the following afternoon, while she was away playing bridge, I went through all her belongings, every one of her drawers and purses, her clothes, boxes, jewel cases—there was nothing I didn't turn inside out. And in a writing case I found something that terrified me, a bill from a psychiatrist dated several weeks back.

"That night I concealed my anxiety as well as I could. When Georgia went out shopping the following morning, I rushed to the address listed on the bill. You can imagine my chagrin when I was informed that the psychiatrist was in Europe and would not be back for three or four weeks. When I demanded to see

my wife's clinical history, the psychiatrist's nurse refused to show it to me, alleging that their records were
confidential. She said I would have to wait until the
psychiatrist returned.

"But I couldn't wait that long; I was so beset by
worry and fear that at night I couldn't close my eyes.
And during the long hours of insomnia, I tried desperately to tie the loose ends together. Not only did I
recall the incident at the party, but others before them.
I remembered that it was Georgia who advised me to
submit my stories to Sonders. When he rejected them,
I was so hurt and disappointed that I refused to send
them to another publisher. There was Georgia's in-
timacy with Sonders at the party, and the incident of
the card at the cat exhibition, and her unwillingness
to look for the penicillin which later turned up in her
purse. Why had she been so fascinated by the blood
running down my cheek? What evil thoughts had
crossed her mind then? Did she want to be rid of me,
perhaps to marry Sonders? And finally, like a great
hammer inflicting the *coup de grâce,* the psychiatrist's
bill. I didn't want to believe it then; I don't want to
even now. But everything pointed in the same direction. Georgia was insane! I was living with a demented
woman who cunningly concealed her condition and
whose sinister intentions I had no way of finding out.

"This terrifying discovery unnerved me so that I
neglected my work. The stack of unfinished stories lay

160

untouched on my desk, while I pursued my investigation. One by one I discreetly questioned all our friends in an attempt to uncover some clue that would point to Georgia's intentions. I only discovered that to every friend we present a different personality, as if we were reflected in hundreds of mirrors each of which returns an entirely different image, and that if we really wish to know a person we must go directly to him instead of judging him by the distorting opinions of his friends. I did learn from two friends that Georgia had met Sonders twice at literary gatherings that I had refused to attend. According to her, for she didn't deny it when I asked her, it had happened accidentally. This only confirmed my suspicion that those two were plotting some horrendous deed against me.

"You couldn't possibly imagine those horrible sleepless nights. Hot summer nights when sweat poured down my back like blood from an open wound. Oh, those endless nights, when my head buzzed as though invaded by angry mosquitoes, while Georgia slept peacefully by my side, or pretended to! Long nights of watching her, waiting for some incriminating word to escape her lips while she slept.

"Many times I caught Georgia staring at me curiously. We hardly spoke to each other any more. Her mouth began to wither, like the petals of a dying rose, and her eyes misted with a veil of sadness. To make things worse, the psychiatrist who could have enlight-

161

ened me prolonged his stay in Europe. I didn't know what to do, how to fight the labyrinthine mystery of a sick mind. And all the time I feared for my life.

"Because I had lost my appetite and refused to eat, Georgia neglected our meals and instead fed me broths and eggnogs, claiming that I looked ill.

"One night, the veil of mystery was suddenly torn asunder. Georgia had gone to visit a sick relative, and I was alone in the apartment when the doorbell rang. Our neighbor, a pale young girl, stood in the hall, smiling.

" 'Is your wife in, Mr. Carey?' she asked.

"When I explained that she was out, the girl handed me a small yellow package.

" 'It's the insecticide she asked me to get her for the bugs on the terrace. Be careful if there's a cat in the house,' she added, laughing. 'It's arsenic and it doesn't discriminate between small and large animals.'

"Mechanically I closed the door, and opening the package, stared horrified at the white, odorless powder. Then, suddenly springing into motion, I rushed to the terrace. The plants were thoroughly sprinkled with a white substance. I ran out into the hall and knocked at my neighbor's door. The same girl with the same wide smile, which she seemed to wear permanently like tooth-braces, appeared.

" 'Pardon me,' I said, 'but is this the same powder my wife has been using?'

162

" 'Yes, Mr. Carey. I lent her some a few weeks ago and she asked me to get her some more. It's very potent.'

"I returned to our apartment drenched in sweat. The loose ends were tied together now and they felt like a noose tightening around my neck. That tasteless powder was so easy to mix in broths and eggnogs! No wonder my insomnia and lack of appetite had been increasing! She had been slowly poisoning me!

"I hardly remember what happened next. It was like a nightmare from which I have never completely awakened. My wife had been trying to kill me. So far she had failed, but when two people live together, there are bound to be many opportunities to commit such a crime. But why? Why did she want to kill me? Did she want to marry Sonders or did she just want to get rid of me? I had no way of knowing and I realized that I would not be able to reason with her sick mind. A sick mind reasons only through its own mysterious mechanism. The actions of a demented person reveal only the right side of the tapestry of his thoughts, not the entangled web, the labyrinth of threads running in all directions on the wrong side, which is known only to the demented person himself. Silently the ivy of madness grows.

"Staggering under the impact of my thoughts, I went out on the terrace again. How many things were suddenly clear! Like the loose pieces of a jigsaw puzzle finally forming a picture, it all fitted together. And the picture before my eyes was terrifying.

"The night was hot. Thirty floors below the terrace Park Avenue was an ever-changing luminous belt, now of rubies, now of emeralds, along which the moving cars cut tiny triangles of light. The smell of dry soil crept up from the flowerpots. The sky had the amber-red cast that precedes a summer storm. From a neighboring terrace the melancholy notes of a blues reached me like the soft flapping of wings.

"Trembling with fear, I clung to the railing. I was in great danger. Anything could happen once she discovered that I was aware of her attempts to poison me.

"Flashes of lightning seared the sky and thunder roared in the distance. I felt it reverberating inside my own head. Suddenly a flash of lightning revealed a silhouette at my side. I jumped. It was Georgia.

" 'I didn't hear you come in,' I gasped. 'They brought you more arsenic.'

" 'Arsenic?' Another flash of lightning lit her profile. Soft and innocent as an angel's—it might have deceived God Himself. 'Oh, the insecticide. The plants are drying out and now the bugs are finishing them off. But what are you doing out here?'

"I didn't answer. She stood so close that I could feel the warmth of her body. More flashes of lightning re-

164

vealed the planes of her face and painted her mouth a livid gray. Our silence, as though it were a sounding board for the elements, made the heat more intense, the flashes more brilliant, brought the clamor of the storm closer. Georgia's hand began to toy with the gardening tools in a box on the ledge, while her other hand softly brushed my cheek like the wing of a dove.

" 'Alvin,' she whispered, 'What has happened to us, my darling? Why have we grown so far apart?'

"She leaned forward to kiss me. There was a flash, and I saw her hand over the pruning shears. . . ."

Alvin Carey finished his story reluctantly. Soon after, I took my leave. As I opened the door I looked back at him. He lay in bed exhausted, wrapped in bandages like a mummy—a rather loquacious, agitated mummy.

Out in the corridor a detective stopped me.

"Doctor," he asked, "did he tell you everything?"

"Almost everything. I want to talk to him again this afternoon," I answered. "Before seeing him I spoke with the physician who treated him. His wounds are extensive, but not serious. He has several deep cuts on the face and arms."

"Why did he plunge through the glass door, Doctor?"

"Who can tell? Perhaps the storm upset him; perhaps he didn't want to hear his wife's scream as she plummeted down to the street. Neighbors who saw the whole thing said that immediately after pushing her, he uttered a horrible scream and rushed headlong at the French doors leading into the apartment."

"Too bad you couldn't see him before you went to Europe, Doctor," said the detective.

"Yes. She shouldn't have waited. When she consulted me about her husband, I advised her not to wait for me, to take him immediately to another psychiatrist. She preferred to wait. It cost her her life. I warned her that he was a paranoiac."

# DATELINE: MUNICH

Shortly after landing in Munich, one December morning in 1947, I knew I had about the most sensational story of the century. I also knew that it would probably never be published.

I began the investigation immediately. I checked my suitcase at the airport, climbed into the car that the Amalgamated Press had waiting for me, and went directly to the old Weissberg Building, where those involved in the assassination were held prisoner.

It was cold. The gray sky was a fitting frame for the shivering, naked city, which still flaunted its smoky ruins as shamelessly as a beggar his sores. The damaged houses loomed shapeless and ghostly in the crude light of dawn. Doors and windows were shut tightly. The few persons on the streets walked with wary steps, eyes cast down, their bodies cringing as in fear. Munich was silent and frightened, like a rabbit that feels the breath of hounds at the opening of its burrow. The people were afraid of the consequences. As though we could punish them! For it was the one crime that could not be punished.

Armed American patrols were stationed on almost every street corner. The only color in Munich was on the cheeks of the boys from Kansas and the Dakotas, pink and shiny as frosted apples in the fall.

The Weissberg Building was surrounded by a cordon of military police armed with machine guns. My arrival nevertheless caused hardly a stir. A guard, his eyes heavy with sleep, and a bored sergeant examined my papers and then directed me to the waiting room. Here an atmosphere of confusion permeated the very walls. Under the baleful glare of the naked bulbs, the benches of dark pine resembled great frozen fish from another planet.

The C.O. informed me sharply that my special pass entitled me to question only one of the prisoners, but that he himself was sick of newspapermen, and besides

168

—what in heaven's name was there to investigate? He added, a note of glee creeping into his voice, that I would not be allowed to choose the prisoner; he would personally do that, and the interview would be taken down, every word of it, and would have to be approved and released by him. He then kept me waiting twenty minutes. Morning cautiously crept through the cracks around doors and windows. Finally a door at the end of the room was flung open and two soldiers ushered in a prisoner.

He was in his middle forties, with a face as creased as a peasant's wedding dress that has been kept in a chest too long, thin mouse-colored hair, eyes of a blue that once may have been bright and clear but was now dull and faded, and a mouth like an upside-down V. His legs and hands trembled and so did his voice when he spoke. He collapsed on a bench and I offered him a cigarette. It was as though I had given him a vitamin shot instead of a Camel. His face brightened a little through the thick spirals of smoke.

His name was Rudolph Zimmer, he said, adding immediately that he was innocent. For weeks he had received the circulars. They arrived by mail once or twice a week. They bore no signature, only a red stamp: "The Revolutionary Committee for a New Germany." They said that a miracle would soon occur in Germany that would bring to an end the bitter tragedy of the German people and restore them to their rightful position as world leaders. One day he received an invitation to a meeting—where moment-ous decisions for the German people would be made, the circular promised—at the "Zum Kleinen Löwen," a beer hall where trade unions held their annual dinners.

After much hesitation, Zimmer's curiosity prevailed and he went to the meeting. Over two hundred people were already seated around the tables when he ar-rived at the hall at nine o'clock. The immense fire-place embedded in the center of one wall cast no warmth, no glowing light, no dancing shadows, and there was no clinking of steins, no singing or laughter. The fierce heads of wild animals lining the walls looked down now upon dimmed lights and whisper-ing voices, and the waitresses silently waded around the tables. At the entrance of the hall, Zimmer had recognized two neighbors, who with five or six other men scrutinized every person entering.

Zimmer sat at one of the tables and shortly after a friend approached him and whispered that a special meeting was being held in the cellar. Zimmer was surprised. The cellar, which could seat three hundred persons, had not been used in years, and he would have thought it to be carpeted with dust and lined with cobwebs. His curiosity stronger than his fear that American soldiers might wander in and surprise them holding a secret meeting, he followed his friend to

170

one end of the hall and down a flight of stairs to the
cellar.

The place was spotless, with row after row of chairs
set in front of a wooden platform, on which stood several chairs and a table with a pitcher of water. People
sat silently, like a concert audience just before the
orchestra begins to play. Candles set along the walls
and on the table lighted the room and filled it with
dancing shadows. Zimmer sat down between two old
men in one of the back rows.

Half an hour later the cellar was filled to capacity.
Many were standing. Then a group of men climbed
onto the platform. Zimmer was too far back to see
them well. He only remembered that, when some uniformed young men snuffed out some of the candles
and a spotlight was focused on the platform, he suddenly felt a wave of nausea, which he wanted to believe
was due to the beer he had drunk too fast and to the
thick tobacco smoke that made the air unbreathable,
but which he knew was really due to fear.

A tall, massive man from Nuremberg, who was introduced as a war hero, addressed them. Because they
were all good Germans, he said, they had been invited
to this special meeting of the Revolutionary Committee
for a New Germany.

"When I heard this," said Zimmer, "I looked toward
the exit in sudden fear, but half a dozen men in uni-

form guarded the closed door, their hands gripping wooden clubs. I realized then that no one would be allowed to leave and I then vowed that if I ever left that place alive I would never attend any more meetings.

"The speaker," Zimmer went on, "turned the platform over to a chubby man, who soon had us gaping. I couldn't see his face clearly, but he had snow-white hair and a long purple scar across his right cheek. He spoke in a deep voice, with long, dramatic pauses that captivated the audience.

" 'A miracle has happened in Germany,' were his first words. People shifted nervously in their seats and glanced furtively at one another. 'A miracle has happened in Germany,' he repeated in a commanding voice, 'and thanks to this miracle the work of this Committee has suddenly become a crusade. For several years the world has believed the lie, spread by England and the United States, that our beloved Führer, Adolf Hitler, was dead. But we knew deep in our hearts that this was not true. No one could prove the death of the Führer. We knew he wouldn't abandon us in our hour of need. We awaited the miracle. Together we have endured shame and humiliation. We have suffered an invasion and a multitude of cruel restrictions. Together we have survived years of punishment and insult. Hope comforted our hearts while we waited. And now the moment has come for a strong hand to raise again the sword of Siegfried from the dust.' "

Zimmer's eyes, staring unseeingly at me, filled with terror as he went on with his story. "There was a pause. The speaker's forehead glistened with perspiration. He spoke again. 'The moment has come again to salute our leader, our Führer, Adolf Hitler!'

"It was like a nightmare. I saw a man step out from the shadows into the spotlight. I rubbed my eyes. I pinched myself. I wanted to shout in terror. It *was* Adolf Hitler. Adolf Hitler, only a few yards away from me, his fists clenched, his head high, the lock of hair over his left temple. The old shabby gray uniform hung limp from his emaciated body, but there he stood, towering above our heads, fiercely arrogant, staring savagely at us. Even from where I sat I could see the flash of steel in his eyes."

Zimmer now went on with the story reluctantly. Deafening applause had followed Hitler's appearance. In vain the uniformed men entreated the people to be quiet. The American soldiers were forgotten. Women wept hysterically and fell to the floor. Caps were hurled high in the air. Cheers sounded like cannon shots. Guards had surrounded the platform and no one was allowed to get anywhere near Hitler.

Once again the voice of the Führer rang out, the same electrifying voice that could make hair stand on end and blood bubble in veins. He had been hiding, said the Führer, waiting for this moment to call good

Germans together to drive the upstart invaders off German soil. The capitalistic forces, allied with communism, would dominate Germany no longer. United, Germans would battle as in the old days. The Old Guard was gone, but he, the Leader, was still there. The voice screeched and hissed like a sharp saw cutting into a mighty tree, and the crowd was enthralled. The voice rolled and thundered and the people listened with bated breath. Nothing had changed. The voice of the little man on the platform had once more cast its spell.

What followed happened so quickly that it seemed to Zimmer that he more perceived it than saw it. A man in the front row suddenly jumped to his feet. Zimmer saw his clenched fist projected into the spotlight as though it were detached from his body.

" 'Assassin! Assassin!' he thundered. 'You have brought death and destruction upon the German people and now you have returned from the grave to lead us to death again. But we won't allow you to do it a second time.'

"Uniformed men," Zimmer said, "leaped from all parts of the room toward the intruder. I saw guards surround the platform, their shadows gesticulating on the walls. A woman's voice pierced the increasing tumult: 'Murderer! Because of you I lost my three sons in the war and now you want to kill the only son I have left.' And turning around toward us, she

174

screamed, 'Are you going to allow this madman to murder us all?'

"There was a struggle up front as several men went to the aid of the first intruder, who now shouted, 'Fellow Germans, let's put an end to this monster who wants to destroy Germany all over again.'

"Almost the entire room, like an army responding to a command, advanced in a towering wave toward the platform. The Führer's face was livid with terror. Men whipped out knives or brandished their chairs high above their heads. Women were knocked down by the pushing crowd. Near me several men kicked two uniformed youths groveling on the floor. An avalanche of men fell upon the platform. It was horrible. Their monstrous shadows cavorted grotesquely on the walls as their hands clutching knives, chairs, and clubs descended upon the body of the Führer sprawled on the platform.

"When American soldiers finally broke down the cellar door, it was all over. Bodies littered the floor, and blood," Zimmer shuddered, "*his* blood, ran down the platform.

"I was seized without effort, but they had to tear the others away from the thing on the platform, at which they were still pounding with a savage fury. The last thing I recall is men wiping their bloody hands on their clothes as they were dragged away."

I left Zimmer with a package of cigarettes in his

175

hands and a look of relief in his eyes, and I headed for the scene of the crime.

A fine rain fell from a steely sky when I arrived at the Löwen. Two soldiers stood with machine guns at the main entrance of the old brownstone building. My friendship with the commanding officer, an ex-reporter, opened the doors for me all the way to the cellar.

The electric lights were not working, so the soldier who escorted me used a flashlight. I couldn't see very well, but I could smell the musty walls, the rancid beer, the stale tobacco and—perhaps I was being too imaginative—blood. The flashlight crept eerily across the room, over the shattered platform, the broken chairs, the dark stains on the floor. Ten people had been killed there, but the blood of Siegfried could not be distinguished from that of his dragons.

I did not stay long in the cellar and once outside I breathed deeply the cold damp air.

I did not go to the morgue. There really was nothing to be seen there. The bodies of Hitler's guards still retained some human semblance, but Hitler's body had been disfigured beyond recognition. Identification, nevertheless, had been scientific and complete.

After an unappetizing lunch at the military canteen, I was on my way to the second appointment that had been arranged for me. No newspaperman had until now been allowed to interview Dr. Abraham Feidern, who was confined to his home in police custody. The little house on the outskirts of the city boasted a bright-green fence around a desolate garden, where some small trees, bare of leaves, resembled bunches of grapes picked clean. The rain had stopped, but somewhere in the sullen skies another storm was brewing.

English and American military policemen stood smoking and chatting at the door. The sergeant-in-charge checked my credentials and warned me that I could only have a half-hour with Dr. Feidern.

The door was ajar and I entered without knocking. An elderly woman dressed in severe black stepped forward, stared at me with hard eyes, and without a word ushered me into an office. Old faded window shades had turned the oppressive gray outside into an even more oppressive sickly yellow. A deathly stillness pervaded the room. It was as if everything there had suddenly stopped: the silent cuckoo clock, the black sleeping cat sprawled on the rug, and the psychiatrist himself, as stiff as a wax figure in his chair behind a desk, an unlit pipe in his mouth.

I greeted him in faltering German. He offered me a hand as cold as his office and pointed to an armchair opposite him. When I lit a cigarette, he lit his pipe. In the dim light of the room his face beneath wild gray hair had been but a blot on which his glasses stood out like miniature moons. The little inferno kindled by the match illuminated his colorless eyes. And I shuddered at the expression of horror I saw in them.

177

"I know nothing. I have nothing to say," he said hoarsely.

But I sensed from the terror in his voice that he had to talk to someone, that if he kept silent any longer he would go mad. It took a good deal of the precious time allotted to me to induce him to tell me his story. My apparent casualness, his pipe, and, above all, his need to talk to someone were my allies.

Dr. Abraham Feidern is one of the two or three renowned psychiatrists who escaped punishment in Germany. Since the end of the war, he has been Chief of Services of the Rahnler Mental Clinic, the fourth-best clinic in Germany. The Director, Dr. Rahnler, is too old now to do anything outside of certain special consultations, and Dr. Feidern carries the burden of the clinical work.

The Rahnler Clinic is where Hans Sieckwitz was interned a few months after his capture in Munich in October, 1945. An American soldier had seen him creeping out of what was left of a bombed building and almost shot him, thinking he was Hitler. No one knows where he was going, for he was already babbling incoherently when he was captured. His clothes were soiled and torn and his body was terribly emaciated. He was placed under medical observation for several months, and when the doctors declared him an incurable paranoiac he was sent to the Rahnler Mental

178

Clinic. After many fruitless attempts by newspaper-men to interview him, he was forgotten.

The English said that with the capture of Hans Sieckwitz the search for Hitler's doubles had been completed. After Hitler committed suicide and his body and Eva Braun's were burned in Berlin, the English and the Americans had instituted an intensive search for Hitler's doubles, who, they felt, should be able to throw some light on the life and personality of the man they had impersonated for so many years. But very little information was obtained. One after the other the doubles were captured. Hacz, of course, had died during the siege of Berlin. Stigler, discovered in Frankfurt, committed suicide before the eyes of his captors with prussic acid, which he carried in a capsule. Reinz was killed in an automobile accident while flee-ing from Hamburg; the police found only his mutilated body, a grotesque doll fashioned in the image of Hitler. And Simmser, who was caught while trying to escape to Switzerland, had very little to reveal about Hitler. All they could learn from him was the method em-ployed to train Hitler's doubles.

Every day, for hours on end, month after month, the five doubles had been made to listen to Hitler's recorded voice, had seen films of him and observed how he walked and moved and ate and talked until they could imitate to perfection every inflection of his

179

voice, every expression of his face, and even the very smallest of his gestures. They had spent little time with Hitler himself, for barring a few indispensable people he wanted no one to know of the existence of his doubles. The five men had been constantly guarded by SS men, who ate, slept, and lived with them, read their mail, and watched them every moment of the day. Except for the occasions when they had substituted for Hitler, they had been kept locked up in a fortress in the country, perfecting their imitations and living the life of the Führer's shadow. Even Hitler's scars and dental structure had been reproduced in the five men.

Twice a year the Führer, to raise their spirits, invited them to Berchtesgaden. There, for several days, they were granted the privilege of listening to Hitler's fiery harangues and to interminable sessions of Wagnerian music. Sometimes they took long walks in the mountains with Hitler. The imagination could hardly conjure up a more weird and frightening vision than that of the six identical men in gray uniforms drifting together through the rolling mist in the lonely mountains like six mirror images of the devil himself.

Simmser finally died in jail of a heart attack. Although the last double, Hans Sieckwitz, was finally captured, he could offer no information, for Hans Sieckwitz was mad.

Sieckwitz had been a quiet patient, Dr. Feidern told me. Many weeks would go by without his uttering a single word. For hours he played Wagnerian records on an old phonograph they had given him. His movements were automatic. His dull-blue eyes reflected interest in nothing except music. The window in his cell overlooked the patio of the clinic, and when he was not playing his music or carving wooden statuettes in the occupational therapy hall, he spent hours with his elbows on the windowsill staring into space.

Now and then he became violent. Suddenly, without reason, he would be seized by violent fits of rage. Once he attacked an orderly with a chair and almost killed him, but most of the time his fury was oral, manifesting itself in a blistering stream of threats about what he would do when he returned to power. Not in vain, Dr. Feidern said, had Sieckwitz been molded in the image of Hitler.

One day Dr. Feidern began to receive, first by mail and later by telephone, messages from the Revolutionary Committee for a New Germany. He never answered the calls, never attended the meetings that were being held right under the nose of the occupation forces. But one morning a visitor was announced, Franz Tresslar, at that time a neighbor of Dr. Feidern and now a prisoner at the Weissberg Building.

Franz Tresslar advised Dr. Feidern at least to cooperate with the Committee, which was organizing patriotic Germans for the purpose of delivering their beloved country from the English and American swine.

"Our plan," Tresslar said, "is simple. We have a group of strong men of action and a program similar to the old National Socialism. But we lack a symbol. With your help, we can provide that symbol. Our beloved Führer. No one remembers the Führer's double, Hans Sieckwitz, but everybody remembers and waits for the Führer. Aren't flags brought out on special occasions to incite the people and then put away until the next occasion? We have a symbol far better than a flag."

"What are you suggesting?" Dr. Feidern cried out, horrified.

"With your help and that of your assistant, Dr. Stemmp, who is one of us, we shall present Sieckwitz to the people and then put him away again once all Germany knows that the Führer is alive."

"You are insane!" Dr. Feidern gasped.

"Only Sieckwitz is insane and his insanity can be of invaluable help to us now. We shall organize three meetings to present the Führer to his faithful followers. The first meeting will be here in Munich, the second in Frankfurt, the last in Berlin. We'll take Sieckwitz to the meetings in a closed automobile, and, on the pretext that his health is poor, we'll return him here immediately after the meetings. I assure you that there is no danger. I swear it. And you'll do Germany a great service. Germany will not forget you when the tide turns."

182

"I cannot let a patient out of the clinic," Dr. Feidern shouted, "most certainly not for such a purpose. I shall not lend myself to such a farce."

"You will do it, *Herr Doktor,* or suffer the consequences," Tresslar replied coldly. "Nothing would be easier than to kidnap Hans Sieckwitz after disposing of you. We're sure, however, that you won't make that necessary. *Herr Doktor,* Germany needs Hans Sieckwitz and you'll be told when he's wanted."

After several agonizing days, Dr. Feidern received an invitation to a meeting of vital importance at the "Löwen." A few lines scribbled at the bottom advised him to expect an important visitor that same afternoon.

Late in the afternoon the visitor was announced. Dr. Feidern sat at his desk as if waiting for the executioner. A gray-haired man of medium height was ushered in. His face was wide and massive, his nose prominent, his mouth like the slit of a piggy bank. His clothes were shiny and threadbare. His eyes bore the glint of steel.

"I have come for Hans Sieckwitz," he said.

Dr. Feidern leaped to his feet. "I will never allow you to take him," he shouted angrily.

The man, unruffled, pulled some papers from a shabby portfolio and spread them on the table. "Look at these papers, *Herr Doktor.* I am Herman Sieckwitz, Hans' brother. Hans will come with me now. Hundreds of good Germans are waiting for a great message.

Tonight they will see the Führer. I shall bring my brother back here immediately after the meeting. Hans will not be allowed to speak. He'll be presented for a few minutes only as a symbol of hope and courage. I haven't seen Hans in three years. I live in Hamburg. I was afraid to communicate with him. But when the Committee informed me of their plans I immediately agreed to come for Hans and take him to the meeting.

"It is useless to protest, *Herr Doktor,*" he continued inexorably. "We know that only Dr. Stemmp and two interns are here now and they are with us. Let's go upstairs."

Like a condemned man Dr. Feidern ascended the stairs to the second floor. When they reached Hans Sieckwitz' door, he stopped. "Are you aware," he said, "of the enormity of this thing you're making me do? Not only does it outrage all medical ethics, but it is also treason against the occupation authorities."

"Germany comes first, *Herr Doktor.* Open the door!"

Hans Sieckwitz stood by the window, staring out into space. Herman Sieckwitz walked slowly toward his brother, who turned around and stared suspiciously at him. Then, suddenly, Herman Sieckwitz fell on his knees before the sick man, seized his hand, and pressed it against his own heart. "Führer!" he cried out. "Führer! Führer! Führer!"

The blood froze in Dr. Feidern's veins. Closing his eyes, he leaned against the wall. When he opened them again, Herman Sieckwitz, now standing up, was saying vehemently, "Führer! Führer! You were not dead. I knew you were waiting for the right moment to come back. You would never forsake the German people. Führer! The German people will rise up as one man when they learn that you are alive. With you, our Führer, we shall once again know victory."

Despite the invisible hand clutching at his throat, Dr. Feidern stepped between the two men. "Have you gone mad, too?" he demanded of the visitor. "Why do you say these things to your brother?"

Herman Sieckwitz glared at Dr. Feidern. "This is not my brother. My brother Hans died in Berlin with Eva Braun. This man is Adolf Hitler."

During the dispute that ensued, Hitler uttered no sound. Warily he stared at the two men arguing, his body tense, like a tiger about to spring upon its prey.

Dr. Feidern refused to believe Herman Sieckwitz. Had Adolf Hitler deceived the psychiatrists, the police, the coroners, the visitors, just as he had once deceived the whole world? Was his paranoia only make-believe to gain asylum? Impossible! He refused to believe it.

Hitler himself put an end to his questions. What happened then practically robbed the psychiatrist of his own sanity. Facing the two men as if they were a

185

vast audience, Hitler launched into a blistering ha-
rangue that boomed like a cannon shot in the small
room. Words tumbled frenziedly from the shriveled
lips, conjuring up hair-raising visions of an archangel
of vengeance wielding the sword of Siegfried over the
treacherous invaders of Germany.

The old oratory had not changed. The words were
the same. Only a hell-engendered fury had been added.

Utterly stunned and paralyzed, Dr. Feidern listened,
for how long he could not say. When he saw Sieckwitz interrupt Hitler to "take you to the German people anxiously waiting for you," he could not move.
Later, much later, he went to the beer hall, where he
was arrested.

I left Dr. Feidern's house and was wondering what
sort of a story I could fashion from the inadequate
and confusing information I had gathered so far, when
suddenly the radio in the military car that was taking
me back to Munich announced that Herman Sieckwitz
had tried to commit suicide in prison. Strangely af-
fected, I asked the driver to take me back to the
Weissberg Building. Once more we crossed Munich
under a fine rain that was slowly turning into snow. It
was night when we arrived at the old military prison
where I had held my first interview. The rain had
given way to snow, a wet drifting snow.

The prison hospital was deserted and quiet, with
the silence of a tomb. There is nothing more silent

186

than the deserted corridors of a hospital at night. It is as if the whole universe had stopped pulsating. And when one hears the moaning of the sick, it rings like the wail of a soul in anguish.

A nurse, pretty and friendly, informed me that Herman Sieckwitz had attempted suicide with a razor blade. He had lost much blood and despite the transfusions they did not think he would live. "Besides," she added, "he keeps repeating that he wants to die."

No one was allowed to see him, but I finally coaxed the friendly nurse into helping me into a long white coat, and with a white mask partially covering my face, I passed the two soldiers dozing by Sieckwitz' door without difficulty. I did not know why I wanted to see Sieckwitz. I only knew that when I heard over the radio about his attempted suicide, I felt I had to see him.

Now, leaning over his bed, I did not know what to do. I gave him a drink of water from a glass on the night table. He looked at me with eyes as withered as dry leaves. It was all I could see of him in the dim light cast by a small night lamp near the bed—a pair of eyes deeply set in a face as white as the sheets of the bed.

"Who are you?" he whispered.

"I'm a friend."

"Are you German?"

"No. I'm American."

187

"I'm dying," he said. "I want to confess. No, don't go," he said, misinterpreting a gesture of embarrassment on my part. "I don't want a priest. You're a doctor. You won't tell. You're not German. You won't tell the Germans. I don't want them to know."

I dared not speak. His chest heaved, and the air was filled with his harsh breathing.

"I must confess before I die. You won't repeat it to anyone. Swear it! I killed my brother Hans. I killed him. It was horrible."

"But your brother died in Berlin," I exclaimed.

"No, no," he said painfully, 'my brother died here. The German people killed him. And I betrayed him to them."

"That was Adolf Hitler."

"No. It was Hans, my brother."

"I don't understand."

"Hans was interned after the fall of Berlin. He was insane. I wouldn't see him. I hated Nazism, I never forgave my brother for being Hitler's double. A few days ago I learned that they were planning to use Hans as a symbol, a symbol that had once ruined Germany and would ruin her again. I decided to sacrifice my brother for Germany. I offered to fetch Hans from the clinic. Don't you see? They wanted to cart him from one meeting to another and lead Germany into war again. I could not allow such a fate for my country and my brother. Hitler the man was dead, but

188

Hitler the myth remained. The myth had to be destroyed. There was no way but to destroy my brother and with him the myth. If the German people themselves didn't kill Hitler, he would live forever in their hearts as a martyr.

"When I saw my brother, I pretended that he was Hitler. I knew he would seize the opportunity to play the role of Hitler. The rest was easy. The Committee did not expect Hans to speak, but they didn't try to stop him. They didn't know what was going to happen. It was I who first shouted against Hitler. The people reacted as I had expected. It was horrible. They went out wiping the blood on their clothes.

"I had to do it. The German people are tired of wars and death and hunger and misery. Hitler's body died in Berlin, but I made them kill his spirit in the person of my brother. Now the man and the myth have died. Germany can look ahead."

Herman Sieckwitz was dying when I left his room. "The German people must continue to believe that *they* themselves destroyed their Führer," he had said.

I went out into the cold night. It was snowing heavily, pure white snow. Munich was white and silent. I knew then I would never publish my story.

# CODE OF HONOR

At five o'clock in the afternoon the small caravan stopped for the night near a cluster of bleached rocks, which in the vast expanse of desert, under a still-smoldering sun, looked like great loaves of bread hot from the oven and sprinkled with sugar. The sky, an unbroken glaring blue, described a sweeping arch toward the horizon, which stood in the distance like a line traced by a child's finger on the golden sand of the desert. Under the

crushing weight of massive blue, the desert lay flat
and prostrate. There was fire both in the air and the
earth, as though these three elements in violent self-
assertion wished to compensate for the utter absence
of water. Only a few sparse patches of weeds and some
insects were to be seen anywhere.

Three men and a woman dismounted from their
horses and proceeded to unload knapsacks and bun-
dles. One of them, a tall dark Indian, unsaddled the
horses. The other three travelers looked at one another for the first time in five hours of continuous
riding.

"Tired, Rowena?" one of the men asked the woman.

Rowena removed her white pith-helmet and shook
loose her long copper-colored hair, which under the
last sunlight glowed like burning coals. In her riding
clothes she looked incredibly tall and slender. As she
smiled at the man, golden sparks leaped from her wide
amber eyes.

"Not as tired as that horse," she replied. Placing two
very dusty arms around the man's powerful neck, she
stood on her toes and kissed his lips. "And how is my
husband?" she asked.

"One kiss from you and no more fatigue. A shot of
whisky now and I'll be a new man."

The third man, who was busily brushing off the
dust that covered him from head to foot, looked at the
embracing couple.

"They say," he remarked smiling, "that one shouldn't drink anything but water in the desert, Burt."

"Nonsense, Paul," Burt laughed. "I've broken that rule a thousand times and nothing ever happened. Antonio predicts that we'll reach the spring tomorrow. He says it's only a few miles from here. If we weren't so exhausted we could go on to it. Anyway, we have enough water, even if we wake up with hangovers, and I'm sure that at least Rowena and I will have hangovers tomorrow."

"Speak for yourself, Burton," she said. "I acquire my hangovers only in night clubs, from champagne chilled in silver buckets, with bowing waiters around me and crystal chandeliers overhead."

"That's my Rowena. I, on the other hand, require only a bottle of whisky and good company. With my wife and my best friend here—the occasion calls for a celebration."

"Celebration?" Paul asked stiffly. Although the younger of the two men, his face, thin and gaunt, was more lined, and his eyes showed great fatigue. "What is there to celebrate in the middle of a desert, three men and a woman looking for a ghost mine?"

"We have been holding out on you, Paul. What with this pack trip and everything else, we haven't had a moment since we met at the airport in Chicago to tell you the news. Anyway I didn't want to break it to you all at once. Rowena and I are married."

192

"I know that. Congratulations," said Paul, leaning down to tie his bootlaces.

"But that's not all. This is going to be our wedding night."

The silence that ensued was as intense as the heat. Paul straightened up slowly. He was almost as tall as Burton but much thinner. Without looking at Burton he turned to the woman, who, holding up a small mirror, was brushing the dust from her face.

"You didn't tell me that, Mrs. Fanton."

"How formal we have become all of a sudden," Rowena said, with a forced smile. "I thought I was Rowena to you. I told you at the airport that Burt and I were married. I didn't see any reason to give you physiological details."

"Of course not, but I just don't understand why you chose this godforsaken spot for your wedding night."

Burton, laughing loudly, extracted a large leather flask from his saddlebag.

"Nobody chose this godforsaken spot. I assure you that we had no intention of spending our wedding night in the desert, nor in company, for that matter. But things turned out this way. We decided to get married right after I told Rowena that you and I were going to Yucatán to investigate the mine. I would have waited until our return, but she wanted to come along. Unfortunately, we had time for nothing but formalities before meeting you at the airport. We had planned to spend a few days in Yucatán, but that was impossible when we were warned to lose no time in getting started because others were already searching for the mine. I couldn't ask you to go alone, and Rowena refused to remain alone in Yucatán. How about some whisky?"

One after the other they took a drink from the whisky flask and then from the water canteen.

"How about giving some to the guide?" asked Paul.

"We're not wasting good whisky on an Indian." Burton screwed the top back on the flask.

"Don't talk so loud," said Rowena, "he might hear you. I think he knows English."

"What do I care what he knows or what he hears? Anyway, Paul, now you know how it is between Rowena and me."

"I'll try to disturb you as little as possible," said Paul, picking up his knapsack and going off in the direction of the Indian guide.

"What the devil is the matter with Paul?" asked Burton, sitting down in the shade of a rock and pulling Rowena onto his knees.

"Nobody likes to be around on someone else's wedding night."

"We don't expect him to watch us. We have our own tent and whatever we do inside is our own business."

"Maybe we should wait," she insisted, trying to extricate herself from his arms.

"Wait!" he shouted. "That's out of the question. If

he doesn't like it, let him pitch his tent somewhere else."

Seizing her head between his hands, he kissed her fiercely on the lips. When he looked up, the guide, Antonio, was standing nearby staring impassively at them.

"What the hell are you doing here? Come only when you're called," shouted Burton, releasing Rowena, who immediately moved away.

"Don't start an argument, Burt. I'm glad he came. Saved by the bell. Don't you know that no woman would like to be mauled in this suffocating heat?"

"We'll discuss that later, Rowena. What are you doing here, Antonio?" he asked the Indian in Spanish.

"Señor Fanton," said the Indian, unruffled and expressionless, "the horses are now secured. I need some help with the tents."

"Why the devil didn't you say so before?"

"You didn't give him a chance," Rowena interrupted. "Go and help him."

When Antonio had walked off, Burt seized her wrist and said sharply, "There is only one person giving orders here. Me. Understand? Not you. Not Paul. Me. One boss is enough. Don't forget it."

"Understood, my lord and master. I was only trying to avoid a scene."

"Rowena, let *me* cope with the Indian and the desert—but first, give me another kiss."

"In this heat?" she protested, evading his hands. "I

195

wouldn't think of it." She went off toward Paul and the guide.

After the tents were up and Antonio had started a fire, the two men and Rowena sat down, using the saddles as chairs. Burt brought out the flask of whisky and set it down with the water canteen and three tin cups in front of them.

It was only six o'clock, yet night was descending suddenly, as though the lights in the heavens were being quickly turned off one after the other to allow for a change of scene. A sudden breeze swooped down over the hot, tired bodies of the travelers like a cool, clean sheet.

"To the money we hope to make and to the happiness that is already mine," Burt toasted.

"The money first, of course," Rowena remarked sarcastically.

"If it weren't for the money, we wouldn't be here, nor would you and I be together now," he snapped.

"Now you're talking to me as if I were the guide," she said.

"This sounds more like a twentieth anniversary than a wedding night," interposed Paul. "It seems to me that we have more important things to talk about."

"What, for example?" asked Burt, pouring more whisky into his cup.

"Tomorrow's plans."

"I plan to do nothing except locate the mine, make

196

sure it's loaded with ore, and register it immediately. Right after that, my little pigeon and I will be off on a real honeymoon. And you, Paul, what are your plans?"

Paul absent-mindedly traced arrows in the sand. "I don't know," he replied, without looking up. "All this was so sudden. I have no plans. But if the mine Hank discovered just before his death is worth anything, I shall hand full powers over to you and return to Chicago. If we make money with the mine, I'll give up hospital work and I'll concentrate on research."

"Allergies?"

"Yes. That's what I've been doing all these years."

"Paul, I don't understand you. There are so many productive things a man like you could do, but all you want is to shut yourself in a laboratory and make rats cough."

"Every man to his own taste. You have fun making money, I have fun in a lab."

"Money hurts no one."

"Of course not, and I hope all this will bring me the money I need. The difference is that to me money means freedom, but to you it means slavery, because you'll keep on trying to make more and more."

"Not slavery, strength. The rich are strong—the richer, the stronger."

"What do you think, Mrs. Fanton?" Paul asked Rowena, who was combing her hair.

"Mrs. Fanton? Again? Very well, I'll call you Dr.

Lester. But all this formality with the wife of your best friend is ridiculous."

"Rowena is right. Why all the formality?"

"Very well. Rowena, I asked you what you thought of your husband's measuring a man's strength by his bank account. Is that the way women figure masculine strength these days?"

"I don't know about other women, but a man who doesn't make money can't be very smart."

Paul poured some water into his cup. "That's possible," he said, "but can you imagine what the world would be like if all the people cared about was making money? Well, it's already night and we have a big day ahead of us. How about some dinner?"

"Good idea," said Burt. "Antonio."

A shadow stepped out from the darkness. The light cast by the fire revealed an angular face with very brilliant eyes and a tall figure wrapped in a poncho.

"What do you wish, Señor Fanton?"

"Something to eat."

"We do not have enough wood, Señor Fanton."

"Damn! Didn't we bring enough wood to keep the fire going?"

"We left most of it behind because we were overloaded, señor."

"And what kind of a guide are you to let these things happen? What are we going to do?"

"About ten minutes' distance from here I remember

some fallen logs near some rocks. They would do."

"Go and get them, then."

"I would be glad, señor, but I need help to bring enough for the whole night."

"I'll go with him, Burt," Paul offered.

"No. Let him go alone. You don't speak Spanish and wouldn't understand him. For heaven's sake! It's his job. We shouldn't be bothered with these things."

"You ordered him to leave the wood behind," Rowena interposed.

"You're butting in again. Well, let's not argue all night. We'll both go with him, Paul."

"I will not be left here alone," protested Rowena.

"In this desert, my pet, there isn't even a mosquito on the prowl."

"I don't care what there is. It's what I imagine, all alone, expecting all sorts of things to leap out of the darkness. Not me!"

"But you can't come with us and leave all this alone."

"Why not?" You said there isn't a living thing around."

"Somebody might come."

"Ha! And you want them to find me? No, I won't stay alone."

"Burt, the easiest solution is for me to go with the guide," Paul insisted.

"No. I wouldn't trust that Indian for a second. He might just slip off in the dark. You stay here. I'd rather go and keep an eye on him. And if he tries anything, I'll take a shot at him."

"Are you serious? This man was recommended to us as the most trustworthy guide around."

"Beware of recommendations! When you have lived most of your life, as I have, on plantations and in mines, you learn that these people have respect for nothing but brute force. Anyway, it will only take half an hour. *Vamos,* Antonio."

A moment later the two men were off on horseback in the direction from which they had come, their lanterns slicing in the darkness two small golden triangles, which finally became mere pinpoints of light in the distance. Paul and Rowena sat in silence staring at the fire.

"Another whisky?" Paul finally said, holding out a cup.

Rowena looked at him over the glowing coals. Shadows danced on Paul's face, checkering it with streaks of light and darkness. To Paul it seemed that the last cinders of the fire had leaped into her eyes. With a fierce movement she knocked the cup out of his hand.

"Is that all you have to say to me, Paul?" she cried, "do I want whisky? Go on, speak. We're alone now. Get it off your chest. Insult me. Don't hold back anything?"

"I have nothing to say, Mrs. Fanton."

"You think you're insulting me when you call me that. Well, you are not. I am proud to be Mrs. Fanton. Were you surprised, Paul? I purposely wouldn't let Burt tell you that this was our wedding night. It could have been *our* wedding night, Paul—yours and mine. But you were already tired of me. When a man has had his will with a woman he has no desire to marry her. Isn't that true, Paul?"

"You know that's not true, Rowena. You know that I loved you, that I wanted to marry you."

"Really? Is that why in Chicago, at The Drake, when I begged you practically on my knees to marry me, you refused?" Her voice had risen to a hysterical pitch. "Remember? We were drinking Martinis. There were flowers and music and fine crystal and silver and bowing waiters—the beautiful world that I love. We could have been there now, you and I. Instead, I'm having my wedding night with another man in this horrible desert. And you'll be only a few feet away. But that doesn't bother you, does it?"

"You forget," he said, "that the cocktails at The Drake came after another, much more disagreeable, scene. We didn't part when I told you that I wouldn't marry you because you could never be happy with me. We parted when I showed you my tiny laboratory, when I explained that that was my real life, for which I had sacrificed everything. And you were afraid. The modestness of it all, the hardships that you might have to endure, terrified you. Your love wasn't strong enough to give you courage and hope. So you gave me an ultimatum. I was to work with your uncle. I was to be a fashionable doctor under his orders, a money-maker like him. I was to give up my research work. That night I didn't sleep. I thought all night of you, and I concluded that you didn't love me, that you loved no one but yourself, that even if I did what you wanted because I loved you so much, we would never be happy, not for long."

Paul had talked fast. He wanted to finish before Burt came back. Now he got up, and looking down at her, said gently, "At The Drake I didn't reject you; I only tried to explain what I have just told you."

"And I offered to marry you anyway, under any circumstances," she said passionately.

"That was only an emotional impulse. You know that. The night before you were your real self. You showed me plainly that I could not give you the kind of life you wanted, the kind of life to which your uncle had accustomed you. You would have been miserable trying to live on my hospital salary."

"I asked you to marry me, Paul," she screamed, "I asked you. Do you hear me? I asked you again and again."

"If you shout like that, Burt will hear you."

"What do I care? What you won't admit is that you were tired of me. You had all you wanted of me for

202

a whole year and you were tired of me. You were afraid to admit it."

"I had no reason to be afraid, Rowena. I didn't force you into anything you didn't wish. As a matter of fact, you chased after me. You did the wooing and actually pushed me into making love to you. But all that is not important. What is important is that I fell in love with you. I still love you. But out of loyalty to Burt I shall never again say it. Your revenge is despicable, you know. First you pick my best friend, and then you cunningly arrange to spend your wedding night where I can be only too aware of it."

"Your reproaches are typical of the narrow-minded scientist, the bookworm, the weakling," she cried. "Go on, tell me more, tell me everything. Tell me that you wouldn't marry me because there was another man before you. Tell me that your stupid puritanism would not allow you to marry a tramp."

"Rowena, you're mad! Stop shouting! I can see lights. Burt is coming back."

In the distance two lights darted to and fro like giant fireflies.

"You're going to hear me out, Paul. You will listen, and I don't care if my words echo over the entire desert. You are a weakling. You always have been. I was too much woman for you. Only a strong man could understand a woman like me. That's why I married him, your best friend, your boyhood idol. He's strong.

203

He's a real man. You are not. That's why you have always envied him, since childhood. He was strong and you were a weakling. He has succeeded in life. He's wealthy and powerful. But you are wasting away in a laboratory puncturing rats. And tonight he will have me."

Paul's face stood out stark white in the darkness.

"That's enough, Rowena. I'm going to meet Burt."

"Don't move! You are going to hear me out. You don't like being told that you're weak, that—"

"Good-by, Rowena." He started to walk away. With a short anguished scream, she leaped forward, falling headlong with her arms around his boots. She lay there, clutching him, her face pressed against his legs.

"Paul, don't go—don't leave me—don't ever leave me. I love only you. I couldn't bear having him near me tonight. I love you, only you. Let's ride off. We still have time. Let's go. I'll get a divorce and we'll get married. Paul, I love you so very much and you hurt me so—that's why I married a man I don't love."

"Rowena, let me go! You're crazy! They're almost here."

"Paul, let's go. I beg you on my knees, let's go. Leave him the mine, leave him everything. We'll have each other. I know that what I did was crazy, but we still have time. Let's go, my love."

His face drenched with perspiration, Paul struggled to free himself from Rowena's arms. In the flickering light from the fire, her loose hair heaved at his feet like red-hot molten metal.

"Paul," she pleaded, "let's go. Why don't we go? Are you afraid of him?"

He stiffened up. "I'm not strong in the way you understand strength, but I'm afraid of no one if I'm in the right. Burt is my best friend. I could never do this to him. I only regret that because of me you have treated him so shabbily."

"Paul, for the last time, let's go away before he comes."

"It's not my idea of honor to rob my best friend of his wife. Rowena, does Burt know that we were lovers?"

"No."

"If he had known he would never have married you. Women can't understand friendship between men."

"He would have married me anyway," she shouted with renewed fury. "He cares nothing for your stupid code of honor. You could never forget that there was another man before you, but Burt doesn't care about such things."

"It's useless. Let me go or I'll have to use force. They're very close. I can't do this to Burt."

"Of course you can't," she hissed, her face distorted with rage. "Only a real man would fight for the woman he loves, and you're only half a man, you—"

He didn't let her finish. Pushing her forcibly, he walked away, leaving her sprawled on the sand, her red hair a small shimmering pool near the dying fire.

Paul advanced resolutely toward the two luminous points bobbing in the darkness like the riding lights on a ship's rigging. When the shadows behind the lamps were clearly visible, Paul cried out, "Burt!"

"Paul, what happened? Where's Rowena?"

"She had a headache and retired to her tent. I thought you might need help."

"The horses are loaded with wood. Antonio can give you his horse."

"No thanks, I'd rather walk. You go ahead. I'll see you later at the camp."

The two horses passed him, stolidly plodding through the sand toward the fire glimmering a few yards away. Paul trudged behind them, his feet heavy, as if unwilling to return to the camp.

When he arrived, Burt was pouring out a whisky and Antonio was pouring water into a coffee pot, which he placed on the now blazing fire. Rowena was nowhere to be seen. Paul dropped onto one of the saddles, taking the whisky that Burt offered him. He was about to drink it, when he saw Antonio's face bending over the fire. His right eye was swollen and his upper lip was bleeding.

"What happened, Burt?" he asked, placing the cup untouched on the sand.

206

"Nothing. Antonio stumbled and bashed his face against a stone."

"But—"

"It's not important."

"Burt, why did you hit him?"

"Look, Paul, you've got to teach these Indians to respect you."

"Was he insolent?"

"He dared think that he knew better than me and took his time about obeying. He won't do it again."

"A guide is a friend, and besides—"

"Look, Paul, you're a scientist; you don't know about these things. You came along only because Hank's will stipulated that you should. You don't care how things are done as long as you can retire to your ivory tower. Let me lead this expedition and everything will work out fine."

The appearance of Rowena from one of the tents interrupted the conversation. Burt gave a long whistle.

Rowena had changed into a blue satin gown more suited to a Park Avenue drawing room than to the desert. When she walked, it shimmered and clung to her long, slender legs. She had tied back her hair with a silver ribbon. Her eyes were slightly red, but her face was composed, even serene.

"Has your headache gone?" Burt asked, helping her to sit down by the fire.

"Completely," she replied. "I'm ready to do justice

to the dinner. Paul, I'll now take the whisky you offered me before."

Without looking at her, Paul picked up her cup, let Burt fill it, and then passed it to her.

"To love," Rowena toasted.

Only two cups were lifted; Paul left his on the sand.

"I propose that we include someone else in this toast, someone indispensable to our success and entitled to a bit of love, which, after all, should not be restricted to you two."

He went over to Antonio, who was squatting near the tents and unpacking provisions, and offered him his cup.

"Have a drink," he said.

"Paul," Burt called, "you're drunk!"

"I wish I were," he answered, and to the Indian, "Go on, drink. It's for you."

The dark face nodded and smiled, *"No, gracias, señor. No es bueno beber en el desierto."*

Burt broke out into guffaws. "There's a lesson for you, Paul. We've run into a puritan Indian."

Paul squeezed the Indian's shoulder and then silently drained the cup.

The meal was quiet and cheerless. Paul and Rowena scarcely touched the food that Antonio placed before them. Only Burt did justice to the meal and the whisky. When they had finished their coffee, Antonio

208

picked up the dishes and went off to put them in the knapsacks. Burt got up and stretched noisily.

"It's time to retire from society, Rowena," he said, winking at his wife.

"I'm not sleepy yet."

"Neither am I. That's exactly why we should go to bed." He passed his hand over the nape of Rowena's neck. "I'll go and get ready. I'll expect you in a minute. Good night, Paul."

"Good night, Burt."

Paul and Rowena sat staring at the fire. The silence was so profound that they could hear each other's breathing. One of the tents lit up inside, and Burt's shadow loomed like a monstrous anthropoid on the canvas. Antonio, huddled in his poncho against his saddle, resembled a carved idol. Paul wondered whether he was awake, whether a heart beat inside the stony figure. He turned his eyes to Rowena, and this time they looked at one another without rancor or bitterness. Each saw in the other's eyes fatigue and a sense of discouragement and futility.

"Paul," she whispered, "we can still go away."

"I'm sorry, Rowena, please believe me, but I can't possibly do this to Burt."

"You prefer to sit here and listen to our panting—"

"Bitch!"

The word and the blow were simultaneous. Rowena,

more surprised than hurt, held a hand to her forehead where Paul had struck when she tried to avoid the blow. She rose silently, her hand pressing the smarting spot, and slowly entered Burt's tent. Paul glanced at the Indian and saw his eyes close quickly.

Paul remained seated, his gaze fixed on the fire. Inside the tent Rowena suddenly burst into shrill laughter, and on the canvas two shadows embraced. Paul jumped to his feet and walked away into the darkness.

Paul never knew how far or in which direction he walked. He walked blindly, without stopping, until the camp became a handful of sparks in the night. Walking fast in the darkness gave him the curious feeling that he was rushing headlong toward an invisible wall against which he would be smashed any minute, but, instead, the darkness constantly opened in silent resiliency, shrouding him in an opaque gelatinous mass. When, finally exhausted, he dropped on the sand, the camp was a mere speck of light, a fallen star, in the distance.

Fatigue invaded him suddenly and relentlessly, as though it were the precursor of death, and he fell into a stupor. When the cold awakened him, after pommeling his numb body back to life, he decided to return to the camp for his horse and slip away, far from that nightmarish spot.

The return was difficult. The first morning gray

streaked the horizon, making it difficult to see the pinpoint of fire in the distance. His teeth chattered from cold, and a great fatigue that seemed to rise from his very heart made it painful to walk. The wan light of dawn was upon the camp when he arrived. The two tents resembled paper birds dropped on the sand by a tired child. Close to the fire, the guide still squatted in his Aztec idol position, as though he had not stirred all night.

Paul was about to tiptoe toward the horses when suddenly a piercing scream rent the serene morning air. Without a moment's hesitation, as if propelled only by his reflexes, in a few leaps he stood before Burt's tent and threw back the canvas flap. The Indian, springing out of his lethargy, followed him.

The interior of the tent was in semidarkness, but Paul saw Rowena's half-naked body paralyzed in a reclining position, her eyes wide with horror, her hands clutching the sides of her cot. Burt, also partly nude, sat on his bed, one leg under the bedclothes, the other dangling out as if he had been held back on the verge of jumping out of bed, a large camping knife in his hand, his eyes riveted to the foot of his wife's bed. Paul and Antonio remained motionless at the entrance, staring in horror at the coiled mass lying like a great bracelet near Rowena's bare leg. Atop the coils a small head oscillated back and forth, watching the newcomers with beady little eyes.

211

"¡*Vibora! ¡Vibora!*" the Indian whispered, his voice choked with terror. Except for the darting head of the deadly desert viper, everyone in the tent seemed petrified.

"Paul!" Rowena called in a hoarse whisper.

Paul glanced at Burt, who looked as though he had been suddenly turned into stone, his hand clutching the knife so hard that the knuckles stood out white and swollen. Then, again propelled by his reflexes only, Paul leaped toward the bed, seized the snake just below the head, and hurled it against the ground outside the tent, where it lay writhing. Suddenly his lips parted in a cry of surprise and he stared with horrified eyes at the blood trickling down his finger.

In a daze he saw Burt bend over Rowena, who lay unconscious, and he saw the Indian take out his machete and with a swift stroke chop off the head of the viper. For a moment he stared at the long dark body squirming grotesquely on the sand. Suddenly, seized with panic, he squeezed his finger to force out the poison, his eyes darting helplessly from one to the other. The look of pity in the Indian's eyes made him hesitate no longer. Snatching the machete from the guide, he stumbled out, dropped on his knees by the fire, placed the finger on one of the stones, struck it off with a single blow, and then thrust his bloody hand into the fire. Violent nausea overtook him. Sprawled on the ground, he cried out in agony. Black clouds swooped down upon him, and slowly he sank through bottomless darkness.

He was awakened by cold water on his face, a piercing pain in his hand, and whisky burning down his throat. The Indian bent over him, his face as impassive as ever. A few feet away, holding onto the flap of the tent, Rowena stood half-dressed, horror still stamped on her face. Next to her stood Burt rubbing his face with his hands.

"Paul," she cried, unable to move.

"I—I don't think," Paul stammered, "that—that there is any danger now."

Burt took a step toward Rowena, but the sudden hatred on her face held him back.

"You didn't come to my help," she cried.

"You didn't give me time," he shouted. "And you called Paul instead of me. Why did you call Paul? Why?"

His eyes, filled with fury, darted from Rowena's waxen face to Paul, sprawled on the sand, pressing the bloody stump to his chest, and then to the Indian, who was wiping off the machete, unmoved.

"You bastard of an Indian," he hissed. "You didn't tell us there were snakes around here." Picking up a leather thong that had dropped from a pack, a cruel look on his face, he approached the Indian with slow deliberation, like a hunter stalking an easy prey.

Despite the pain that racked his body and paralyzed

213

his mind, Paul was suddenly acutely aware of how absurdly theatrical the whole scene was. The middle of the desert for a stage, the great arch of gray sky for a canopy, and four puppets, one mutilated and bloody, another with a wax-doll face, the third with his features distorted by cruelty and rage, and the silent Indian forever impassive, like an ageless Aztec idol far above the picayune dramas of mere mortals. "None of it is real," he thought, "none." But the pain in his hand was excruciating, and nausea gripped his stomach like a vise.

Burt never reached the Indian. Rowena, pale and haggard, interposed herself between them.

"You would blame this poor Indian," she cried. "You're a coward and I despise you. Shall I tell you why I called to Paul and not to you? Because I hate you. I loathe you. I married you only because Paul refused me. Your coarse hands last night degraded my body forever."

The leather strap fell upon her again and again until she dropped to the ground shrieking with pain. Then, blind with rage, Burt lashed viciously at the Indian. Paul, crawling toward them, his arm outstretched to stop Burt, saw him suddenly fall down to his knees, his hand on his chest, his eyes horribly dilated, and then crumple up grotesquely like a huge rag doll. Even before Paul touched him, he knew that the Indian's knife had pierced his heart.

Incapable of motion, Paul watched the Indian pick up his saddle and walk toward the horses. The bloody knife on the sand was a vivid red against the all-gray setting of sand and sky. Rowena, sprawled on the sand, stared into space with vacant eyes. The bleeding welt emphasized the pallor of her face. Paul crept up to her.

"Rowena," he whispered.

She stared at him vacantly. "It's our fault," she murmured. "My lack of honor—your stupid code of honor. You should hate me as I hate you."

They lay exhausted, the silence broken only by their heavy breathing. The sky flushed with the pink of dawn. The sound of hoofbeats made them look round. The Indian, as indifferent as an eternal force of nature, rode away slowly in the direction from which they had come. Not once did he look back, as in silence they watched him grow smaller and smaller against the flaming horizon.

Paul fell back on the sand, conscious of the pain that with a thousand sharp points was tearing at his whole body. Rowena rose slowly. At her feet, Burt was but a crumpled rag on the blood-soaked sand. Rowena stared at him, then at Paul, clutching his mutilated hand in agony. Picking up a flask of water, she knelt down to wash Paul's wound.

## DON'T BLAME ANYBODY
## FOR MY DEATH

W HEN LIFE BECOMES UN-
bearable, it's time to quit. Only death by my own hand
can deliver me from my dishonorable life. Don't
blame anybody for my death."

Roger Lenison finished copying these words on a
clean sheet of paper and then affixed his bold, angular
signature beneath them. He hesitated an instant, picked
up the pen again and added the words, "The End."
Then, one by one he began to tear into tiny pieces the

pages from which he had been copying. When he came to the last page, the uneven, sprawling signature under the words he had just copied arrested his eyes. He smiled scornfully, then quickly tore up the page, placed all the pieces of paper in a large ceramic ashtray, and with his gold lighter set them on fire. When the fire had died out, he took the ashtray over to the fireplace and emptied out the small heap of ashes.

Looking up, Roger Lenison saw his face in the mirror over the mantelpiece and smiled. Nobody would have believed that he was eight years older than the thirty-nine that he told everyone was his age. Thick blond hair framed a high smooth forehead (regular massages with rich oils had kept the wrinkles away), the eyes were large and clear, and a small geometrical mustache was perched smartly above the narrow mouth. It was indeed more the face of a movie star than that of a famous author.

"And now I can have a drink," Roger Lenison said aloud.

He crossed the thirty-three-foot living room. The late afternoon sun tiptoed through the large window, diffused a soft glow over the multicolored jackets of the books that lined the walls from ceiling to floor, and exploded into a myriad of rainbow sparks on the glass top of the elegant red leather bar. He poured a good shot of bourbon into a tall glass, drank it down in one breath, poured another, added some soda and

217

ice, and picking up the glass, walked over to the window.

Twenty floors below, the murky water of the East River was a shimmering scarlet under the setting sun. Echoes of hoots and whistles drifted up. Roger looked at his watch. Five thirty. He must telephone his typist about the manuscript.

Roger Lenison always took the same precautions: he copied the original stories by hand, then destroyed the originals, and finally had his secretary copy *his* manuscripts. This system prevented all possible complications.

He dialed Adele Crawford's number and then realized he was frowning—the situation was beginning to trouble him again. Fortunately, the movies had bought the last three stories, and he was certain that he would get twice the usual amount for the story he had just copied.

Someone in Adele's rooming house finally answered the telephone, and Roger gulped down his drink while he waited for Adele to be called. And then, "Adele? Roger Lenison." He liked the suave sound of his own name.

"How are you, Mr. Lenison?"

"Fine, Adele, fine. I've just finished another story and I'd like you to type it this evening."

There was a short pause, and then, "I'll be delighted, Mr. Lenison. When do you want me to come over?"

"Right away. It won't take you more than a couple of hours. I'm sure you'll like it. It's called 'The Only Way Out.'"

"The what?"

"'The Only Way Out.'" There was no reply. "Adele, are you still there?"

"Yes, Mr. Lenison. I'll be over shortly."

Roger stretched out on the sofa to wait for Adele. He was vaguely disturbed about recent developments, but his mind soon drifted to more pleasant thoughts. He liked Adele. He had been very lucky to find her immediately after his former secretary had rushed off to Florida in an outburst of temper because she was tired of being his "mistress at a ridiculous secretary's salary." It was an old trick of Roger's to combine his secretary's duties with extracurricular diversion—and all for peanuts.

The doorbell interrupted his thoughts. He jumped up, dashed over to the mirror, smoothed his hair, passed his fingers over his mustache, and then opened the door.

Adele Crawford entered in her usual timid way, which Roger found so enticing. Because she was so shy he had made no advances as yet. He did not want to frighten her away.

She was dressed in a tailored tan suit. Her long chestnut hair, combed back severely from a center part, was caught in a clip at the nape of her neck. Her large green eyes were bright and clear, and she had a wax-like oval face. She smiled at him—a schoolgirl smile—and without saying a word, went to the typewriter and began to arrange paper and carbons.

"Here is the manuscript, Adele," Roger said, handing it to her. "It's the best story I have ever written. Excellent material for a film." Adele glanced through the manuscript.

"You know what, Adele? It's after six. How about something to eat before we start working? After dinner we'll come back here and really get down to work. Let's go," he insisted, observing the look of indecision on her face. "We can discuss the manuscript over dinner," and he picked it up and put it in his pocket. "Otherwise, we'll have to interrupt our work right in the middle to have dinner. There's a little Italian restaurant nearby. You'll love Donatello's. They have the best *zuppa di pesce* in town and their *calamari* are superb. They also make wonderful Martinis."

When she picked up her bag and gloves, he congratulated himself on his strategy. After she had typed the story, there would be a long evening ahead of them.

Donatello's had a charming little patio with a brick floor, ivy on the walls, bright red geraniums in white pots, and blue and white checked tablecloths. A delectable aroma drifted in from the kitchen.

Roger was surprised that Adele made no protest when he ordered double Martinis.

"To the success of the story and of our association," toasted Roger.

She smiled and raised her glass also. Both downed half their Martinis. "Wow!" thought Roger. "It's hard to figure out these quiet little pigeons. I bet this one has been around after all."

"Tell me about yourself," he said, lighting a cigarette.

"There isn't much, Mr. Lenison. I work as a secretary during the day, and at night I do extra work, such as yours."

"That's crazy. A pretty girl like you shouldn't work herself to the bone that way. And why don't you call me Roger?"

"All right, Roger. But life in New York is very expensive. My mother is ill in Albany and I help pay the doctors' bills. But I'm not complaining. I don't mind the work and I manage to save something."

Roger finished his Martini in one gulp and ordered another without waiting for Adele to finish hers. Once he started drinking, he could not stop.

"Very soon, Adele, I'll be able to ask you to devote yourself completely to my work. As soon as the contracts with Hollywood are signed, I want you to be my private secretary, and you'll earn twice as much

221

as now." It didn't cost anything to make promises, and Adele was looking more attractive than ever.

"It's very nice of you, but it wouldn't be right for me to be alone with you all day in your apartment."

He laughed. "You come now for an hour or two—what difference would it make if you came for a full day? We're not in Albany, you know. Here in New York nobody pays any attention to that sort of thing."

The soup interrupted the conversation, and an excellent Chianti was an excuse for more toasts.

"What do you do on weekends to amuse yourself?" he asked, after they had finished the *calamari* with garlic sauce.

"The same thing all girls do: movies, read the papers, watch TV, take walks, look at shopwindows, visit friends—girls," she added smiling.

"Only girls? How dull! A girl like you should have dozens of boyfriends."

"I don't have any."

"Don't be modest. Your trouble must be in getting rid of them, not in finding them."

"No, I don't have any. I had one not long ago, but it's all over now."

"He must have been crazy to leave you—for someone else?"

"No. He died of a heart attack."

Even through his alcoholic haze Roger could see that the girl was very upset.

222

"Adele, I'm sorry. Forgive me for bringing it up."

"That's all right," she said. "Excuse me for making a scene. You wanted to discuss the manuscript. . . ."

"Not now," he interrupted her. "Let's have a bottle of Lachryma Christi. You'll love it."

But neither his jokes, nor the delicious wine, nor even the Chartreuse cordial succeeded in cheering up Adele.

"Mr. Lenison—Roger," Adele said, after the check had been paid, "I'd like to go for a short walk to wake up a bit. Do you want to come with me, or shall I meet you later at your apartment?"

The bourbon, the double Martinis, the Chianti, the Lachryma Christi, and the Chartreuse were doing a mad dance in Roger's head. Perhaps the walk would do him good, he thought, and then an intimate finale in his apartment.

"I'll come with you," he said with a thick tongue, "and you can tell me all your troubles."

They walked toward the river. It was a warm night. The starless sky had a reddish tinge—somewhere a storm was brewing.

"Good idea to go down to the river," Roger said, leaning heavily on Adele. "It'll be cooler there." When they reached the East River, short intermittent flashes of light cleaved the dark sky. The electric storm made the air oppressive. People had vanished from the streets. Alone in a small square beneath the street level, Adele

223

and Roger watched the lightning compete with the blinking neon signs on the other side of the river. At their feet was the river, around them silence and darkness. Suddenly an outburst of lightning seemed to illuminate the whole world. Roger, startled, turned around quickly and caught a glimpse of the empty wooden benches with their warped iron backs and the lonely lampposts with their broken bulbs—unhappy targets of the neighborhood children.

"Why did we come here?" he asked, shuddering.

"This spot holds memories for me," she answered. "Now it looks as dismal to me as it does to you, but a few weeks ago this little square was heaven. I used to come here with my fiancé." Violent flashes illuminated the pale face of the girl. Distant thunder followed.

"My fiancé," she continued, "was a writer, too. He had talent, but he couldn't sell his stories. He came from a little town in Illinois and didn't know anyone here. We met in an employment agency while we were both looking for work and we fell in love.

"One day he went to see a writer who was looking for a secretary. When my fiancé showed him his stories, the man promised to help him and asked him to leave a number of the stories with him. Then one evening he told my fiancé that the only way he could succeed was to publish one of his stories under the name of someone with influence and connections. On the verge

224

of starvation, my fiancé agreed and the writer gave him a few dollars for one of the stories. The man published it under his own name. It was a great success.

"A few weeks later, another of my fiancé's stories appeared in a famous magazine under the same writer's name. My fiancé demanded an explanation, but he was cleverly put off with promises and another check for a few dollars. The same thing happened again and again.

"My fiancé called on the editors of the magazine that published the stories. They thought he was crazy. The famous author threatened my fiancé with the police. The night that happened, we came here. He had a heart attack right here. He died in my arms."

The murmur of the river was audible at their feet. Roger Lenison was trying desperately through the haze in his head to make some sense out of what he had just heard.

"Mr. Lenison," Adele said softly, "let me have your manuscript."

Automatically he pulled it out of his pocket and handed it to her.

"'The Only Way Out,'" she whispered, pressing the manuscript against her heart. "It was the last story he wrote. To kill or to die. He had decided it was the only way out. But he died before he could kill. He told me that you were looking for a secretary. He also told me that you were afraid of the water, that you couldn't swim, that you loved to drink. The only problem was to get you here. . . ."

Firmly she pushed him with both hands. Roger Lenison disappeared in the dark waters. The girl saw his head, then a hand clawing at the air.

When the final ripple had disappeared, Adele tore the last page from the manuscript. Under the continuous flashes of light, she read, "When life becomes unbearable, it's time to quit. Only death by my own hand can deliver me from my dishonorable life. Don't blame anybody for my death."

Roger's signature under these words was bold and angular.

Adele picked up Roger's hat from the bench where he had dropped it, but before she tucked the sheet of paper in the hatband, she tore off the top of the page bearing the number 13 and the lower half with the words, "The End."

# TRIANGLE

ONE PALE AFTEROON I VIS-
ited my secretary Tina in the hospital. She had broken
one of her lovely legs while skiing in Sugarbush a
week ago. As I was about to say good-by, my attention was caught by a silver-haired woman who was
sitting beside the bed of another patient at the end of
the ward. She had a perfect cameo profile.

"Whom are you looking at?" Tina asked, turning
her head in the direction of my staring eyes.

227

"For a minute I thought I knew that visitor over there."

"Oh, she's no visitor. She's a volunteer worker. She comes around almost every day and reads to the patients. Sometimes she runs short of reading material and then she tells some far-fetched tale about an ex-schoolteacher, a Cuban, and a dead husband. She's told me the story at least three times. Mrs. Hannaway means well, but that story she tells is simply unbelievable." Tina shook her head.

"What did you say her name was?"

"Mrs. Hannaway. Why? Do you know her?"

I knew her, and the story was not unbelievable. As a matter of fact, *I* was part of it.


It began in 1948 on the Champion—New York to Miami express—when I was on my way to Havana to write a series of articles for a magazine. At about eleven o'clock, tired of sitting, for I had not moved since the Champion's departure from New York early in the evening, I walked to the club car.

Most of the passengers in the cars I passed through were already asleep. Probably bound for Florida for long-planned vacations, they lay crumpled in their seats, their heads lolling grotesquely on pillows, their clothes askew, their faces sagging with vacant expressions.

Laughter, singing, and harmonica music carried to

a deafening pitch greeted me as I opened the door to the club car. Thick smoke stung my eyes.

I sat down at a table near the bar, ordered a drink, and looked around. About twenty persons were drinking and smoking, but barely half a dozen of them were responsible for the commotion. Two young men, the stamp of salesclerks all over them, were furiously playing harmonicas to the delight of their girl friends, who with their brassy blonde hair would have stood out even in an overcrowded Madison Square Garden.

A tall white-haired man and a short, grotesquely shaped dark woman were cavorting wildly in the narrow aisle between the tables, encouraged by cheers and laughter from their companions.

"They are disgusting!" remarked my neighbor, a short chubby man with a startling orange-colored bald pate.

"They have been carrying on like that for three hours," said the stout lady at his side, with a wifely air of agreement.

Making no comment, I took a sip from my glass. Through the bottom of the glass the ice cubes against the smoke-filled background looked like miniature icebergs in a heavy fog.

The white-haired man was evidently going through his entire repertoire of comical antics. He crooned in Italian, hobbled up and down the aisle on one foot, covered his mustache with beer foam, held a kerchief around his backside and danced a rumba, and finally wound up jitterbugging, leaping, and jumping with astonishing vitality. Then, whooping like an Indian, he dashed across the car to the opposite end, where a group of young fellows and girls made him sit down and have a drink with them.

I took advantage of the relative calm to order another drink. A woman sat down next to me and ordered a Tom Collins. From the corner of my eye I could see her pale profile, like a cameo against the clouds of smoke. Suddenly, resounding barks were heard, and the white-haired gentleman leaped by on all fours, followed by the two bleached blondes, who were lashing him with a red belt.

"Revolting!" said the woman with the cameo profile.

"Every man to his own taste," I replied. The white-haired man went by again, this time with a blonde on each arm and the imprint of red lips on both his cheeks.

Suddenly craving solitude, I went to the smoking car, which fortunately was deserted, and making myself confortable in one of the big leather armchairs, with a sigh of relief I lit my pipe and soon became immersed in thoughts about the articles I was planning to write. Vaguely, through the smoke from my pipe and my far-off thoughts, I saw the people from the club car file by and the conductor turn off some of the lights. Soft shadows now capered around me, and the muffled noises of the train, uniform and rhythmic, sounded like the humming of a gigantic bee.

"Have you a match, please?" The soft voice pulled me back to reality. I raised my lighter, and the tiny quivering flame leaped into wide green eyes that peered at me from under a mass of auburn hair graying slightly at the temples. The cameo profile had small, delicate features.

"Thank you," she said. "Am I disturbing you?"

"On the contrary. I have been dreaming all by myself and I was beginning to be bored."

"I'm glad. I wanted to be alone—no, please don't move. I was about to say that I wanted to be alone with someone else. All that noise back there made me dizzy."

It was easy to see that the noise alone had not made her dizzy. Her tongue was trapped in the thick net that one too many whiskies can weave in one's mouth.

"Yes," she continued, reading my thoughts, "for the first time in my life I have had too much to drink. Oh, not enough to make me drunk, but enough to warm my heart a little after that vulgar spectacle."

"By the way," I said, "I wonder what happened to the white-haired clown. I believe I saw everybody pass by except him. There's no noise in there now."

"He's still in there," she answered distantly, holding her cigarette as if she were holding a candle over a dead thought. "He's snoring. He'll snore for hours." She placed her cigarette between her thin lips, now free of lipstick, and withdrew it without taking a puff. "One of his blonde playmates is sleeping on his shoulder."

"I wonder what drives a man to such disgusting behavior."

"Would you really like to know?" she asked, nervously stroking her hair.

"I'm a writer by profession," I said. "I'm interested in people."

"I'm interested in this man, too, but for a different reason. He's my husband."

Trying to remember whether I had said anything offensive about her husband, I remarked hurriedly, to hide my confusion, "I guess then you have never known what it is to be bored. He's so full of life!"

She shrugged her shoulders. "Geoffrey is like that only with strangers. He's very quiet at home. Actually he's a highly respected executive of a large manufacturing firm."

"Such a double personality is to be envied," I volunteered, without much conviction.

"You don't mean that. It'll be much worse in Havana, where fun comes first."

"That can be easily remedied," I advised. "Enjoy yourself with him."

232

"Like that!" she cried, pointing toward the club car. "The way you saw him!"

"If you join him from the beginning, perhaps he won't go so far."

"When it comes to having fun, Geoffrey always excludes me. He really does nothing bad. He just becomes a mischievous little boy and he likes to have his fun alone. It's not that he doesn't love me. In his way, he does." She let out a deep sigh and extended her cigarette for me to relight it. "Well, the only thing that matters is that we're going to Havana. I've been dreaming about returning there for the past eighteen years."

"You must have gone there as a baby," I remarked.

"You must be Spanish. Latin men never miss an opportunity to be gallant."

I laughed and introduced myself.

"I'm Isa Hannaway," she said. "I was a schoolteacher in Trenton until I married Geoffrey ten years ago."

"Then you went to Havana during a summer vacation?"

"Yes. I'll never forget that vacation. Few people ever get a chance to see Havana the way I saw it, thanks to Alfonso Varela, my guide."

"You must have liked it very much if you have been dreaming of going back for eighteen years."

"I would rather go to Havana than to any other place in the world. Señor Varela would come for us every morning at the hotel. For fifteen days he was an inseparable companion. When the other tourists in my group were tired of sightseeing, Alfonso—I mean Señor Varela—would take me to places all over the island, where he had never taken anyone else."

She sat motionless, but her face was alive with memories. In the windowpane on my left I could see the reflection of her profile, a wax mask floating through black space. In the darkness beyond the row of windows, an endless parade of lights flashed by. My pipe had died out in the ashtray.

"I don't know why I'm telling you all this," she continued. "Perhaps I'm a little high, or maybe I just feel so humiliated that I must fight the present with the past."

"You're too young to speak of the past."

"I'm forty," she said flatly. "I don't look it, people tell me. I have lived, loved, and suffered. I knew paradise in Cuba eighteen years ago."

"Aren't you afraid to return and find the doors closed? They say that the doors to paradise are opened only once."

"Just the same I prefer to return, come what may. New illusions, disillusion—what does it matter? I only want to convince myself after all these years that it was not a dream. I want to visit the same enchanting

234

places, walk the same quaint streets, see the luminous blue waters once more."

"Who'll show you around this time?"

She looked at me sharply, but the flash of anger vanished as quickly as it had appeared. She laughed. "No, I shall not be angry. You hit the nail on the head. But then you're a writer. No, we won't have Señor Varela as a guide. I have no intentions of seeing him again."

"But I thought you had been very pleased with him," I said innocently.

"Very much so. That's exactly why I should not see him again. Anyway, he probably wouldn't know me after all these years."

"I'm sure you have improved with the years. Women always look best in their late thirties and forties."

"I have changed a great deal. He too must have changed. Perhaps he's married, has children. No, that chapter is finished and it's better to turn to a new one."

"I dare say you have reread that chapter many times."

"Yes, I have. Thousands of times. It has been my only consolation during many bitter hours. Why deny it? If I did, I would have to cry and there are no more tears left. Life with Geoffrey has been a tragedy. I'm not ashamed to tell you. You're a stranger and I probably shall never see you again.

"When I married Geoffrey he was handsome and seemed so very romantic. Even his name recalled to

235

mind the hero in a book of chivalry. Yes, the little teacher from Trenton, tired of teaching arithmetic and bored with school, was only too happy to marry the handsome businessman from New York. I believed he was going to open wide the doors to a world I knew only through the books I used to devour at night alone in my little apartment. How very stupid of me! The only romantic thing he ever did was to marry a poor small-town girl.

"I soon found out that my husband was the acme of the very things I wanted most to escape from: order, routine, even mathematics. Except when he drinks. Then he behaves as he did tonight. He resents me then. There is nothing I can do. These years have brought me nothing but humiliation and bitterness. That is why I insisted on this trip to Havana. It's the only thing that can bring a ray of light into my bleak existence.

"I intend to see no one in Havana, believe me, no one I know. It will suffice to feel the soft warm breeze on my cheeks, to stroll on the Malecón and watch the sea turn into shimmering silver under the rising sun. At night, in the silent little squares, the moon turns the old stone façades into lace, and one has the feeling that soon a tall figure wrapped in a cloak, a touch of white lace at his throat and a gleaming sword at his side, will step from one of the ancient Spanish iron doors. I only want to make sure that I'm not dried up

236

inside, like the leaves in autumn. I must find out if under the layer of ice over my heart there is still a little bit of spring."

"Your visit to Havana seems to have left very beautiful memories," I said.

"Yes. Señor Varela was in love with Havana. He saw it with the eyes of a lover and extolled it with the tongue of a poet. He was proud of his beautiful island. He was steeped in the traditions of his ancestors. His images, though fantastic, were exquisitely beautiful. He had the singular power to impart warmth and beauty to everything. I listened entranced to every word of his. Aware of this, he took pains to show me the quaintest places. Under the spell of his words the little restaurants in out-of-the-way corners, the narrow cobblestone streets, the old crumbling stone walls, the ancient little churches and squares—all acquired a bewitching charm that seemed to emanate directly from his fabulous Spanish ancestors, as if he had brought them back and they were there with us, speaking to us.

"On my last evening in Havana he took me on a boat ride. The moon was huge and radiant. He said that in the moonlight I looked like the silver virgins in their old churches, that in the daylight my eyes were the soft green of moss, and in the moonlight they held all the sweet promise of love. We talked, we laughed, but often we were just silent."

She had been talking in low tones, as if to herself, staring all the time at her reflection in the window. Suddenly she picked up her purse and rose.

"You have been most patient and kind, and I much too talkative. I may regret it tomorrow."

She offered me her hand. It was hot and moist. In her eyes I saw the desire to say something more. She hesitated. "Are—are you going to Havana yourself?" she asked, staring at the map on my lap. When I answered in the affirmative, she asked, "Will you do me a great favor? You may not like it, but it means so very much to me."

"Then, I can't possibly refuse."

"Thank you. Next week, whenever it is convenient for you, will you please go to the Agencia Transmundo on the Prado and ask for Alfonso Varela? Tell him that I asked you to say hello for me. Give him my regards. That is all. I will not see him, but I'm curious to know how he is. Call me at the Nacional. My husband will be away mornings on business. Please let me know then how Señor Varela is. I believe you can understand this feminine curiosity to know what has happened to the man who for two weeks generously shared his romantic dreams with me and forever endeared his country to me. However, under no circumstances do I want him to know that I am in Havana."

"What if he should meet you on the street?"

"He won't recognize me. I was only twenty-two then. Should he recognize me, I won't know him. I'm married now. I don't want a dead man to come back to life. I only want to know what his life has been like."

She opened the door to the club car. Her husband's snores were audible above the noise of the train as she disappeared behind the slowly closing door.

My first few days in Havana were so busy that I forgot all about the schoolteacher. It was May, and the city was gay with spring. Noisy crowds thronged the streets. The dresses of the women were as brilliant as flowers. In the sidewalk cafés people joked and laughed.

One hot afternoon I was crossing the Prado when two words spread across the front of a two-story building caught my eyes. In the windows brightly colored posters promised all the joys of paradise to those with time and money. The young man behind the counter informed me that Alfonso Varela had not been with Agencia Transmundo for the past three years. He now was a private guide. He gave me Varela's telephone number, and I called him then and there. After several rings, a child's voice answered.

"Señor Varela?" I asked.

"Who is Señor Varela?" said the little voice.

"Señor Varela, the guide."

There was no answer except a noise that sounded like lips sucking a lollipop.

"That is my father!" screeched the child suddenly. "Alfonsitooooooo!"

Another, more mature, voice said, "Yes?"

"Señor Varela?" I asked again.

"He is my father. I am sorry; Pedrito, my little brother, picked up the telephone. My father is taking his siesta. I will call him if you are a client."

"No, I'm not a client, but I have a message from a friend of his in New York."

There was a pause while perhaps Alfonsito pondered whether he should disturb his father's siesta. Finally he said, "One moment, señor, I will call him."

The third voice sounded as if it came from the depths of the earth. "Who is calling?"

"You don't know me, Señor Varela. I bring you greetings from someone you know in New York."

"A client?"

"I can only tell you personally. May I call on you?"

"All right, but please come immediately. I have a client later." He gave me his address.

The taxi was like a furnace under the scorching sun. The streets reflected the light as though asphalt and stone were lined with glass. The pale sky glared down without mercy, and in the distance there were sudden flashes of indigo blue from the sun-drenched Caribbean.

The taxicab stopped before a small white house with a red tile roof glowing in the sun and stunted green vines creeping up the walls. A black dog lay panting

240

in a shady spot. The doorbell tinkled frostily through the hot air. The door swung open and three youngsters, with dirty faces and undershirts hanging over thin naked legs, stood in a row staring at me with large smiling dark eyes. Silently they stepped aside for me to enter. Inside, standing in the middle of the room, was the man from which the three miniatures no doubt had been copied.

Alfonso Varela offered me a large, hairy, perspiring hand and then motioned me to an old stuffed armchair. A rocking chair, a dresser, and an old table with a blue vase containing three red paper carnations completed the furnishings of the room. A thin ray of light sneaked in through the lowered blind.

Señor Varela looked middle-aged. He was tall, with a massiveness more common among pachyderms than among human beings. His white cotton trousers had numerous deep wrinkles, as if they had been folded many times and then pressed with a hot iron. His shirt was stained with perspiration. He had powerful hairy arms and a thick neck like a Roman emperor's. Beneath coarse, unruly black hair there were large laughing dark eyes, and the long aggressive nose above an untrimmed mustache resembled a sea gull with outstretched black wings. His mouth was sensuous, and the yellowed teeth denoted the inveterate cigar smoker.

"An old client of yours in New York, Isa Hannaway, asked me to call on you and give you her regards."

241

He offered me a cigar, which I refused, whereupon he bit off the end, spat it out, lit it, and blew out a mouthful of smoke. He said indifferently, "I do not remember her, but then I have had many clients."

"This was eighteen years ago. Besides, it just occurs to me that Hannaway must be her married name. But her first name, Isa, is not common. She was an American schoolteacher from Trenton, New Jersey. It seems that in the two weeks she spent here you went out of your way to show her the most romantic places in Havana. She remembers you quite well."

He puffed heavily on his cigar and the smoke floated like torn pieces of veiling in the sticky, confined air of the room. The smell was sickening. Somewhere in the house a woman was scolding the children.

"I remember now," he said, in the same indifferent tone. "Isa Smith, the schoolteacher. Such a foolish romantic girl! Never have I met a more attentive listener than the little schoolteacher. And what legs! I was just beginning to work as a guide and I was young and foolish and as romantic as the tourists themselves. At first I enjoyed taking them around. They were so grateful you would have thought Havana was my garden and I their host. Isa was like that. She received very special attention."

He winked an eye, leaned forward, and lowering his voice so that no one else might hear him, said, "Is Isa Smith a friend of yours?"

242

"She's Mrs. Hannaway now. She was married ten years ago."

He burst into loud coarse laughter that seemed to increase the heat in the room. "So, she got married? Well, is she a friend of yours, yes or no?"

"I can't say that she is. I met her accidentally a few days ago."

"You are in no way interested in her?"

"Certainly not."

"Then I will tell you an amusing little story to compensate you for coming here in this heat. When Isa came to Havana I was not yet thirty years old. I wanted to be a poet. Instead I earned my living as a guide. God gave me an eloquent tongue and an attractive face. I made the best of both. I had interesting little speeches all prepared for the tourists. For people like Isa I had poetic ones. I turned them on and off like records. Tourists. Bah! Cattle! Nothing more, nothing less. But I was charming, I was courteous, and the tips were large. I made a good living. After a while I hated it. It kept me from what I really wanted to do.

"Isa. She was so thrilled and I was so amused! The little teacher had read everything about Cuba she could lay her hands on and she spoke excellent Spanish. I told her such fantastic stories about the island. I showed my admiration for her and constantly flattered her, and she accepted it all as if it were part of the tour.

"One night I took her on a boat ride. There was a full moon, and I whispered such foolish things in her eager little ear. How easy it was to make her come to my room!"

He took a noisy puff from his cigar. I remembered the sad cameo face and, disgusted, I stood up abruptly.

"You are annoyed," he said, surprised, stretching out his huge arms as if to embrace me. "I asked you if you were interested in that woman and you said you were not and I believed you. Let me tell you the end of the story. You will feel better. Sit down. There, that's better. Well, that night the joke was on me. When Isa left my room, her eyes radiantly green and her face glowing like a Madonna's, I was in love. She was no longer a stupid little tourist on whom I had played a trick. She was a young innocent girl and I was her first love. I was a poet then. Yes, I fell in love with Isa. I wanted to marry her, but I had no money and she had to return to her country. She promised to wait until I could send for her. I wrote her many burning letters. I reminded her of her promise. The months went by. I stopped writing. Finally she, too, stopped writing.

"One day I tore up her letters. You know how life is. I got married and now have three children. Isa, I forgot a long time ago." He lowered his voice to a whisper and winked again. "I wouldn't mind seeing her again, for a little while, just to change my daily diet—oh, *diablo!* This cigar is damp. It does not pull. Excuse me while I get another."

When he disappeared into the next room, I rose and hurriedly went out, craving a breath of fresh air. As I walked away, I looked back once. In the yard alongside the house I saw a dark plump woman, sleeves rolled up to her elbows, scrubbing a child in a tub of water.

Back in my room, I called the Nacional. Not until I heard her voice did I realize that it was already late afternoon and she had asked me to call in the morning.

"It doesn't matter," she said when I apologized. "Geoffrey is downstairs at the bar half-drunk already. Have you seen Alfonso?"

I regretted then that I had not planned what I should tell her. With an instinctive aversion, I had refused to think about my conversation with Varela from the moment I had left his house. Now it was too late. I decided quickly that, rather than prolonged treatment, surgery was the best cure.

"I saw Varela. You didn't tell me all about the entire affair."

"That's not important," she answered impatiently. "You must have guessed it all along. I regret nothing that happened then and I don't care if you know it. It has been the most beautiful thing in my life. Tell me about him. How is he? What did he say?"

"It's better for you to forget him. He's married and has three children. He was in love with you once. Your innocence kindled a spark of decency in him. But that was a long time ago. The poet no longer exists. He has grown fat, ugly, brutish, unscrupulous. There is nothing left to love. You must forget him. I know this may sound cruel, but it should help you to forget him."

"Did he mention my letters?" she asked, ignoring everything I had said.

"Yes. He destroyed them after a while."

"I still have his," she sobbed. "I always keep them near me. They're here with me now."

"Mrs. Hannaway, you must stop this madness. You're living with a dream that is dead and gone."

"That's not so," she shouted. "You're lying. I'm going to see Alfonso."

"That would be madness!" I cried.

"What would you suggest I do? Stay cooped up in this room while my husband gets drunk? I know now why I wanted to come to Havana. I've been all alone in this room for days, alone with my memories, waiting for your call. I must see him again. I don't care what he looks like. I don't care about his wife and children. I won't take him away from them. I just want to see him once more, for just one minute."

"Mrs. Hannaway, please wait for me," I shouted into the telephone. "I'll be there in a few minutes and we'll talk—"

The click of her receiver was sharp, definite, final, like a court verdict.

Half an hour later I was knocking at Mrs. Hannaway's door. When there was no answer, I pushed the knob and flung the door open. Standing by the night table, staring at some letters in his hand, was the white-haired man. There was a look of surprise on his face. When he looked up at me, he did not seem to see me.

"Mr. Hannaway, you don't know me, but we traveled on the same train to Miami. Your wife—she asked me to locate some friends of hers. I have come to tell her about them."

He stared at me vacantly. His eyes were a deep blue and his skin as pink as a baby's. He must have been drinking heavily and was now making a great effort to understand what was happening. He pointed to the letters in his hand. "Were you helping my wife to meet this man?"

"No, no. I tried to persuade your wife on the telephone to forget him."

He staggered to a chair. When he looked up again there were tears in his eyes. "It doesn't matter. She would have found him anyway. You seem to know all about this. Look! Love letters!" and he tossed them on the floor. "I come up looking for my wife and instead I find these and this piece of paper with an address. She is with him now. I know now why she could speak of nothing else these past ten years but her visit to Havana. She was always so far away. It was like living with a ghost. She thought I was a bore. That's why I started to drink and when I'm drunk I behave like a fool. And she, so proud, so dignified, so unapproachable—she was thinking all the time of her cheap little adventure." He leapt to his feet. "So, I have the dull mind of an accountant! I'll show her—" Pushing me aside, he staggered out of the room, the scrap of paper with the address crumpled in his hand.

I ran after him, calling, "Mr. Hannaway, let me come with you. You'll find things a lot different from what you expect—"

"Thank you," he interrupted me sharply. "I don't need you. This is a family affair. You have intruded enough. Good-by."

I stood in the hall, not knowing what to do, watching the white head swaying atop the bright-red neck until it disappeared into the elevator.

I saw Isa Hannaway again late that night. A detective called for me at her request.

On our way to the police station the detective told me what had happened. After talking to me, Mrs. Hannaway obtained Varela's telephone number from the travel agency. Varela asked her to meet him at a certain address, which turned out to be a house of ill repute. In her excitement, or perhaps not caring any longer, she left Varela's letters and the paper with the address on the table near the telephone, where her husband found them.

Hannaway found his wife and Varela talking on the sidewalk in front of the house. He pulled out a gun. Varela grabbed his hand. In the scuffle, the gun went off, killing Hannaway.

In the waiting room at the station Isa Hannaway sat like a rag doll dropped by a tired child. The unshaded bulbs cast a baleful glare over the hard wooden benches and the naked walls, on which dampness had traced sinister-looking spots. Two policemen stood motionless at the door. In the center of the room a long narrow table with a stained marble top stood bare, as if waiting for a corpse. In a corner a child was cuddling a kitten.

Mrs. Hannaway's auburn hair was the only note of color in the grim room. Her long thin hands were clenched on her lap. She looked at me. There were no signs of tears in her eyes. The two green pools had gone completely dry. In barely two hours numerous tiny wrinkles had crept around her mouth and eyes. She now looked much older than forty. Her lips twitched.

"How horrible! How horrible!" she moaned, twisting her hands.

"You must calm yourself."

"Never again will I be calm," she sobbed, "never again. You were right. That man is revolting. For eighteen years I have lived with a dream that is dead. Eighteen years!" Her lips parted into a twisted little smile. "How very funny! I thought my husband dull, stupid, but he really loved me. He was jealous. He came ready to kill for me. Just like one of the stories I used to read as a young girl."

Her eyes were sunken and lifeless in her withered face. "I want to cry and I cannot. I want to cry for my husband, for Alfonso, for myself. But suddenly we are all dead."

As I walked down the steps of the hospital and signaled for a taxi, my head was still filled with the story of Isa Hannaway, one of the living dead.

# THE LIVES OF LEONARDO

*A Renaissance Tale*

Florence
May, 1504

G OD KEEP YOUR EXCELLENCY
Don Luis de Vergara, Grandee of Spain, and our
Most Exalted Majesty the Queen, Doña Isabel la
Católica.

I, Don Lope de Medina, of the Order of the Knights
of San Jaime de Compostela, the humble servant of
Her Majesty and Your Excellency's envoy to Italy,
consider the first part of my mission fulfilled and beg
to render an account to Your Excellency so that I may

be given further orders and pursue my assignment to a satisfactory conclusion.

In compliance with your instructions, I traveled from Madrid to Milan. Milan is a lovely city of great culture, although our own cities in Spain far surpass it in beauty and learning.

My first night in Milan I spent at the Osteria della Bella Spagnuola. While ambling through the lonely narrow streets in search of a suitable lodging, that name, which under the full moon shone as though incrusted in silver on the board above the door of the inn, called to me like a voice from my distant country. It was late. At the inn, an ill-humored, sleepy-eyed proprietor served me a loaf of hard bread and some tough mutton. But the red wine was good and the embers in the fireplace gave forth a pleasant warmth, for the nights here chill the air. While I was eating my humble repast, the innkeeper joined me in a glass of wine. With the flickering candlelight dancing wildly on his unshaven face, I proceeded to question him along certain lines of great interest to both Your Excellency and me.

Like Florence, Milan is going through a period of relative calm. The people of Florence still recall with horror the stakes set up in a public square for Savonarola's execution, and heretics still tremble when the monk's name is mentioned, although six years have passed since he left this world. But right now Cesare

Borgia provides so much to talk about that soon all memory of the past should be wiped out.

The innkeeper was the first person to speak to me of Leonardo da Vinci, the object of my mission. He himself had never spoken to Leonardo, but many years ago he lived in Florence, and every day Leonardo passed his house on his way to the atelier of Andrea del Verrocchio. The innkeeper vividly evoked Leonardo's corpulent figure clad in black velvet, without sword, dagger, or any other weapon, walking slowly, his eyes looking right through people. It is a pensive Leonardo the innkeeper remembers. He recalled Leonardo's stopping to scrutinize a damp spot on a wall or to stare as though in a trance at the fat white clouds in the Florentine sky, which he then sketched in a notebook. When I was quite convinced that the innkeeper knew nothing of importance about Leonardo da Vinci, I retired to my room.

The next day I went to Piero della Sagazza's shop. Your Excellency will recall this painter, some of whose canvases hang at the Court in Madrid. He is both painter and sculptor and has his own atelier, where he gives classes in painting and deals in pictures with the great lords of the various duchies in Italy.

The letter of introduction that the painter Pedro Berruguete gave me in Madrid was of great help. Piero della Sagazza, a great admirer of Berruguete's work, immediately offered me his hospitality. We spent a pleasant evening in his atelier, surrounded by bronze busts and pink marble torsos, onyx boxes and green jade figurines, lamps and jugs wrought most consummately in silver, and canvases in all stages of completion. Piero is not only the master of the secrets of fresco painting, but also of tempera and oil. The room smelled of fresh paint. Through the open window we could hear a lute nearby playing one of those plaintive compositions so dear to the hearts of the Milanese. A table had been laid with silver bowls of dried fruit, a wheel of cheese, and flasks of Neapolitan wine, of which Piero is very fond. As it grew darker and the square of sky outlined by the window was dotted with stars, Piero told me many things about Leonardo da Vinci.

Leonardo was born in 1452 and is today fifty-two years of age. He has now come to that dangerous period in an artist's life when he must either surpass himself and reach for fresh laurels, or give up everything and follow the humble path to a monastery. Leonardo is passing through a period of such melancholy that few are those who are allowed to speak to him. Only a few intimate friends may enter his home, where he rarely sleeps, in order to avoid surprise visits. He has greatly changed since the days he was in the service of Ludovico Sforza. He would no longer be able to spend ten years on a statue as he did on that of Ludovico's father, Francesco Sforza. Piero thinks that

Leonardo is now going through that crisis inevitable in the life of all men who, ignoring the limitations of the human being, embrace the entire universe, suffer a tragic disillusionment, and become overconscious of their shortcomings. His natural misanthropy has deepened of late. Only work seems to alleviate his anguish at not being able to extend his creative genius beyond the limits he has reached.

Thirty-five years ago Piero was a young man of twenty and one of Verrocchio's pupils in Florence. In those days Leonardo himself went often to Verrocchio's studio. He was a fine-looking young man with auburn hair, a lofty brow, and eyes the color of the sky on a clear day. Piero especially remembers Leonardo's fondness for anatomy. Other disciples still cultivated the manner of Giotto and painted as though their figures were meant for medieval altarpieces, but Leonardo was obsessed by the human body. He loved Masaccio's "The Expulsion from Eden" only because the subjects looked to him like an ordinary Florentine middle-class married couple with all the imperfections of naked flabby flesh, and he went into ecstasy over Fra Filippo Lippi's plump Virgins and robust little angels. Piero thinks that Leonardo admired Verrocchio because of his realism. His Virgins have tranquil countenances, long slim fingers, and a well-defined anatomy, and his children are chubby and exude good health. Leonardo also liked the naturalism of Donatello's bronzes and the violent emotions implied in the faces of Signorelli's Virgins.

In Verrocchio's atelier, Leonardo, with amazing anatomic precision, modeled clay figures, which he then painted on canvas, imitating relief with his brushes, thus introducing into his painting the sensation of bulk and solidity. When his fellow students saw his early work, "The Adoration of the Magi," they admired and praised his knowledge of anatomy.

Piero recalls those years with nostalgia. Leonardo was a good friend to all of them, but his kindness and gentleness were detached, sometimes even remote, like the dates on a palm tree. No one dared mistreat an animal in his presence. Behind his back people made fun of his mania for buying caged birds in the market and, after kissing their palpitating breasts, setting them free to fly on their swift wings into the morning air.

"No," Piero told me, "no one ever knew whether Leonardo had a mistress or was ever interested in a woman. No one ever saw him in the company of women except when he was working on a painting, and even on such occasions he treated his models with great reserve. He was a loveless youth. 'He who does not control sensuality,' he used to say, 'becomes an animal.' Of course—" Piero paused and got up and walked to the window. With his back turned to me, as if he wished to avoid looking me in the face, he continued, "Of course, it was all slander, but because he was so often seen in the company of fair adolescent boys there were many nasty rumors and finally the authorities had to intervene. They even suspected his relationship with the master Verrocchio. The hearing lasted three months, but he was found innocent of the heinous crime of which he was accused. There could have been no other verdict."

According to Piero, Leonardo has been a man of pure heart and unimpeachable morality all his life. To doubt his virility was an outrageous insult. Still, Piero does not believe that Leonardo has ever loved a woman. Love in any of its plastic manifestations strikes him as repulsive and degrading, and that is why he depicted it the way he did in one of his sketches, which a friend has put away as one of those creations that can be shown only when its author has passed into the world of shadows. It is said that Leonardo loved only once in his life, and even that was more like a scientific experiment. He prefers to live with a free soul and to cultivate the dreams of a timid man enamored of an ideal.

Piero della Sagazza promised to show me one of Leonardo's wall paintings called "The Last Supper," which is in the refectory of the monastery of Santa Maria delle Grazie in Milan. Since I was too impatient to wait for the next day, we set out through the deserted labyrinth of streets under a sky already covered with stars. When we reached our destination it was quite late, and even the church bells were sleeping.

The monastery before us was a mass so great and black that it seemed as though the night had frozen it into a solid block of darkness. We knocked at the door several times. A little peephole opened. Piero whispered to the monk who kept watch; the door opened, and we entered the courtyard of the monastery. The moon embroidered our cloaks in silver. We could hear the gurgle of water in an invisible fountain. We crossed another doorway. More darkness. Long corridors. Our boots wakened a thousand sleeping echoes. Finally, guided by the monk, we entered a large room. The stale smell of cooking and moldy bread assailed my nostrils. The monk struck flint and steel over tinder and lighted a candle; the bluish flame projected a series of dancing shadows on the walls. The pale face of the monk was like the end of a wax taper. We were in the refectory of the monastery. In a corner stood a mound of hay. Painted on the wall separating the refectory from the kitchen was "The Last Supper."

I could not see very well and I was then sorry that I had not waited until morning to visit the monastery, although the monk told me that even when the sun is high the light in the refectory is poor. Vague figures, licked by the flame of the candle, oscillated before my eyes. I drew closer until my face was almost against the wall. I could see the cracks in the painting caused

258

by the heat from the kitchen. Piero spoke enthusiasti-
cally about this work. Exhaling warm breath into my
ear, he whispered that Leonardo had spent many days
staring at the painting, unable to do Jesus' face. Finally, one day he finished the painting. I raised the
candle, and in the pale light the face of Jesus glowed
with all the gentle fortitude of the Savior. Against the
surrounding shadows the golden countenance stood
out, as though suspended in mid-air, radiating a dia-
mantine light. When I finally moved the candle away,
I could still feel the eyes of Jesus looking at me.

Out on the street again, dogs barked at us and a
cock crowed, heralding the first light of dawn.

On the following day, Piero introduced me to Francesca, a native of Vinci, the town where Leonardo was
born. She is a little old woman with gleaming silvery
hair and a face as wrinkled as a dried leaf and veiled
by that golden down that comes with great age. She
has a fruit stand, and the rich merchants of the district will buy fruit from no one else. When we approached her stand, the fruit wagon had just left,
and Francesca stood surrounded by large straw baskets
overflowing with porcelain-like fruit, among which
had sneaked a few leaves still sprinkled with dew.

Francesca greeted us warmly, for Piero has done
her a few favors and also buys from her. When he
told her that I was seeking information about Leonardo because I was considering commissioning him

to paint a portrait, she grew even more friendly and begged us to taste her exquisite plums.

Francesca had been a servant in the very same inn where Caterina, Leonardo's mother, had worked. She recalled with nostalgia the inn in the small town of Vinci, on the slopes of Mount Albana, not far from the city of Empoli in Tuscany, between Pisa and Florence. Perched on the mountainside, the few houses of the town of Vinci (Francesca has a poetic soul) are like doves poised for flight. The surrounding hills are fragrant with thyme and lavender. Francesca said she shared the work of the inn equally with her good friend Caterina. At dawn both would get up and stuff the fireplace with ginger sticks to make the fire smell sweet. The spacious kitchen was lighted by the oil contained in typical wide-necked clay vessels. ("Everything is Etruscan in Tuscany," Piero interjected, smiling.)

A notary named Piero da Vinci used to come to the inn. A love affair blossomed between the gentleman and the serving maid. The fruit of their illicit love was Leonardo, who spent his childhood at the home of his father's parents until he felt the urge to go and seek his true destiny, which began in Verrocchio's studio. Caterina later married a laborer, who could have never been, not even by the widest stretch of the imagination, Leonardo's father. Francesca's eyes dimmed with tears as she recalled Leonardo's devotion to his mother.

Leonardo was fond of Francesca and occasionally he would walk past the fruit stand and stare at her with a deep nostalgia in his limpid blue eyes. Sometimes he drew flowers and birds on walls to amuse the children who came to buy fruit. The things that Leonardo could do! He made a scale for Francesca so that she could weigh her fruit; he gave her several sketches he made of her, full-face and in profile, and a special knife, which he made in less than an hour, to peel fruit without damaging the pulp. On another occasion he brought her a machine he had made to suck the dust from her stand into a bag that could then be emptied very easily. "Yes," said Francesca, "Messer Leonardo is a good man, humble with the humble and proud with the proud."

On my first evening in Florence I had dinner at the palace of the Duke of Pavoneda. The other guests were a doctor and mathematician from the court of Cesare Borgia. With me was Piero della Sagazza, whom I had persuaded to accompany me to Florence.

The atmosphere was intimate, the food delicious, the table service of the purest gold, the music of lyres heavenly, and the wine red and warm as blood. Oriental tapestries hanging in profusion from the walls muffled all sounds to such a point that our voices sounded like murmuring, which lent the conversation a confidential tone. As soon as we finished supper, the Duke excused himself on the grounds that the Duchess was indisposed and he must return to her side. But an elegantly gowned lady with her face veiled, whom I saw in a mirror as she quickly crossed the hall beyond the dining room, was probably the real explanation for the Duke's sudden departure. We were then alone with Messer Paolo Crivelli, the mathematician, and Doctor Bertoldo Rinozzi. Servant girls, after clearing the table, brought us several jugs of wine, bowls with figs and nuts, and a vase of roses so red that they looked almost black. The music ceased, and without further ado I began to question both men about Leonardo da Vinci.

"A clever charlatan," remarked the mathematician.

Messer Paolo Crivelli had been in the service of Ludovico il Moro at the same time as Leonardo. Evil tongues say that he never forgave Leonardo for winning Ludovico's favor with a silver lyre in the form of a horse's head, which Leonardo himself had made.

Leonardo had offered his services to Ludovico il Moro as an inventor of war machines, constructor of light movable bridges and a kind of armed wagon, military engineer, expert in artillery and the art of laying siege, sapper, sculptor, and painter. It was at Ludovico's court that Leonardo triumphed over Paolo Crivelli and other courtiers in a dispute on paleontology and geology. Later, when Crivelli was temporarily in Ludovico's service, the two men met again. It seems that Leonardo completely ignored the mathematician and even manifested some scorn for his knowledge, which aroused hatred for Leonardo in Crivelli's heart.

Leonardo, Crivelli told me, never cast the equestrian statue of Francesco Sforza, the first Duke of Milan of the Sforza dynasty, despite the fact that the model was ready ten years ago. He "wasted his time" on innumerable technical problems "of no importance whatsoever." He constructed a revolving stage for theatrical production, took part in the competition to construct the dome of the cathedral of Milan, sketched fortifications for cities in Lombardy, and studied the system of canals and locks that regulated river traffic in the most active province in Italy. At the same time, he was often seen feverishly filling notebook after notebook with sketches and notes on mathematics, astronomy, physics, architecture, botany, and geology.

"It was impossible to read his notes," Crivelli said, "because he wrote them from right to left, with his left hand, and only with a mirror could one read them. Leonardo thinks he can master everything because he believes he is endowed with divine omniscience. There is no science he has not attempted to master. He does not realize that one science alone—mathematics in my case—is more than enough to occupy an entire lifetime. His pride has no bounds. They say that he has submitted plans and maps to Cesare Borgia purporting to change the course of certain rivers and isolate entire cities from the sea."

What most infuriated Crivelli was Leonardo's audacity in attempting to construct a flying machine. When still a young man, they say, he built a machine, a sort of bat heavier than air, with which he tried to imitate the flight of birds. This strange contraption now lies covered with dust in a corner of his studio, together with all sorts of strange things on which he has worked at one time or another, such as models of war machines and cannons, ships for sailing under water, machines for excavating earth, diving dress, airtight chambers, crossbows, bombs that would reduce the universe to ashes, vehicles propelled by their own motive force, and many other such chimeras. But, above all, flying was Leonardo da Vinci's obsession.

"It almost seemed," said Crivelli, "as though he wanted to escape from men to the heavens, or perhaps to snatch from our Lord the secret of the heights, which belongs only to Him." And Crivelli, rubbing the rubies with which gout has ringed his fingers, grew silent and pensive.

As it was now rather late, I arranged to meet with Doctor Bertoldo Rinozzi the following day.

I found the physician in his study, standing by a window, holding a tube of amber liquid up to the light. In spite of the heat, he was wearing a short fur-trimmed coat.

Doctor Rinozzi's study was spacious but dark. The light of an eight-branched candelabra shone on the golden spines of the huge volumes enclosing all of medical knowledge. On a table *The Canon* of Avicenna and Galen's treatise on hygiene lay open, together with flasks containing the viscera of animals in alcohol, glass jars with crushed herbs, amulets, and several anatomic plates showing the best areas for bleeding the human body, undoubtedly for the edification of the Doctor's barber.

After greeting me, Doctor Rinozzi promptly took out from an intricately carved Spanish chest a bundle of papers, which he placed on his desk for me to see. There were hundreds of pages of various sizes, all covered with a tiny, cryptic, unintelligible writing. Among them were all sorts of anatomic illustrations. I know nothing about medicine—I am not even a very learned man—but even I realized how marvelous the sketches were.

Doctor Rinozzi said they had all been done by Leonardo. They were found in his atelier one day when the crowds incited by Savonarola, who suspected Leonardo of practicing black magic, assaulted the atelier. Compassionate hands rescued the papers, and when they saw that they dealt with anatomy they gave them to Doctor Rinozzi for safekeeping.

"I do not know Leonardo," said Doctor Rinozzi, "and therefore cannot return them to him personally, although I crave the opportunity to do so. Meantime I am aware that this is a treasure which one day science will fully esteem. Look at this, and this, and this! More than fifty sketches on the heart and the motion of the blood. Of course, there are many errors, for Leonardo is so bold as to contradict Galen's theories and even to replace his 'vital spirits' by mechanical forces. His study of the mechanics and hydraulics of the heart is incomparable, although I do not understand his theories completely. He says that the function of the heart is to create body heat. Contrary to Galen's, Avicenna's, and Mondino's theory that the heart has only two ventricles, Leonardo says it has four. He claims that the heart is not made of special tissues but that it is a muscle, and he even describes its valves. He must have dissected and studied many cadavers to have been able to reduce the dimensions of the organs to mathematical formulae. Look at these drawings of bones, muscles, nerves, arteries, cross sections of the brain and liver, and these sketches of the faces of men condemned to death, of monsters and dwarfs. It is a pity that this man—who is not, I am sure, an atheist or a sorcerer, but a mystic in love with all living things—has such scorn for us physicians that he calls us liars and destroyers of life. When Duke Gian Galeazzo died and his disciple Andrea Salai became ill, Leonardo threw all the medications prescribed by the doctors out the window."

266

Doctor Rinozzi, pausing, looked at me pensively. "This Leonardo da Vinci," he resumed, "is a very courageous man. Let me tell you an incident I have never told anyone. I saw him in church one day, when Fra Girolamo Savonarola was delivering a terrifying sermon to a vast crowd of people. With fiery words he was painting a horrendous picture of hell with its thousand torments for all sinners. The people, petrified on their knees, began to scream, 'Mercy! Mercy!' Over the sea of trembling people prostrate before that implacable voice announcing the Day of Judgment, I saw Leonardo da Vinci, a solitary figure standing erect among the masses of kneeling religious fanatics, pencil and notebook in his hands. His face was of almost feminine delicacy, his beard heavy, his hair soft and wavy as a child's. He wore a black mantle down to his knees over an ankle-length red tunic. I drew close to him and, when I saw what he was doing, I trembled with admiration and fear. Leonardo was calmly drawing a grotesque caricature of Savonarola, the priest feared by all!"

Since I felt that I should not attempt to speak to Leonardo da Vinci before learning Your Excellency's opinion, I begged Piero della Sagazza, who was still in Florence, to at least point out the master to me, even from a distance, so that I might add my own impression to those I have garnered from others. Piero promised that as soon as he found out how and when we might see Leonardo, he would let me know.

Two days went by. I visited every important church, museum, and palace in Florence. I attended two diplomatic banquets and became acquainted with the ever-growing intrigue in high circles. On the third day, a messenger brought me a note. It said: "Today, at sundown, follow the bearer of this note and you will find me." It was signed, "Piero."

Impatiently I waited for sundown. It was one of those afternoons when the Florentine sky, as though washed by the angels, shines with pristine purity. Closely wrapped in my cape, I followed the guide. Soon we left behind the main thoroughfare, where only a few bold people still lingered, for after sunset hardly anyone dares venture on the streets for fear of bandits.

We were already outside the city gates when we reached our destination, a very old house with a garden surrounded by a wall. A tower bell nearby tolled six strokes, the sound of which quivered through the air and hung as though entranced in the stillness of twilight. Evening was languidly descending upon the ancient yellowed stones. A black martin suddenly took flight and then remained suspended in mid-air above our heads, like a bird of ill omen. We entered the garden through a discreet little door. The fragrance of roses promptly enveloped us. On the other side of

268

the door stood Piero della Sagazza, his forefinger raised to his lips enjoining me to silence.

"I succeeded," he whispered, "in bribing a maid to let us enter. From behind a curtain you will see the master painting a portrait. Do not speak; make no noise. We could be arrested for housebreaking."

"Where are we?" I asked.

"This is the home of Ser Piero di Batto Martelli, deputy of the *Signoria,* where Leonardo da Vinci is painting Lisa di Antonio Maria de Noldo Gherardini, a Neapolitan lady. She is the wife of Francesco di Bartolommeo di Zanobi del Giocondo, one of the twelve *buon' uomini* of the city. It is said that he will soon be a *priori.*"

Silently we crossed the garden past fragrant flower beds and murmuring fountains. From the house came the faint notes of a sad Florentine melody.

"Leonardo has been working on this portrait for three years," Piero whispered. "He never works on it before twilight because it is then that the face yields its most subtle expression. Mona Lisa comes to sit daily."

On tiptoe we slowly advanced through a dim corridor ending with a doorway hung with thick curtains. Carefully, Piero pushed aside a corner of the drapes so that we could see the studio clearly. Mona Lisa was already seated. Nearby stood the man I had come to see: Leonardo da Vinci.

Mona Lisa is about twenty-four, with a well-proportioned, voluptuous body and a soft, delicate face. Her beauty is elusive, of antique mold, like the vague scents that rise faintly from the depths of an ancient chest. Although far from the autumn of life, she is already a ripe woman. I could almost smell the aroma of tuberoses that her body, in its premature fullness, suggests. Limpid, dreamy eyes attenuate the sensuousness of her countenance. Her hands, like enamored doves, lay crossed on the arms of the chair. Mona Lisa! Her sad face fascinated me, for every woman smiles at some time or another, but this was the face of a woman who never smiles.

Holding my breath for fear of being detected, I looked at Leonardo.

He is tall, with the corpulence of a wrestler, but his hands are too delicate, his gestures almost effeminate. Judging by his alert eyes and his quick movements, Leonardo is still at the height of his physical and intellectual powers. His body is that of an athlete (they tell me he is an expert horseman), but his hands are more those of a lyre player (they tell me he is that too) than those of Hercules. His soft blue eyes hold a promise of friendship, but the weak chin discernible beneath his beard indicates withdrawal. His is the countenance of a man tormented by deep anguish, a man who craves to do great things and cannot do them, who, tired of doing what is possible, dreams of doing the impossible. He is a dilettante who, because he desires so much, can achieve so little. His profound melancholy, his tremendous yearnings are all visible in his smile, infinitely sad and full of renunciation. When the lutist stopped playing, in the silence that followed, I could suddenly feel the vibrations in the air—like a tenuous hum, like the beating of wings —between the painter and Mona Lisa. It was as though the nostalgic lady and the melancholy painter were silently reciting to each other the endless psalm of their sadness.

And then Leonardo moved away from the easel and I saw the painting of Mona Lisa. And I staggered under the impact of a sudden revelation. The portrait of Mona Lisa was that of Leonardo da Vinci himself!

Were my senses deceiving me? Was my interpretation completely mad? No. Leonardo da Vinci *was* painting himself with a woman's face. The face, the body, the clothes, were all Mona Lisa's, but the expression of the lips, the remote melancholy in the eyes—they were Leonardo's. And then I noticed something that sent shivers down my spine. The woman in that room, as I have said, was a woman who never smiled, a woman of eternal seriousness. But the woman on the canvas was smiling, and her smile was the identical gelatinous smile that never left Leonardo's lips while he painted Mona Lisa.

I am so profoundly perplexed that I find it impos-

271

sible to express my feelings to Your Excellency clearly. But this I believe to be the truth: for years Leonardo has been painting a woman who is only a mirror of himself. In her face Leonardo is painting his own face, and especially that strange smile that never leaves his lips, but which I dare say has never crossed the lips of Mona Lisa.

I beg Your Excellency to convey, through the Chief of Protocol, to Her Most Exalted Majesty the Queen, Doña Isabel la Católica, this testimony about the man who is today one of the most outstanding artists in Italy. I shall await your orders. My humble opinion is this: Leonardo da Vinci is too close to us for us to judge whether he is a genius or a prodigious charlatan, an admirable artist or a mad visionary. I can personally vouch for his artistic ability. Nevertheless, I earnestly and respectfully suggest that no attempt be made to commission him to paint the portrait of Her Most Exalted Majesty the Queen, Doña Isabel la Católica. Leonardo could never paint our Sovereign in all her glory, for he is too engrossed in his own tragic drama. They tell me that many of his works bear the same smile he has given to Mona Lisa. Perhaps Leonardo bestows that smile on all his subjects so that they may not cry. It is the smile of one who feels that, were he not held down by his human limitations, he could be the master of the universe, the equal of the gods. Even I, a simple man, was greatly disconcerted when I noticed the contrast between the solemn, humorless face of Mona Lisa and that of "La Gioconda," Leonardo da Vinci's smiling sphinx. For the smile worn by the woman in the painting is the smile of the master himself, a smile that hides his deep, silent skepticism about a world that he feels cannot comprehend the magic of his genius.

# THE LADY OF
# THE GREEN JADE LAMP

*A Romantic Prelude*

I JUMPED FROM THE SKIFF onto the sand, which gave beneath my feet like a wet carpet. The night enveloped me in its thick mantle of darkness, pierced only by fat drops of rain. I advanced a few steps and turned around for a last look at the boat that had brought me to the island. I could see nothing in the dense blackness except a red light bouncing wildly. That scarlet lantern, it struck me, was keeping pace with the thumping of my heart.

The oppressive darkness seemed menacing, and for an instant I felt cut off from the world. Between some rocks nearby, the silvery thread of light from my flashlight picked out a tall rusty iron gate standing ajar, the only means of entering the other side of the soaring sea-polished wall of rock.

I crossed the threshold. With a strenuous effort I closed the heavy gate and barred it with the steel crossbar, which made it practically impregnable. I walked slowly along a sandy trail beside the rock wall, unable to see farther than a few paces ahead. Suddenly the path left the wall and swerved between tall slender trees. And at that same moment the rain descended on me with torrential force, like a stage curtain unexpectedly dropping on an unprepared actor. Half-blinded, I made my way between the trees.

I looked up and in the distance I could barely make out the tall wooded hill that by daylight could be seen from the mainland. At its very top, a window, glimmering like some celestial emerald eye, was watching my arrival. The light imparted a phantasmal glow to the vague outline of the castle.

A light and a castle. At last I was approaching Miranda's manor!

For a moment I stood enthralled by the distant window with its promising light. A violent gust of wind almost knocked me down and tore the flashlight from my hand. For a few seconds it sailed through the air

like a glowworm before shattering to pieces against
a rock. The rain enfolded me like masses of drapery.
I plodded on, stumbling over shrubs and vines, losing
the path only to find it again a little later, feeling ship-
wrecked in a whirlpool of wind and rain. Raindrops
pelted me with the force of bullets. But within my
battered body my heart was singing like a happy
bird. That window beckoned in the distance.

The window was in an ancient castle, and in the
castle was a room with a green jade lamp, and in that
room Miranda was waiting for me.

For what seemed an eternity I kept climbing up the
path, made ever more difficult by the plants and
branches tossed all over it by the storm. The rain fell
with such violence that I could hardly see my surroundings. I was guided only by my sense of touch
and the light from the window, which shimmered in
the distance and seemed to contain all the colors of
the rainbow. As the path grew wider I realized that the
light was actually the same misty, faded green that
can be seen in Venice early in the morning, shortly before the sun rises, when the dusty liquid patina of
the canals transforms the water into a mirror sprinkled
with the finest powder.

I finally reached what once must have been a draw-
bridge; there apparently was no longer a moat because
untrimmed hedges and bushes bordered both its sides.
After I crossed the bridge, my hands, piercing the

276

curtain of rain, found a massive knocker, on which my fingers traced the wings of a mythological bird. I struck three resounding raps, and like bats of bronze the echoes winged through the storm-laden air.

The door was opened almost at once, and an oriental servant as tall and massive as a giant Buddha stood staring at me. The dim lamps in the hall intensified the darkness around us. Lights and shadows, dancing across the great planes of his impassive face, made it look like a basalt relief in an ancient temple. His eyes were as brilliant as burning coals. With his head he motioned me to enter. The huge door was shut behind me, and as the bolts were put in place they rang with a note of absolute finality.

We started down a wide corridor with carved oak benches and ancient full-bellied chests along either side. Suits of armor, mighty in their eternal grimness, accentuated the deathly stillness. I could hear the crackling of logs burning in the fireplaces of unseen rooms.

The colossus walking in front of me clad in muted-colored silks did not once turn his head to see if I was following him. The absence of all signs of life, human or animal, in the castle was disquieting. Now and then the polished metal of a suit of armor or the glass door of a cabinet brightly reflected a speck of light. In silence we climbed a magnificent staircase of Carrara marble. The sumptuousness of the castle was being revealed to me in an exquisite statue, a beautiful painting, a magnificent carving on the various landings, or in a sparkle from the silver and crystal chandeliers. We stopped on the third floor. The corridor was thickly carpeted in red, and the walls between the velvet hangings and tapestries bore the traces of many centuries.

Obeying a gesture from the servant, I entered a room lit by several silver candelabra. The Oriental bowed silently and turned his broad back on me. I was left alone.

I looked around. Water dripped from my clothes onto the Persian carpet on the floor. It was a spacious chamber with silk-covered walls, luxurious armchairs, and an enormous bed of ancient oak with four tall posts carved with garlands of flowers. On a table laid with fine linen, there was a silver bowl of yellow roses, majolicaware platters piled with cold meats, cheeses, fruits, and loaves of bread. Crystal decanters glimmered with garnet- and topaz-colored wines. Like the tongue of a great hound, the luminous light of the flickering candles gently licked the spines of the ancient tomes that lined one of the walls. Shepherdesses and princesses in a tapestry portraying a sylvan and courtly scene of the France of Louis XIV looked down from the wall behind the patriarchal bed.

I looked out the window and then opened it. The night thrust a black, damp shoulder against my face.

Quickly closing the window, I approached the fire-place. It was wide, deep, and high, and the flaming logs crackled like a friendly inferno set up for my benefit by kind-hearted spirits.

I opened an armoire as large as a small chapel and found it filled with sumptuous robes. Next to it a door opened into a bathroom, and there a black marble tub the size of a Roman galley was invitingly filled with warm water. I removed my sodden clothes and stepped into the tub. Afterward I dried myself with one of the huge sea-blue towels. From the armoire I selected black Indian-silk pajamas and a scarlet dress-ing gown. I poured a glass of brandy from a decanter and sat in one of the velvet-covered chairs by the fire-place, feeling suddenly relaxed. Soon my thoughts were racing after one another as wildly as the flames in the fireplace.

The sea, the towering hills of the island, and three doors—the gateway at the landing, the castle door, and the door of my present room—separated me from both the mainland and the rest of the world.

I was at the Castle of the Green Jade Lamp. Soon I would be seeing the chatelaine herself—Miranda. And as soon as I saw her, spoke to her, my pilgrimage across the world would come to an end. Meanwhile the pleas-ure of anticipation made its nearing realization all the more attractive.

I don't know how long I sat by the fireplace smoking

a pipe filled with fragrant light tobacco from a sandal-wood humidor I had found on the mantelpiece, beneath a pair of proudly crossed Toledo steel swords. A blue cloud of smoke encircled me completely. My blood raced gaily through my limbs. A pleasant warmth crept up to my heart. I closed my eyes and dropped into a deep reverie.

"Fernando."

Winding around me like a crystal thread, the voice pulled me back to reality. I opened my eyes. The candles had burned down. The only light now came from the smoldering embers, a mass of rubies glowing in the fireplace. I looked around. I was alone in the room.

"Fernando."

The voice came from the scarlet embers! I immediately walked toward the fireplace.

"No, Fernando, don't look for me. I'm a long way from your room. This is an ancient Spanish castle with many a hidden corner from which a voice can be transmitted to other places within the building. We can talk as though we were sitting side by side."

The voice was sweet, warm, deep with tenderness.

"Miranda?"

"Yes, I am Miranda. I've been waiting for you a long time."

"I've been looking for you a long time."

"I know. That is why I decided to bring your search

to an end. I was told that you were on the mainland and sent you a message."

"I received the message and many others which I've been pursuing all around the world. Whenever anyone spoke of you, whenever your name was mentioned, I felt that my impatience to find you would tear my heart out of my body. At last, late this afternoon, in a small tavern by the harbor, I was sipping a glass of wine and watching the lanterns of the fishing boats disappear on the high tide, when a fisherman came in and told the bartender that he would be leaving in an hour to take a passenger to the island. He spoke in a loud voice, looking at no one, and then left the place. I inquired what island he meant, and they told me it was the island of the Castle of the Green Jade Lamp. I went out and followed the fisherman. When he stopped in front of his boat, I approached him. Silently he shone his lantern on my hand and looked at my ring. I have it on my finger now. A gold ring with a broken piece of green jade. He motioned for me to get into his boat. On reaching the island, he left me in front of the gate, the only opening through the rocks. I knew then that I must be expected. But the climb to the castle was difficult. The rain blinded me all the way."

"I wanted you to find the way to this castle. From the time you decided to look for me until now, the light of the green jade lamp has been your guide."

"Miranda, I must see you."

Laughter like the tinkling of fine glass wafted down the chimney. "In the morning, when the sun is shining. A midnight meeting after so many years of looking for one another would be precipitating matters too much. And one thing there must not be in our meeting is haste. Together we shall make time stand still."

"Miranda, I have often seen you in my dreams. Let me now see you in reality."

"Dear impatient man! Your craving for excitement has made you go chasing around the world as though you were wearing seven-league boots. Your yearning to meet me has made you plunge headlong into every fresh sea of adventure you found across your path, hoping to find me waiting in a shell, like a lustrous pearl, at the bottom, and to come back to the surface with your booty between your teeth like the divers of Ceylon. Fernando, you must learn to wait. He who knows how to wait is a gentleman, and he who can wait longer than a gentleman is a philosopher. But he who will wait longer than a philosopher—only he is a real man."

"All my life I have pursued a dream and now that I have found it I fear I may wake up."

"You are awake, I am near you, and the world is standing still on this far shore of the sea. Like so many others, you have come here in pursuit of an ideal. One after another I sent the others away, for in my dreams there is no room for the grossness and tyranny that men consider to be proof of affection. My dream is clear and transparent as crystal, not fragile like Bohemian crystal, but firm and strong like rock crystal. I have waited aeons for you. You have sought me all over the world, and I have sought you in my world. Now that we have met, do not push the hands of the clock ahead. For there is no clock!"

"Miranda, who told you about me?"

"You did. The wild beating of your searching heart reached even the depths of my dreams."

"Miranda, I seek only dreams, and you are the most perfect of them all."

"They say you are a Don Juan."

"Indeed no, nor do I wish to be. I have neither mocked nor worshiped women. I have often played the game of love. Next to Werther's dress coat, which I don in romantic hours, I carry the skin of a faun, which I wear when passion beckons under the light of the moon. I can also clothe myself in the swallowtails of diplomacy for tea dances, and only at masquerades do I wear the scarlet cape of Don Juan. But in my often-secluded life, I prefer the ascetic sackcloth of a hermit. I am neither poet nor mountebank, but I shall be your troubadour, albeit perhaps a somewhat bohemian troubadour. An alchemist of love, I have tried to extract one single drop of perfume from many roses. But now I find myself in the presence of the one rose that makes me wish to be the alchemist no longer. For you alone, sweet rose, I hope to be the gardener. Miranda, open the gates of your soul, your arms, and your heart."

"My gardener of love, the rose is waiting for you. But that would be too easy. When you speak thus, you make me doubt whether you really are what I had so much hoped for. I have lived surrounded by a court of impatient and unpolished suitors. I have often felt like a swan escorted by bears. You come with a universal passport. To you, together with my memories, which are the very sustenance of my soul, I may yield my kisses, which are the promise of my body. Fernando, roses never smell sweeter than under the morning dew."

"Or when they droop in the dark and every petal fills the night air with the scent of eternity. However, I shall respect your wishes. I shall learn to wait. I could even wait my whole life long if only I knew that at the end of an eternity of expectation I would be granted one single hour in your arms, for that would be another eternity in itself."

"Do you know what I look like?"

"I picture you in a thousand different ways, but every man who has ever spoken to me of you has described you differently. I suspect that no one has seen you as you really are, because you have never allowed it. There are in you a thousand mirrors, so that every man sees only the reflection of you that you wish him to see. Every reflection has been different, but all of them have been equally strong in their intensity. Some men have seen you but for a moment, others have held you in their arms or listened to your voice, still others have loved you from afar. All have emerged from the horizon of your witchery with a scar of light on their hearts and an indelible mark on their souls. After seeing you, hearing you, and loving you, life became for them a fleeting present, a past full of luminous remembrances, and a future relieved only by a consuming hope."

"You are right. I have shown myself to no one as I really am. For some, I was an Asiatic princess who dreamed only of the lost glories of bygone dynasties and who made of love an eternal court ball resplendent with pearls, plumes, gold braid, and silks. For others I was a true gypsy, harboring under her tawny skin the accumulated passion of thousands of years of frenzy and rapture, for whom life was a mad ride along the highroads of the world and a crushing embrace beneath an olive tree.

"Sometimes I was the mysterious woman sheathed in resplendent satins, arms laden with diamond and ruby bracelets, sinuously reaching for the gold coins with which they feed the green cloth of the gaming tables at Monte Carlo, a woman whose love was passion

285

as sudden and unexpected as breaking the bank at roulette; and there are some who saw me as a Nordic goddess, with flaxen hair and a strong body, a Valkyrie who skied down the slopes in a whirlwind of snow and made love with a chaste kiss by the firelight. In a Persian town they thought me a fugitive slave from a harem, and I lived on love as only a harem favorite and her secret lover could, teaching the beloved the delights of love learned in the sensuous shadows of the seraglio.

"I have also camped on the mountainsides in Greece, the leader of a guerrilla band, and made love by the campfire, always alert, even in moments of ecstasy listening for the footfalls of the enemy. And I have, from the lofty height of a castle tower, inspired immortal verses in a poet who could reach me only on the wings of his poetry, to which I responded by setting fire to the castle, for the only way for heaven and earth to unite in a kiss is that of fire."

I drew near the hearthstone. My heart had become another blazing coal.

"Miranda, I have seen you in all these forms and many others. You are both fact and fancy, 'half woman and half dream.' I have spoken of you to nostalgic sailors in the isles of the Marquesas, at the hour of dusk, when, enveloped in the smoke from their pipes, they evoked the elusive Lady of Dreams who, real or legend, had crossed the paths of their vessels. A banker, ruined at the tables in Monte Carlo, said in my presence shortly before plummeting from his balcony with a bullet in his temple that the only thing he regretted was not having played an everlasting stake on the wheel of life with you as the prize. A love letter to you was found in the hand of an Arctic explorer who, before his heart and lungs were frozen solid, sought a little warmth with the memory of the fur-clad noblewoman whom he saw but for a few moments at a Norwegian port before sailing for the Pole.

"In a Franciscan monastery in the Carpathians there is a monk who has never left his cell in five years. When I asked him what he had been doing all those years, he answered that he was expiating his worldly sins, to which had been added still one more, that of spending those years of solitude thinking of you. In the art galleries of Florence they vowed to me that your beauty surpasses that of a Titian Madonna; and while on safari in the Congo, a South African hunter told me that your passion was like the wild fury of a leopard. I have also heard the peasants of Alicante compare you with the tawny Virgins in their shrines; and the film stars in Hollywood and Rome say they would give half their life to learn your secret of eternal beauty.

"Miranda, seeking you I have followed the wake of all these creatures who have lived obsessed with the thought of you. And at last I have reached your castle and my heart feels as if it were bathing in the green radiance of your eyes.

"And here is something odd," I continued. "I feel no jealousy. It seems to me that your whole life has been a period of preparation. I believe no one has ever really possessed you. You have been a butterfly flying hither and yon, alighting for a moment on the wandering bow of a gypsy violinist, flitting onward to the crested ring of a duke, then to the pen of a poet, to the brave Toledo blade of a cavalry captain, and onto the cape of a bullfighter. But no one every succeeded in capturing the butterfly. Only a few golden specks of powder remained between their fingers as the butterfly flitted ever faster on its way. Miranda, let me succeed where others have failed. Let me be both your master and your slave."

On the hearth nothing remained now but a faint glow. A pale luminosity was creeping up on the other side of the window.

"Good-by for a while," said the voice from the dying fire. "For now may your dreams foreshadow the dreams to come. Come to me when the noonday sun is shining over the glory of the island."

Morning came, golden, clear, and fresh, like a fine crystal goblet filled with manzanilla. I opened my eyes and they were filled with radiant light. The window, which the previous night had been but a hole overhanging a world of sodden darkness, was now a rectangle ablaze with sunlight. My dreams must have been pleasant, for I felt contented and rested. But suddenly one single thought erased with one stroke all my dreams and replaced them with a reality more wondrous than all that had passed in my sleep.

Miranda!

I was in the Castle of the Green Jade Lamp and Miranda was under the very same roof and it was midday and the sun was shining and in a few moments I would be in her presence.

I leapt from the bed, shaved, faced the quick, freshening attack of a cold shower, and from the well-provided wardrobe selected a country outfit that smelled of fresh apples. And then I opened the door of my room and went out into the hallway.

The scent of roses led me up a flight of stairs. The cooing of doves drifted through an open window. On one of the landings a dark shadow jumped at my legs. It was a fine black whippet. For a few moments he rubbed his noble head against my knees and then disappeared down one of the sun-bathed halls. On the top floor of the castle I found a glass door through which I stepped onto a terrace. A flash of sunlight stabbed me in the eyes.

On the vast marble-balustered terrace, gurgling stone fountains alternated with huge urns planted with masses of blooming flowers. A table was set with glimmering silver and cut glass, and there was an inviting array of cold meats, fruits, and wines. But what enchanted me most was the view from the terrace.

I was not on earth. The castle seemed to be a part of the sea and the sky. The sea spread as far as the eye could see, a deep turquoise with emerald streaks, flecked with scales of silver, fusing in the horizon with the brilliant blue of the sky. In the distance, the white sails of the fishermen's boats were like butterflies perched on a mantle of blue silk. The island on which I stood was but the crystallization of the dreams of the sea.

From the terrace I could see several small patios attached to the lower stories of the castle, flagged with redstone, the walls painted indigo. At the very bottom there was a wooded garden—during the rainstorm the night before, it had loomed in my imagination as a vast untamed wilderness—ablaze with peonies and roses and peacocks of gorgeous plumage. Beyond the garden, an untouched green glade stretched out like a pleasant smile on the face of the earth. And all around was the sea, vast and mighty, yet it did not separate one from things; rather, it integrated them with one's dreams. In the luminous silence the solitude hummed happily. The woods were a noble pagan mystery.

I stood there a long time gazing at the water, the sky, the woods, filling the depths of my soul with light and color. At last, I turned my back on the sea. In front of me, leaning against the marble balustrade, stood Miranda.

Miranda!

Enveloped in a crimson robe that just barely outlined her body as does the damp cloth of the sculptor around a statue, she was like a glowing log escaped from a flaming hearth. A loose, rebellious mass of copper-colored hair framed her face, large and oval-shaped, on which the parted lips stood out. Long dark lashes shaded the radiance of her green eyes. She moved a little, and the full rounded hips became clearly outlined under her robe, contrasting sharply with her small, almost fleshless ankles, the same ankles I had seen on the stone Virgins in Gothic cathedrals.

I approached her slowly. The sun had paused as in ecstasy on the ivory of her brow.

"Miranda, you are more dream than woman."

She broke into a peal of delighted laughter. "I am only woman, right now a very hungry woman. Come, let us enjoy together the sun imprisoned in these grapes."

She held out a plump cluster, every grape swollen with the sweetness of the heavens and the light of the sun.

"Let's begin the day by purifying ourselves with fruit, so that we may be worthy of the clemency of the gods," she said in her rich, warm voice, in which all the sensuality of the landscape seemed to have concentrated.

We sat down at the table and in silence we ate the grapes and drank wine in which a piece of light had fallen.

It was noon. The sky was as pure as the soul of a novice. The sea lay stunned under the dead calm of the day. The fountains in the garden sprayed their water in different ways. In some the water was but a fine dust, rainbow-hued in the sunlight; in others the drops were the size of pearls and fell as in strings; in others it descended rapidly in crystalline streams, and in still others it came down in large splashing drops like frogs in hasty flight. Water and sky everywhere. The sea encircled us like a blue and emerald girdle. I lit my pipe, and soon a plume of smoke rose through the slumbering air as proud and insolent as the plume on Cyrano's hat.

"Why did you leave Spain?" Miranda asked me.

"In Spain I found I was too much of a European, and outside Spain I was too much of a Spaniard."

"Even to your fickleness in love?"

"And even in my faithfulness to one Love."

"You Spaniards have a thousand loves and to you all of them last only too long."

"That's because we so rarely meet our one true love, which would last all too short a time."

"You are a poet and as such a candle of fleeting light."

"And you are poetry itself and thus a star of eternal light."

She smiled, and her mouth was like a red carnation sprinkled with salt.

"Come, I will show you around the castle."

She offered a firm, warm hand and we descended the steps leading to the gardens.

"When I was a little girl," she said, "I always dreamed of living in a castle, and yet when I first came here to live I thought I would never get used to it. The isolation, the solitude, the silence, nothing but sun and salt, sea gulls and cicadas, woods and sea—nothing else."

"Did you come alone?"

"I arrived alone. My husband died on the way here. It was he who turned this castle into an inaccessible love nest. He was a Persian prince, handsome, strong, and cruel as a tiger. He renounced his own people, his customs, his traditions, to come here alone with me. He wanted to learn from one woman alone what he had failed to learn during all those nights spent in his seraglio.

"He made this island impregnable. We are only a short journey from the mainland, but it is impossible for anyone to enter the island except through the gate in the cliffs, which is always kept bolted. If anyone should ever succeed in scaling the cliffs, there are great surprises in store for him. My servants are strong. They can spring upon a man and tear him apart as silently as a leopard does his prey. And there are ferocious dogs on the island. On the mainland they have come to look upon me as a witch, and my name is never mentioned without awe.

"My husband thus intended to keep me away from the world, which his suspicious oriental mind never trusted. He did everything to turn this castle into a paradise for two. We were married on the mainland, one stormy night. The air was charged with electricity. The sky was a livid color, like that in a painting by Van Gogh. After the ceremony, we waited at a café for the motorboat that would bring us to the island. I had met my husband six months before, in Monte Carlo, but I had never been closer to him than the other side of a table. Why did I marry him? That is another story, and this is not the moment to tell it. If I ever do tell it, you will understand. As we were getting ready to leave the café, after we heard the boat's whistle calling us from the harbor, a man walked in and suddenly jumped upon my husband, who fell to the ground instantly while the man fled into the night. I bent over my husband. A scarlet rose suddenly blossomed on his breast. A dagger had pierced his heart. I never knew whether the murderer was a political enemy of the Shah or someone jealous with love of me. I decided to come alone to the island. I have never regretted it."

We had now reached the garden. The island was not really very big, but it had many hillocks, small thick woods, gardens, and streams.

"They say that a very beautiful marchioness once lived here."

"In which case," I replied, "she still lives in the fragrance of the roses in this garden."

We strolled hand in hand, among flower beds and small ponds with dark waters set aquiver by multi-colored fish. Through the branches of the trees, the sun checkered the robe of the radiant creature walking beside me with shimmering light. Every step she took outlined her long slender limbs and made the crystal beads of her Indian anklets tinkle faintly.

The sun was pouring down hot and golden when we reached the cliffs surrounding the island. In daylight, what had seemed an untamed jungle the night before was merely a narrow path flanked by enormous trees and an impregnable cliff polished by the sea and the winds. The blue sea stretched out in front of us. The mainland in the distance was like a scratch made by a fingernail.

"I have here," she said, making a sweeping gesture with her arm, "jungle, prairie, and gardens."

"A worthy setting for drama and romance."

"My life on the island thus far has been neither.

Only a passionate dream broken by interludes of reality."

"Do you ever go to the mainland?"

"Very seldom, and then only for an extraordinary reason: once when I was fleeing from my own thoughts; another time, in pursuit of someone. Do not be surprised at my seclusion. In the first place, I live close to, as well as far from, civilization, guarded by my oriental slaves and protected by the armor of my dreams. In the second place, I have decided to live in a surfeit of enslavement. And here I am, of my own free will, the slave of my dreams."

I looked into the wondrous green gardens of her eyes.

"A slave and a mistress of slaves. In all the corners of the earth, from Belén to Marrakech, from Narvik to Karakorum, I have encountered many men who dream of you without knowing you. I have known others who have gone mad with the yearning to see you once again."

"My dreams make others dream."

"You are the dream of dreams. The odd thing is that in my wanderings I have been at the point of meeting you many times. I remember one evening in Bourbon Street in New Orleans. I was coming out of a tavern where they still play the blues the way they were conceived by the shackled Negroes in their long nights of captivity, sweat, and anguish, under a spectral moon that dotted the darkness with worms of light and clothed the earth in a ghostly shroud. With the last strains of the blues still ringing in my ears, I walked down the street. The hot night had the same fire as the absinthe they served at the tavern. A Negro came staggering toward me. Staring at me with wild eyes, he moaned, 'She just passed that corner and I'd swear I saw her at our last voodoo dance.' Quickening my step, I caught sight of a woman, her hair a blazing scarlet under the streetlight, who suddenly vanished into Pirate's Alley. I could not find her again. Was it you?"

"Who knows?" she whispered.

"Another time, early one morning at a hotel in Bangkok, I heard moaning in the room next to mine. I looked in through the balcony door and saw a handsome blond man sobbing in an armchair. 'She's gone, she's gone away and she'll never come back,' he kept repeating. A strange scent hovered in the air, as if the woman were still there. I went back to my room. A few minutes later I heard a pistol shot. That night, after the body had been removed, I went back to the room. The perfume seemed stronger than ever. On the floor I found part of a photograph showing only two wondrously beautiful eyes. Were they yours?"

"I couldn't say. My eyes have been everywhere."

We walked slowly through the grounds of the castle. Miranda was like a Valkyrie from the pages of an ancient myth. Her arrogant bearing was like the invisible wall that guards the odalisques in a harem, yet the rhythm of her movements promised all the delights of the seraglio. In all her sensual plenitude she was like the month of June, the month that has everything.

A salt-laden sea breeze sprayed the cliffs with all the colors of the rainbow. We sat down on a smooth ledge sheltered from the sun and remained there without speaking, for how long I do not know. The warmth and silence of the afternoon sweetly descended upon us. Drawing close to each other, we sank into a deep reverie that was neither of this world nor of any other, in which we were both our own self and the other's—a complete surrender of self, and yet we continued to retain our own identity. The hours passed gently and slowly, like the passage of the sun across the waters. Miranda's eyelashes were like the wings of a butterfly against my cheek.

When we finally returned to the castle, the late sun was painting the sky a ruby red. At the door, I stood still for a moment contemplating the landscape, now swathed in shades of crimson and gold. When I turned around again, I was alone. Miranda had vanished.

I started back to my room. A clock somewhere chimed six times. The castle seemed to be forsaken by all human life. On the ground floor, through an open door I saw a peacock pompously crossing a terrace, its tail fanned out in a rainbow-splendid ritual. Fascinated, I stepped out and found myself in a patio partly bowered with green vines, through which the dusk flickered with emerald tones. Peacocks proudly strutted among stone urns filled with water on which water lilies and lotus blossoms floated.

"Fernando."

I looked up. She was leaning on a windowsill, her red hair tumbling like a cascade of fire down her bare shoulders. Her flesh was a pagan challenge to the solemnity of the twilight hour.

"Miranda. You vanished as you came, just as the queens appear and disappear in fairly tales."

"It is time to bathe, to shut oneself up alone and let the warm water wash away all fatigue and leave one rested, ready to enjoy the pleasures of the approaching night."

"Miranda, to wait for you is agony."

"You must learn to wait, as I have. Only then will you have conquered the most difficult kingdom of all for impatient lovers. Last night I welcomed you through the chimney, that magic entrance to fairyland. We breakfasted on the terrace in sight of the sirens. We strolled through enchanted gardens. Rest now, and later we shall dine together, and then we shall sit by the fire in the library. And at the witching hour, when on the mainland the wolves come howling down the mountains, we shall enter the chamber of the green jade lamp, where I shall tell you tales such as you have never heard before."

"Why do you want to tell them?"

"You will know later. Don't be so impatient. First you must listen and later you will speak."

"When shall I see you?"

"When you hear a waltz playing. Listen for it and follow it."

The pale shoulders, the flaming hair, the emerald eyes disappeared. The scenery suddenly lost its radiance.

For a long time I remained seated on the terrace beneath the vines, while my mind projected on the sky, as on a screen, dreams of the past and dreams of the future.

An oriental maid clad in blue silk, with a vaporous gray scarf framing her face like a summer cloud, had silently left silver trays of sweetmeats and fruit and several translucent decanters of wine on the black-veined white marble table near my chair. Another maid, also dressed in oriental fashion, had brought a tray with pipes and a small exquisitely decorated copper brazier with burning charcoal. The scene had taken on the quality of a tale out of *The Arabian Nights,* but the sudden cackling of hens from the courtyard behind the castle reminded me that I was on the solid ground of reality and not in the realm of dreams. I finally retired to my room to bathe and wait.

Night had fallen, dark and thick, when I heard the melancholy notes of a waltz. Rested and dressed in flowing Eastern garments, I descended the imposing staircase, guided by the distant music.

Beyond the windows there was only a dark vacuum, filled from time to time by a flash of lightning. The storm, though far off, made its presence known with peals of thunder, which echoed through the halls like the hooves of horses galloping across the distant prairies of the heavens. The music, which at first had been a faint sound, the vague memory of a melody, now grew louder, and I recognized it. It was one of those waltzes that a hundred years ago had been the delight at court balls, where women wore hoops and crinolines and the men tight-fitting tail coats.

I found Miranda in an intimate retreat hidden in a remote wing of the castle. In a corner, lit only by the scarlet radiance from the fireplace, there was a long table covered with an embroidered white linen cloth on which were set exquisite plates and gleaming silverware, tall crystal goblets, chafing dishes, cut-glass bowls, and platters filled with delicate foods of all kinds, and two shining silver buckets, each with a bottle of champagne.

Reclining on a sofa by the fire, her arms and shoulders bare, Miranda was like a marble goddess un-

301

earthed by an archeologist. She offered me her hand. Every movement she made was as seductive as a serenade by Toselli. I drew near and kissed her fingertips.

"That waltz brought you here?"

"You brought me here, Miranda. The waltz only lent me wings. Waltzing is the beginning of flight, the secret yearning to free oneself from the gravitation of life. It is a spheric celestial empire. The waltz isolates us in a vertiginous world of blue shadows and dark-circled eyes, bleached hair and painted lips, piano and violin, in an endeavor to reach the bliss of heaven by the path of music."

We dined undisturbed. The shadows in the corners of the room emphasized the scarlet splendor of the fire-place. With dessert, Miranda lit a four-branched candelabra, which underlined the bubbling blond marvel of the champagne and her red hair, restrained by a golden band. Her eyes were two gems set in the mother-of-pearl translucence of her face.

Waltzes poured from music boxes that had been placed all over the room. There were dozens of them in all sizes and shapes: small chests and miniature pianos, tiny houses and silver bells, boxes of sweets and crystal balls. All were as ancient as the waltzes they played, melodies that belonged to a remote past, full of nostalgia for a long-gone world. At first they

mingled together in bizarre confusion, but one after
the other they stopped, until there remained only one
large box, whose strains went on and on, slow, soft,
tender, more the music of angels than of human beings,
a music as fleeting as the bubbles of champagne, as
fugitive as the reflection of the moon on a lake.

After eating, we sat on a tiger skin in front of the
fireplace. Rain began to beat and bounce on the windowpane. In the bottom of our crystal goblets, the old
Napoleon brandy mirrored the leaping flames in its
golden surface.

"Miranda, tell me, when shall we find meaning to
my presence on your island? When shall we know if
we are to fulfill the dream that may turn the re-
mainder of our lives into an eternity, that may convert
years of love into centuries of intensity and these into
fleeting instants in the immensity of time? Why have
I ranged the whole planet searching for you? And
now that I have found you, will I find the solution to
the riddle of the sphinx of love, which has been de-
nied to man for so long? When will you yourself learn
whether your search has come to an end, whether
everything that went before was but a prelude and
the future but an epilogue to a present filled with
revelations of the mystery of the relativity of love—
love which can stretch in all directions and imprison
the past in memories and the future in hopes? When

shall we open our hearts to each other and reveal the marvels that lie hidden therein as in a sacred treasure chest?"

Miranda smiled.

"How divinely impatient you are! But before we explore the secrets of love, there's a long road to travel, of confessions and confidences, of secrets and revelations. I have tried to place myself in a sanctuary so that I should become unattainable to the philanderer and the ravener. Like the lioness, I have always spurned apes and jackals. I have given much of myself and then decided to give, like a vial of perfume, no more than a fragrance, until I met someone who would know how to discover my secret."

"You are too much of a woman to make your lover subsist on a fragrance. I don't know where you come from. At this very instant you have all the fascination of a Cordovan beauty, worthy, like the Andalusian moon, of bewitching all the midnight hours of a caliph. Yet, you might be Diana waiting in the forest, surrounded by the rustle of the wind in the foliage, to hear Pan's own pipe."

"Don't rush to the end even before you have started. Wait. Savor the anticipation. At my age, revelation does not take the form of empty words of love or a stolen kiss or a transient embrace. There is fire in my heart, and to keep it in rein I carry ice in my hands. Filled with hopes and illusions, I have waited for you, but you must make yourself worthy of me. It is not enough that you are a poet. You must be a man in love, a man who can curb the mettlesome charges of his instincts. I shall be either your whole future or nothing. You will give meaning to my existence or be nothing at all to me."

Miranda now remained silent, and her ardent yearning reached me as the expression of a woman of that exquisite age when flesh and soul drift together like the scent of a rose. In the fireplace the logs crackled in time with the beating of the rain on the windowpane.

The magic of the hour was making me a captive. In my imagination, so I told her, the castle became a coach standing in a dark street in the middle of the eighteenth century, the coach of Manon Lescaut and the Chevalier des Grieux, with its rich golden carvings and velvet curtains, shadowed and intimate, an invitation to discreet yet passionate love.

"Come," said Miranda on the stroke of midnight. "The time has come to tell you my tales."

In the midnight silence we climbed the grand staircase, lighting our way with a candelabra, the rose-tinted wax running down the candles like fat teardrops. Our shadows danced silently on the tapestried walls. We reached a remote wing of the castle.

With a little gold key Miranda unlocked a gilded door, and we entered a beautiful room hung with silk brocade. A magnificent bronze brazier stood on four exquisitely carved Gothic leonine paws. In a bookcase richly bound books stood slumbering in the shadows. We stepped into another room walled with nostalgic mirrors framed in gilt and then into still another room filled with trophies of the chase and travel. With another golden key Miranda unlocked a door concealed under a tapestry and we walked in. Our steps were cushioned by thick carpets. Miranda blew out the candles, and a tenuous milky light crept through the window.

"This is the chamber of the green jade lamp," said Miranda. "Before I light the candles again, breathe in the atmosphere of the room."

There was no need for her to tell me. I was already inhaling the scent of exotic perfumes and fragrant woods, cinnamon and lemon, sandalwood and myrrh, nutmeg and patchouli. They were an invitation to adventure.

Miranda's fingers reached out in the darkness, and a moment later a lamp was shining in her hands, a small lamp suspended from a chain of gold. A lamp of carved green jade.

I suddenly felt that my life was being endowed with sense and meaning. The lamplight sparkled with gold and green jade. The jade was dark, translucent, of imperial magnificence.

Miranda raised the green jade lamp and what I

saw made me gasp. The room was a treasure chest out of *The Arabian Nights*. Piled up in magnificent disorder lay damascened swords, bejeweled mandarin hats, carved ivory figurines, temple coffers encrusted with precious gems, rare censers, gold and silver narghiles, gorgeous lacquered trays, intricately chased vessels in precious metals, carved woods glowing with the patina of centuries, oriental robes embroidered with rare stones, agate snuffboxes, Ming vases, Manchu ivories, and Tibetan jades.

"What is all this?" I asked.

"The ebb tide of a lifetime. Trophies, gifts, tributes, keepsakes from princes and sailors, emperors and monks, merchants and highwaymen, who with these things tried to show me their gratitude for a word, a glance, a gesture, or an alms of love. The world of marvels that life has revealed to me is symbolized by all these things here. Every midnight I come here, and in the light of this green jade lamp I spend hours dreaming among these treasures, whose material value I do not know, but whose sentimental value is, for me, beyond any price. This room is the symbol of my life and my soul. Here time and space have no boundaries and reality has yielded to the wondrous."

"Why did you bring me here?"

"Look at this green jade lamp, Fernando. It is closely bound to all the strange stories collected by me during my travels. In fact, at one time or another, it figured in the lives of all the men and women in the stories. Like a thread, it joined them together. How it came into my possession I shall tell you some other time. First, you will listen to my tales of the green jade lamp, and then you will tell me how you came to possess that piece of green jade in your ring."

I looked at my hand. In the light of the lamp, the green jade in my ring shone like the green eye of a cat. She turned the lamp around and pointed to one of its corners. It was broken and a small triangular piece of jade was missing, the same piece that was set in my massive gold ring, which for so many years had never left my finger.

I had no time to express my astonishment. "Be quiet and listen," she bade me. "By day we shall enjoy this enchanted island of dream and mystery. By night, here, in the room of the green jade lamp, I shall tell you tales in which real life yields to illusion, which is always more real than life itself for the same reason that the reflection of a rose on the limpid waters of a pool is more real than the rose itself. When I have finished telling you all my stories, you will tell me about your ring, and then, perhaps, the thousand-and-second night will have arrived for us. Now let me be your Scheherazade."

Miranda set the green jade lamp down on a chest. A green-gold circle of light spread through the room. Silks, woods, the centuries cast their exotic scents